BLACK CLOCK no. 18
SPRING/SUMMER 2014

EDITOR Steve Erickson
SENIOR EDITOR Bruce Bauman
MANAGING EDITOR Orli Low
ASSISTANT MANAGING EDITOR Joe Milazzo
PRODUCTION EDITOR Anne-Marie Kinney
POETRY EDITOR Arielle Greenberg
SENIOR ASSOCIATE EDITORS Patrick Benjamin • Jessica Felleman
ASSOCIATE EDITORS Emma Kemp • Adriana Widdoes
EDITORIAL ASSISTANTS Lauren Artiles • Ani Bakhchadzyan • KT Browne • Allison Conner
Anna Cruze • Regine Darius • T.M. Semrad
COMMUNICATIONS EDITOR Chrysanthe Tan
ROVING GENIUSES AND EDITORS-AT-LARGE
Anthony Miller • Dwayne Moser • David L. Ulin
ART DIRECTOR Ophelia Chong
ILLUSTRATIONS Ophelia Chong
AD DIRECTOR Sara Gerot
GUIDING LIGHT AND VISIONARY Gail Swanlund
FOUNDING FATHER Jon Wagner

Black Clock © 2014 California Institute of the Arts
Black Clock: ISBN: 978-0-9836625-6-3
Black Clock is published semi-annually under cover of night by the
MFA Writing Program at the California Institute of the Arts,
24700 McBean Parkway, Valencia CA 91355

THANK YOU TO THE ROSENTHAL FAMILY FOUNDATION FOR ITS GENEROUS SUPPORT

One-year subscriptions (two issues) can be purchased at
blackclock.org/subscribe

Editorial email: info@blackclock.org

Distributed through Ingram, Ingram International, Bertrams, Gardners and Trust Media.
Printed by Lightning Source

BLACK CLOCK no. 18

tom carson   FRAN KUKLA'S PARTY

jonathan lethem   THE EMPTY ROOM

aimee bender   A SLICE OF LEMON CAKE

susan straight   FOR SALE: BABY NIKES, NEVER WORN

brian evenson   THE OPEN CURTAIN

geoff nicholson   THE LOST NICHOLSONS

janet fitch   A SHRINE FOR UNBELIEVERS

diana wagman   BIG SHOES

michael ventura   TO NAME AND BE NAMED:
ELIA KAZAN AND HUAC APRIL 14, 1952

greil marcus   SHAPE OF THINGS TO COME

david l. ulin   LABYRINTH

rick moody   THIRTEEN STORIES

joanna scott   UNTELLING

THE DIRECTOR'S CUT

This is an age that defies the definitive. The era encourages an entropy and multiplicity that are synonymous with liberation, including the artist's; in a time when a movie exists in theatrical, DVD and various digital incarnations, the concept of the "Director's Cut" has become familiar to every buff as an ever elusive grail—the flawed work in a more flawless form, or the great work in an even greater or at least purer form, from Touch of Evil *to* Apocalypse Now *to* Blade Runner.

The "author's edit" doesn't have the same ring as the Director's Cut and, just by the nature of the business, writers are less likely to get second chances without creating among readers the confusion on which moviegoers, with their hyperventilating attention spans, thrive. Nonetheless most authors have buried in their cyber-catacombs the book that got away, even when it's just a less compromised version of the published magnum opus that's stained with the blood of those darlings every writer learns—as a rite of passage into creative maturity—must be killed. In another life or at the hands of some publisher born to indulge my follies, two novels of mine, called The Sea Came in at Midnight *and* Our Ecstatic Days, *will be published in one edition as the single work I've since convinced myself they always were meant to be, and this issue of* Black Clock *is the playland of such authorial dreams (though not mine).*

It includes anthologies that turned into extended meditations, meditations that turned into novellas, novellas that turned into novels, elaborations that still resemble the original and other elaborations that elaborated themselves into something else entirely. Thus this edition of Black Clock *represents the resurrection or final resting place, depending on how you look at it, of editorial decisions reconciled, rued or regretted, the excision of some cherished artistic detour that finally was necessary for the sake of the whole, or a relinquishment that every writer is bitterly waterboarded into at one time or another, against his or her desires if not better judgment.*

After all, if editors really knew anything about writing, they'd be writers, right? Says the writer writing this (when he's not being an editor).

Steve Erickson

tom carson
FRAN KUKLA'S PARTY

tom carson

As it happens, the notion of a "director's cut" reissue isn't hypothetical in my case. My 2011 novel *Daisy Buchanan's Daughter* was an extravagant tour of the so-called American Century as (mis-)remembered by the book's octogenarian narrator—none other than Pamela "Pammie" Buchanan, the only child of *The Great Gatsby*'s Tom and Daisy. Frightening off potential readers in a way I hadn't calculated, the original edition of the book was 628 pages long, and that was after Paycock Press honcho Richard Peabody and I had cut some 20,000 words from the manuscript.

Nowhere except in my most stabbable heart of hearts did deleting all those extra jokes, sideshows and other curlicues mar the novel's mood or theme. There was only one full scene Peabody marked as expendable, and it's this one.

Part Three of *Daisy* is concerned with my heroine Pam's experience of midcentury Hollywood. She's had previous lives as a Jazz Age infant, an uncomely schoolgirl during the Great Depression, a Stalinist playwright's New York bride and a war correspondent who waded ashore on Omaha Beach and witnessed the liberation of Dachau. The "Bill M." she mentions as a friend is my homage to the great World War Two GI cartoonist, Bill Mauldin—the secret love of Pam's life, at least so far as men go.

Now here she is in her mid-thirties in 1950s Los Angeles, married to kindly Noah Gerson. He's a onetime MGM exec convinced by his faith in television's democratic vistas to take a job with Rik-Kuk Productions, purveyors of crappy TV Westerns and bad sitcoms to a network I call One Eye. The Queen Mab making Noah's joiner-squirrel life hell is Fran Kukla, famous star of *That's My Fran*—in which she plays the mewlingly celebrity-besotted wife of an expat French bandleader she met as a wacky WAC in Marseille. Fran's dipsomaniac husband, former OSS man Gene Rickey, has hired Gerson to add quality programming to Rik-Kuk's roster.

Gerson obliges by cooking up a prestige series called *Proscenium* that re-creates celebrated stage performances of yesteryear. Woe is him when Fran—craving an Emmy for drama, not comedy—claims the lead part in its debut episode: a simulation of Sarah Bernhardt's legendary Hamlet. Her improvised slapstick turns *Proscenium* into a smash

hit. The show's burlesques of classic plays end up as a much-loved exemplar of the Golden Age of TV.

Most of this is in the original *Daisy*, but shorn of a political dimension I was fond of. The scene Peabody marked for cutting was a celebratory garden party at Fran and Gene's Brentwood digs before the *Proscenium* version of *Hamlet* airs. That Fran's promotion of herself for impersonating someone else playing Hamlet would double as a fundraiser for the Democratic Party's 1956 presidential candidate appealed to me. Giving my heroine a deflating encounter with Adlai Stevenson struck me as a good capper to Pam's disenchantment with the marzipan 1950s—a projection, needless to say, of her unhappiness about her own incipient middle age. I have her trying to compensate for both by writing a Barbara Tuchman-style book about the American Revolution's birth pangs called *Glory Be*.

Anyhow, I did get to restore "Fran Kukla's Party" to *Daisy* when some kind friends in New Orleans offered to reprint the book. Their press—River House— was first conceived to publish novelist David Lummis's three-part *The Coffee Shop Chronicles of New Orleans*. That inspired David and his partner Csaba to suggest printing *Daisy* in two volumes, a far more manageable format than the original's 628-page bulk. I tried not to go nuts about sticking my jettisoned pearls back in, but including "Fran Kukla's Party" was the one mulligan I begged for.

To understand Fran Kukla's ego—and said ego's interplay with self-knowledge, self-doubt, self-delusion and base cunning—is a job for a shrink or a saint. I'm neither, but here's a tip for any saint or shrink trying. Start with the fact that the big Brentwood bash she threw to celebrate her triumph on *Proscenium* ("Fran Kukla IS Sarah Bernhardt as Shakespeare's *Hamlet* tonite") took place *before* the show's broadcast.

By then—late September?—I was wild for *Glory Be*'s imminent appearance in bookstores. As many-eyed Qwertyuiop looked on with arms proudly folded, the pale tender scruff between the virgin's parting shanks was in view. But for Gerson's sake, I put on a print dress and went along to Fran Kukla's.

Adlai Stevenson was there. Or reputed to be, and tall bald men with weak chins enjoyed sunshine's spotlight. But I did like the house, a French-windowed and turreted, blancmanged and simpatico *echt*-Twenties smorgasbord built in silent days by none other than a budding pudding's favorite moving-picture star, Victor Muet. Relinquished to screwball comedienne Gabby Chatterton when *The Jazz Singer* did

Victor's career in, it was now Fran and Gene's trophy. By the late Sixties, a rock star had it—and some people will tell you L.A. has no history.

Years earlier, in a book recommended to me as the bleak truth about Hollywood by that old monkey's paw Claude Estee, I'd come upon a more ominous view of the city's architectural kickshaw and motley. "Few things are sadder than the truly monstrous," its author opined, and I knew I was supposed to be impressed. (Isn't the pretense of *compassion* marvelous?) But I'm afraid I just grunted "Oh, take a hike, Nathanael" before pitching his rubbish across the Gerson garden at a thrumming, perfectly innocent cicada. Honestly, what kind of man gets that aghast at droll housing? Is it because it's unfettered in a way that must threaten him?

Even so, when a Pam stumped for anything to say to Gene Rickey complimented him on the Muet house, he looked wary. Never leaving well enough alone was a Kukla-Rickey trademark, and they hadn't *done* anything to it yet. At a loss equal to my own, he offered this: "Well, we're working on the esplanade."

"Esplanade?" I said, since I couldn't see either a likely site or a use for one.

"Yep. Franny's got a lot of esplanadin' to do. Don't you, Fran?"

"Hello, you two. Yeah." Clutching and munching from a box of chocolates, her hair a bright orange firework, gaunt in a sprigged gown that ill became either a lawn party or her own bony sternum—not that I'd ever been chesty, but I did know what not to *emphasize*—the most renowned TV comedienne of the Fifties had traipsed up to us.

"Gene, can't you shut that fucking brat up? I know *I* sure didn't invite her," Fran railed. "Where in hell's Carmen?"

"Carmen's busy with Sherry, I think," said Gene. "Brandy! Go play in the side yard," he called to a diapered child lost in sobs amid white trousers, tray-hefting waiters and Democratic donors. "Your mother's got a lot on her mind today."

"Damn right I do. Noah, where in hell do you get off?"

"I'm sorry. Off what?" my husband said, meekly but tightening his grip on his drink. Unfortunately, he hadn't been given one yet, and so much for subtlety.

"Giving Mamie Dwight my old trailer. Is the show called *That's My Lou?* That old bitch'll be screwing my hairdresser next. You watch."

"Fran, you know perfectly well I don't handle such things," Gerson said as I tried hard not to be interested in Gene's fleetingly reflective look. "It's in my *contract* I don't handle such—"

"Yeah, well. Perfectly well, yeah!" Fran looked wildly around the teeming

lawn. "I can't find him. Gene, what's that sorry SOB's name? I'm Fran Kukla, Fran Kukla! Doesn't that ring a bell for *anyone* here? And I'm going to be Sandra Birnham tonight. Am I still a crummy day player back at TKO, for Chrissakes? Is this still that twat Gabby Chatterton's house and not mine?"

"Sarah Bernhardt," Gerson murmured in pain, audibly not for the first time. But she'd already stormed off.

Things esplanaded downhill from there. The band kept reprising the *That's My Fran* theme, alternating its Gene-composed brassy hopscotch with "Happy Days Are Here Again." The broad dance floor laid over the mansion's swimming pool stayed barren. With nothing better to do, I played spot-the-Stevenson awhile.

Not that Pam was ablaze to lay eyes on the real one. Gerson and I had duly mailed in our check, and of course voting for Eisenhower—and Nixon!—was unthinkable. But our 1952 fervor in chorusing "You pray, I pray, we all pray for Adlai" had cooled a good bit by the rerun. We'd both frankly been fonder of Estes Kefauver.

My God: those names. Adlai, Estes, Ike, Milhous! My God, were Gerson and I really facing our third presidential campaign? It honestly hadn't seemed that long. Dyed-in-the-wool Democrat or no, Mrs. Gerson or no, the banner on the mansion and the giant poster crowing back from the lawn—the first proclaiming ADLAI STEVENSON FOR PRESIDENT, the second FRAN KUKLA IS SARAH BERNHARDT AS HAMLET—suddenly made me feel a mite weary of the Nineteen-Fifties.

Gerson had been kidnapped by the One Eye delegation. Victor Muet, fleetingly the only man here I wanted to meet, was long in his grave. Nearby, Fran was loudly explaining her interpretation of the melancholy Dane: "Well, hell! Ghost, my ass. He's just gone from being a nut people put up with to one they all of a sudden don't. That's what's driving him crazy. Just like all those dopey bastards with egg on their tonsils when sound came in." Carrying a wan bouquet of wildflowers and weeds, her daughter trotted back up. See, Mommie? I went to the side yard.

It's never pleasant to see one's own childhood caricatured, especially when the setting's already grotesque. From now on, my memories of my mother—already stylized by time's never-leave-well-enough-alone stylus—would be unwelcomely wrenched by moments when she was played by Fran Kukla. When I'd been Brandy Rickey's age, Warren G. Harding had just died and turned someone named Coolidge into something called a president. I was thirty-six and only Qwertyuiop could bring virgins to my bower.

Needing Gerson to anchor me, I came upon him remonstrating with the actor who played Fran's husband on her sitcom. Like the rest of the *That's My Fran* cast, despite their grumbles, he wasn't in the *Proscenium* version of *Hamlet*, Gerson not being that big a fool. But he'd been roped into this lawn party anyway, like anyone else over whom Fran and Gene had any control.

"Why is it any *different*, Hy?" Gerson repeated, dumbfounded. "Are you serious? It's the only country in history—the only one besides this one, but that wasn't in my lifetime by a long shot. The only country that's ever been founded on an *ideal*. Not just some mess of pottage with a flag stuck on top for convenience, an ideal."

Recognizing the topic, I was less surprised by his vehemence than his audience. He'd told me once that discussing world events with an actor was like talking about the weather to a turtle.

"Yes, yes, yes. I know that," Hy Lector—the former Hippolyte Lecteur—said rapidly. "I think it's a danger, that's all. Tell me, when do we learn the difference between ideal and illusion? *Ah, oui*"—this to a waiter—"gin and tonic, please. When? At death, I suppose." Then added with a swift glance around him, "Impossible. In that case I'd know it right now."

"Hy, I didn't mean to bore you," Gerson said a bit stiffly.

"Not you, Noah. You're exempt, I assure you. But between you and me, Lafayette? *Comme il en doit rigoler.*"

Gerson had no French at all, but the tone gave him the gist, causing his eyes to widen slightly as mine, still unobserved, narrowed. For one of the Marquis's compatriots to confirm my husband's Ferris-wheel pessimism about America's happy, plump slide into soap-flakes masking fungus was something I could do without right now, not at the last minute before *Glory Be* burst into bookstores and changed Gerson's and everyone's opinions of everything.

Damn you, Hippolyte Lecteur! Haroun Pam-Raschid wanted to stalk over and reel off chunks of my text at the top of my lungs, but I couldn't usurp the occasion. This was *Proscenium*'s day: however dimmed now by Kuklafying, still Gerson's hope and not mine. I retreated instead to the open-air bar near the covered swimming pool. Ended up waiting in the slow-motion scrimmage there next to one of the imitation Adlais.

Tall, bald and weak-chinned, he was holding a wan bouquet, which made me think well of him. If I'd been Brandy Rickey, I'd have wanted someone to accept it too, and I decided to thank him by showing some wry solicitude of my own. "You must be

sick of people thinking you're Stevenson," I said.

"Yes, I am," he agreed as his voice and the crinkle of a horrifically recognizable smile snapped his face into focus. "I'm just not sure what I can do about it."

I gaped. "Oh, Governor! I am so sorry."

"Not at all, not at all. G & T?"

"My God, anything. I mean yes. Oh, please."

Deftly chucking Brandy's bouquet under a rhododendron—I only hope she didn't find it there later—he took his glass and handed me mine. "I don't think we've met. And you might be?"

"Then again I might not," I pleaded. "I don't suppose I could tell you I'm Fran Kukla. Could I?"

"I'm sorry. Her I have met. There can't possibly be two."

Rather sexily, our eyes seemed to decide no further comment was needed. Taking my arm once I'd said "Pam Buchanan"—not "Pam Gerson," as usual—he led me away from the bar to the dance floor laid over the swimming pool, a sure indication he wanted to enjoy my company undisturbed.

"Shall we dance?" he asked with eyes twinkling. "The band's on a break. It's our chance."

So it was true he could be seductive. I shook my head, though: "Two left feet."

"Croquet, then." He jerked up a mallet from its wheeled rack nearby. "Though I've never been sure how you win."

"You won't find out today."

"Two left hands?"

I pointed. "No balls."

"Are they really so vital? I think not. Perhaps we can fake it." Surprisingly limber for a man I mistrusted, he swung the mallet at grass. "I'm ahead."

But I'd recovered somewhat. "Um, Governor? I don't mean to be rude. Not *again!* But there's something I've been hoping to ask you."

"Of course." The mallet wheeled happily, disturbing some flies.

"It's that story everyone knows. When the woman called out at one rally, 'Governor, all thinking people are for you!' And you said—"

"'That's not enough, madam. I need a majority.' Oh, it's true. When I said it, the whole room just roared."

Beaming, he gulped gin and tonic as if briefly confusing it with a dais's water

glass. Then shook a finger he'd freed from his other hand, now a wig-wagging worm above the mallet's striped pendulum.

"And no, Pam—she wasn't a plant. That's been asked many times. No, completely spontaneous! I give myself credit for that."

"No, that wasn't—"

I wasn't sure how to explain. I hadn't expected to meet him, let alone watch him turn a croquet mallet into a soft-shoe act's prop on a Brentwood lawn. While thinking most Americans were cretins might be rational in all sorts of circumstances, Fran Kukla's winging included, it hadn't struck *Glory Be*'s author as a seemly idea to voice—much less to get laughs with in public—by a man asking them for their vote.

To too many of the people unrequited by Ike's grin I'd heard quoting that crack, I knew the imbecile category included some women miners I'd met in Riceville, Tennessee, and a nameless GI who'd made an unknown Dachau inmate laugh with jokes and dumbshow about Spam's inedibility. I'd told Bill M. in Chasen's that he couldn't love them as much now that they weren't heroic, and God knows I'd often felt the same. But that was a far cry from calling them fools, and neither of us was running for President.

Unhooked from his neck, the mallet was merrily corralling some clouds over his shoulder. "Do you know, after every campaign I'm asked by a publisher to compile my best jokes? Even FDR never got that. Can you imagine walking into a bookstore to ask for 'The Eisenhower Wit'? Or 'The Kefauver Wit,' since I'm among friends he—oh, Lord."

Clunk. We'd both turned an instant before her knees buckled to see a bewildered Fran Kukla clutch her orange-frizzed head and go crosseyed. Nimbly ditching the mallet, he caught her on one side; ruefully tossing my drink, I grabbed the other. And even though Jack Kennedy was never the thigh-slapping, helpless, roaring-with-laughter type—more New Yorker than Irishman, really—I sure kept him entertained when we shared that table at the Waldorf after *Glory Be* came in second to *Profiles in Courage* in the 1956 Pulitzer sweepstakes.

People were coming up fast, but Gene Rickey was fastest. Not only did he size up his wife's state—goggling, hence conscious—but his eyes quickly flicked from me to Adlai and back before he rushed to take over Pam's share of our rubber-legged burden. "It's all right, I've got her. If you would, Governor, let's get her back to the house. Slowly, slowly! Carmen! *Chinga* the kids. Ice bag! Doctor."

"I don't know why she hit me," Fran moaned.

My own husband's face in the crowd went from baffled to crumpling. "Pammie, for God's sake! What—"

"Later!" I said a bit impatiently. "Don't worry, though, Gerson. It's all right."

We left before Stevenson spoke, were told he'd been witty. The reports of Fran's later behavior sounded mental even for her. But our last sight of Fran Kukla before we tuned in *Proscenium* that night was forlorn. When we started on foot up the hill to the mansion's back gate, she'd just emerged from a long gallery's side door, an ice bag clapped to her head.

Ignoring the tiny daughter who'd wandered to meet her, she made her way through her hordes of oblivious guests as if increasingly surprised and appalled at their numbers. She was wading obliviously toward the American flag that fluttered indifferently over both *ADLAI STEVENSON FOR PRESIDENT* and *FRAN KUKLA IS SARAH BERNHARDT AS HAMLET* from its tall pole near the top of what sky we could see. The famous first three notes breaking slow and mournful as if to keep pace with her, the band started the *That's My Fran* theme.

But even those who agree she was a horror also acknowledge that Fran was a trouper. Well, of course! That's like saying Napoleon was always a soldier. They had what draftees don't: motivation.

It's not just that she did appear as Sarah Bernhardt in *Hamlet* on live TV that night. When she phoned me a few days later—a definite first, no less definite last—she didn't apologize for framing me in The Case of The Flying Croquet Mallet. But she did say, "You know I had to. If the story got out it was Adlai who beaned me—"

"Oh, Fran, it's nothing!" I assured her. "Christ, I understood that right away."

"Hah! Gene, I was right. It's okay. I wonder why we aren't friends, Pam. Well, I guess I wonder that about everyone sooner or later. *Fuck off, Sherry! Just fuck off,* will you? Oh, don't think twice about it! The little one doesn't speak English. A few words of Mex and that's all. Well, goodbye."

jonathan lethem
THE EMPTY ROOM

jonathan lethem

There isn't a whole lot of drama or mishegoss lurking in the tale of this "director's cut" version of "The Empty Room." I wrote the story to my perfect satisfaction and sent it to Lorin Stein at The Paris Review and he took my breath away by cutting the shit out of it in galleys. I'd never had anything quite—or remotely—like it happen before, but I love and trust Lorin and found myself fascinated with how much could be lopped out. The comparison reminded me of the before-and-after-Gordon-Lish drafts of Raymond Carver's stories. Besides, Lorin wrote an accompanying note brilliantly calibrated to make me insecure about the possibility I'd wandered way off my game, and he was simply trying to help me come to my senses. Something about how I was turning into an old, overwriting fuddy-duddy and should try to recall my fierce chops from when I was an instinctive idiot savant hotshot kid. Maybe I shouldn't love and trust Lorin; maybe I should be very suspicious. The cut was severe enough that the earlier version looked and felt like something different, even if it was something rendered unnecessary, useless by definition. Then Steve got in touch, and here you go: "The Less-Empty Room" had a home. Someone else will have to be the judge.

The empty room. Silence and mystery attached to the phrase from the beginning, yet the notion was also covered by the air of amused indulgence that surrounded all of my father's enterprises in the life of our family in that period. I don't remember a time when my mother and younger sister and I weren't players in a script of benign exasperation toward my father. Like anyone, I took my family as it was given. So too, the empty room.

I do remember the apartment we left behind, on the thirty-somethingth floor of the tower on Columbus Avenue, the tumult of shelves lining every surface, home to my father's disarranged collections. It was this apartment's place to serve as the anxious symbol that made the empty room necessary. Earliest memory: father tripping on strewn toys, hopping with toe outraged, mother's rolling eyes inviting Charlotte and

me to judge him complicit with what he decried. For my father had toys himself. He once brought home a traffic light. This elaborately sculptural artifact, its taxi-yellow gone matte from pendulum-years above some intersection, and crackled like a Ming vase's glaze where bolts had been overtightened and then eased, sat to one side of the coffee table it was meant to replace, as soon as my father found an appropriate top. In fact, the traffic light would follow us up the Hudson, to Darby, to the house with the empty room, though it never escaped the garage.

Another memory of life before departure from Manhattan: my playmate Max's parents had borrowed, from mine, a spare set of china plates. I spent a lot of time visiting with Max and, when he let us inside his room, Max's older brother, who kept collections of his own, of Batman miniatures, and Edgar Rice Burroughs' novels arranged by the numbers on their spines. So I was present the afternoon when my father destroyed the china set. Max's family lived in a duplex, the basement and parlor floor of a brownstone, a palace of abundance to the eyes of a New York child raised in a one-bedroom with low ceilings, a half-kitchen, and burdened with my father's collections. Max and his brother had separate rooms, and a backyard. All this would pale beside the spaciousness of our Darby farmhouse. That was its point.

The return of the china had become a running joke between our two families, Max's parents persistently trying to return them, my father explaining that we really had no use for the second set; he claimed that they'd been a gift, not a loan. In this my father struck them as facetious, when he was actually not only sincere, but losing patience. My father's theatrical gestures doomed him to being taken for ironical when his temper flared.

This day my father had swung by on his way home from Penn Station to pick me up. His work was taking him to Albany more often. While they stood in the kitchen, waiting for me to extricate myself from play, Max's father took my own by surprise, placing the stack of scrupulously cleaned china into my father's free hands.

"You really don't want them?" my father confirmed, in his dry way.

"No, please," said Max's father.

"Well, then, we'll just do *this*," declared my father, releasing the plates from his hands. I doubt he added any thrust to gravity's pull, but he didn't need to. The plates exploded, slivers finding every corner of the kitchen and the living room carpet beyond. There, memory halts. Max and I were reduced to pen pals when my family moved.

The New York State Department of Housing and Urban Development

was my father's employer, and we went upstate to be closer to his work. The move, though, was sold as a kind of bodily impulse on my family's part, like that of salmon spawning, to reject the hectic, compromising city in favor of a place where we could *live*. Charlotte and I were bribed with the promise of separate rooms, like those of Max and his brother. I was old enough to fantasize about the teenagerish collections of who-knows-what I'd cunningly display and how I would exclude Charlotte and her friends from my sanctum, and then how, later, with great ostentation, I *would* allow them to enter.

The movers poured our belongings into the new home. Its hugeness, the endless closets, the fact of the barn and garage: these performed a magic trick on our stuff, and on my father's accumulations, which now dwindled as if viewed through the wrong end of a telescope. Charlotte and I ran through the house in a fever, counting the doors, including those of closets, attics, cellar. We lost count at sixty. We then chose our rooms. One room was declared a den, then another a guestroom. My father singled out a room downstairs, formerly the doctor's consulting office (my parents had purchased this house from the estate of a retired country optometrist), with one door and one window, otherwise a simple rectangle outlined with plain molding, and declared it the future site of the empty room. The room was empty now. It would stay so.

"What's it for?" asked his 11-year-old son, the utilitarian.

"Anything we want it to be," my father said. "It's a free room, free even of definitions."

"Can we play there?" asked his 8-year-old daughter, the pragmatist.

"As long as you take your toys out with you when you're finished, yes."

The empty room was my father's defiant reply to his past sins. It wasn't just that it would take a worse man than he to clutter up a ten-room farmhouse; it required a genius of amplitude to conceive the legislation of a *permanently empty room*. He explained by means of a series of exclusions. I asked whether we could go inside and close the door. "There are no rules," he said. "But—" I began. "Except that it stay empty," he interrupted. "Can I eat in there?" I asked, a few days later. "There's nothing you can't do in there," my father said, mysteriously. "Our family eats together at the table," said my mother. Charlotte asked if it was my father's room. "It doesn't belong to any of us," he said. "It's just a part of the house. In the same way that Arfy lives *with* us but doesn't belong *to* us." On moving upstate we'd gained a puppy, to prove we had a backyard. "Is it Arfy's room?" asked Charlotte, perhaps misunderstanding. "Arfy, too, is free to use the empty room," said my father. Again, this emphasis on freedom,

as though such an esoteric substance could be trapped inside a house, the way my father had brought a traffic light indoors. "If Arfy poops in there who has to clean it up?" I asked. We all glanced at my mother.

Then came a ritual cycle of first occupations, Barbies and G.I. Joes each soberly scattered and collected under my father's gaze. My mother ignored it. One Saturday morning she slept in, and my father led us in to sit cross-legged for a breakfast picnic on the smooth, cold floorboards, our hot toaster pastries raised above our heads to keep them from Arfy's nipping bounds. These episodes were grim and perfunctory. Mostly the empty room sat empty.

At summer's end Charlotte and I were captivated by the challenge of Darby's sprawling public school, an isolated compound encompassing a terrifying twelve grades, at which we negotiated fresh alliances and distance from one another and our parents. When we brought a new friend home the room was glossed as a symptom of our in-progress expansion into the vast house, or, as a "famous" oddness of my father's, worth an instant of snorting, but no more than might ordinarily be given to any of the older generation's lame feints at charisma. Within a year, though, the empty room was a social asset, like my father's collection of comedy LPs or his back issues of *Playboy*, like my mother's attractiveness and her willingness to provide fresh-baked blondies during wintry *Gilligan's Island* and *I Dream of Jeannie* marathons. Ironically, it felt as if the empty room counted among the "cool" things imported from my urban existence, rather than being the symbolic opposite of that vanished life.

My father created a sign-in sheet at the empty room's door. My mother's afternoons became occupied with management of the room, the first thing she complained of when my father slogged in for dinner. If he arrived in time to personally hound kids from the room, always checking to make certain we'd faithfully emptied the space of baseball cards, *Archie* anthologies, Slim Jim wrappers, what-have-you, he'd honor us with an arched eyebrow and one of his verbal captions: "Multifarious Doings, I Presume," or "Goings-On, Unspecified, Ensued." Once, cigarette smoke was detected, residue of a spontaneous radical act by my friend Mike's annoying friend Buzz, the empty room now the default hangout for a clan of Darby High boys I hadn't even particularly wanted to impress. My mother flushed us out, Mike and Buzz to their homes and myself to my "real" room. When my father returned, she sent him in for a sniffing tour of the room's corners.

"This fails to pass muster at any number of levels," he began. "The empty room is like a living organ in our family's house. It won't do to pollute it with this kind

of residue, which flunks the standard of *leaving nothing behind* in the most insidious sense." My father's interpretive monologues were getting arcane. We tuned him out before he'd finished articulating nuances of some new policy. We'd never dispute his jurisdiction, but though it was he who'd dragged us from Manhattan to Darby, my father's fifty-odd weekly hours in Albany shrank his grasp of what our lives had become. "The lung could be seen to be the empty room of the human body, not mere negative space. By filling and emptying with the stuff of the world it stands as the most *aspirational* organ, in a literal sense. By keeping this room empty, we've kept it *full*—of potential, for this family's future, and of our private aspirations too…." Charlotte, hanging on this night's dissertation in hopes of seeing me dramatically punished, quit the scene in an arm-flapping show of vexation. My mother, too, wandered off.

The room embodied conceptual distance, like a horizon dragged indoors. As a destination for dark nights of the soul it was nearer than a hotel room or a friend's house, yet much farther than the living room couch. My father was an early riser. We rarely caught him rolling his pillow into his sleeping bag, yet his bindle's position on the laundry room shelves was altered anytime one cared to check. His cheerfully gnomic greetings over the coffeemaker as we staggered out for breakfast gave nothing away.

Under the Reagan cuts, Hugh Carey's administration reluctantly disassembled HUD. In the months before my father was fired my mother colonized the empty room, setting out on her great delayed project of transcribing the oral histories of our grandmother and seven great aunts, whom she'd tape-recorded for her thesis in anthropology at Hunter. Charlotte and I ceded the room readily. We'd situated our lives elsewhere, mostly in the cars of our friends with cars, or in the booths or parking lot of Darby's donut shop, which served for the town's teenagers as much more than a donut shop. My mother, wearing large headphones and operating her special tape player by foot-treadle, labored on her project with an air of private fury like that of a sweatshop seamstress, in solidarity with matriarchal martyrs of the Lower East Side, though she never failed to meet my father's criterion for the empty room by setting up and removing her desk each time she worked.

I was months from departing for college when my father quit driving to Albany each day. He'd been haunting "the corridors of power" in his words; more specifically the lunch counter of Allworthy's, the greasy spoon where the department had lunched, and where some of his colleagues now convened, mourning careers they'd taken for granted. He'd begun scouring the capitol's dusty junk shops, from

evidence of the haul amassing in the attic rooms and garage, and the gilt-framed, Hudson-River-school-knockoffs cluttering the walls of the living room. Yet there was a lackluster quality to this postlude. Soon my father was drawn to the sacred vacuity of the empty room, the one pure accomplishment of his life.

He brought little inside: a Penguin Graham Greene, leaving a slim vacancy in one of his obsessive bookshelf rows; a saucer stacked with five Oreos; a vintage transistor radio with a miraculous bent for receiving Bob Murphy and Lindsey Nelson's Mets broadcasts all the way from New York, albeit wreathed in crispy static. For a brief angry spell it was my parents who reactivated the sign-in system, vying over the clipboard at the door, my father's original hand-ruled grid now a grainy blur in umpteenth-generation photocopies. When his claim on the room ultimately trumped my mother's she set up an office in the guestroom, upstairs. This was more logical than having to reconstitute her station each time, yet her attitude said she'd been relegated at a cost. If a smoke detector had gone off in the kitchen she might have pitched her body through the guestroom window to dramatize her identification with victims of the Triangle Shirtwaist fire.

I registered this in passing. After I left for freshman orientation at UMass, my calls home became a lifeline for my sister, or so I imagined, and therefore made short work of whichever parent answered the phone, then asked them to pass the receiver Charlotte's way. The extra length of cord my mother had installed meant the wall-mounted kitchen phone could be stretched, barely, to slide under the closed door of the empty room. I heard Arfy whining and scratching at the door.

"It isn't the fact that he's always *in here*," she said. "Or that half the time *she's* upstairs in her pedal-operated time machine. It isn't that they never speak a word to each other. It's that every time either one tells me what to do they start with 'your mother and I feel' or 'your father and I want you to understand' or some other stupid fucking bullshit that makes me want to puke."

I convinced them to pack Charlotte off on a Trailways bus to visit me during Fall break, claiming we'd be treated to Thanksgiving dinner at a Northampton hotel by my girlfriend Deanna's family. In fact, Deanna and Charlotte and I spent that week scuffling around the vacant dorm corridors, eating fast food and ramen noodles, listening to R.E.M.'s *Murmur* and smoking marijuana morning, noon and night. Deanna was the first person I'd met who smoked marijuana like it was cigarettes; she was the first person I'd met who did a lot of things. I'd been certain she and Charlotte would get along. I felt my first pang of jealousy at the bus station, just instants after

Charlotte pulled her duffel from the undercarriage.

"So you're the fun one," said Deanna, putting her hand into Charlotte's hair and mussing it upward into a tangle. "No wonder your brother likes me."

"I can think of a bunch of reasons why he'd like you."

"You wanna let me do something about that hair?" Deanna mimed scissors. Charlotte widened her eyes.

Deanna, I saw, would help Charlotte as she'd helped me, to find a self-definition outside either our family's convoluted myths or the dull nullifications of those myths possible in the parking lot of Darby Donuts. Deanna had come of age in a crumbling, wine-smelling brownstone, with parents as ostentatiously "in love" as the parents in *The Addams Family*. Visiting there, Deanna had allowed me to understand that my attachment to New York City needn't be routed through my own parents. The city was part of me, and it might not actually be true that we'd taken the best of it with us when we'd packed my father's Barbicide jars and complete runs of *Horizon* and *Eros* magazines off to Darby.

On Thanksgiving the three of us took psilocybin mushrooms and sprawled on a dirty, marijuana-seed-infested section of carpet in the middle of Deanna's dorm-room floor. Occupying Deanna's room for the drug trip, while the rest of the universe, so far as we knew, enacted a normative Rockwellian Thanksgiving, recalled my father's notions of the suspension of ordinary life within the bounds of the empty room. But Charlotte and I didn't speak of this. For dinner we'd bought cans of Chef Boyardee ravioli, just for the squalor, but felt no particular appetite. At four in the morning our flaming synapses crumbled and we sagged on the carpet into catlike slumber. We'd forgotten to phone my parents, but the next day they forgave us easily, asking no prosecutorial questions to expose our flimsy cover stories. They were probably just grateful to know that Charlotte, who'd been escorted home a few times by Darby policemen, was alive and in my care.

Charlotte unsuccessfully veiled her tears at the bus station an hour later. For a few weeks more, before the fatal New Year's visit, I could flatter myself that my parents' world was a place both immutable and dull, a snow-globe I'd been lucky enough to escape, and which remained Charlotte's misfortune to endure. I was the one engaged in chrysalid transformations, the wonderlands of drugs and sex through which Deanna ushered me. These made early December seem as remote from September, when we'd first met, as Darby's mileage from the moon. What right did my parents have to do anything but stand stock-still for my barely-attentive scorn?

When I called to say I'd be spending Christmas with Deanna (we would visit New York this time; Deanna's parents had since high school granted her unpatrolled use of their whole top story, with its wrought-iron four-poster bed tucked deep between dormers, so the daylight was always angled, and the privacy absolute) my mother's voice rose to a key I was slow to parse as sobbing. The women of my family were on a crying jag. "Well, you can't have Charlotte this time," my mother said, astonishing me. I heard my sister in the background, saying "Let me talk, Zoe." Charlotte had begun calling them by their first names around the time of my father's firing. I still said "mom" and "dad."

"You have to come back," said Charlotte. Her voice was cold. "No," I heard her say, with the mouthpiece covered. "No, he can't have the phone, I don't care. Tell him to come out if he wants the phone."

"What's going on?" I asked.

"Rupert wants to talk to you." My mother's bird-like cheeping evaporated from the background.

"What's taking him so long?"

"He's getting dressed."

My father appeared. "Okay, college boy, I've been deputized to insist you give us a gander at this lady of yours. I've heard good things, but I'd like to see the new paradigm assert itself under my own roof." My father's flippant mode was even more ponderous than his ponderous mode. I promised we'd come for New Year's. My sister called from the parking lot of Darby Donuts the next day, to confirm it: Rupert had implemented a new policy of shedding clothes at the room's threshold. Zoe had detected a corroded dribble down the clapboard outside the window: urine.

I'd called from New York on Christmas day, then treated my parents to radio silence. They believed we'd be traveling up from New York City, but Deanna and I had closed ourselves again in the quieted dorms, needing nothing but our versatile bodies. When the last day of December brought a snowstorm we set out hitchhiking Route 9 at one in the afternoon—early enough, we thought. But rides grew scarce in the whiteout, and the sky was dark by three thirty, our feet frozen from trudging with our rucksacks out of the centers of villages, seeking an acceptable spot to begin thumbing again. Too many of our rides had been in the open backs of pickup trucks, and so to get warm we quit for a while in Pittsfield, and spent the last of Deanna's parents' money on dinner, open face roast beef sandwiches "au jus," at a place called Dewey's. I couldn't know if my parents understood how long ago I'd run through the funds for my daily needs at college.

Deanna and I began working the diner's parking lot, petitioning drivers there to spare us trying the open road, where a translucent slushy inch made braking hazardous, unlikely even for those inclined to give us a lift. Within an hour, though it felt much longer, we found a merciful soul, a middle-aged man in a bowtie and hunter's cap, to drive us into Darby, three across in his pickup's cab, our bags, already drenched, bungeed in the back. Shame sealed our lips, the journey home a surreal plunge through a cyclone's-eye of white, soundtracked by radio hymns.

Neither Deanna nor I wore a watch, but the samaritan's dashboard said it was twenty before twelve as we disembarked. Was this a plan? No, it never was. Some unplans are destined to be remembered as if they were conspiracies. My father must, at sight of the headlights in our driveway, have rushed from the empty room and begun dressing in the hallway. He stood in the corridor buttoning his cuffs when Deanna and I stomped out of the mudroom, through the kitchen door.

"Happy New Year, revelers!" said my father. Arfy clung to my leg.

"Where's Charlotte?" I asked.

My mother perched on the staircase. "When you didn't show up she called some friends," she said. Then: "How do you do, I'm the mother." Deanna went far enough up the stairs to take my mother's hand and bow. I said, "Well, we did show up!" trying to meet my father's exuberant tone, failing.

"Your sneakers are soaked," my mother said. This was true of both of us; Deanna plumped down beside her rucksack to pry them off, though she had difficulty even undoing the laces. "Actually, everything's soaked," I said. Our jeans hadn't dried despite the samaritan's blasts of engine-fume. "You feel like throwing this crap in the dryer?"

My parents were stilled by the petulance of this request. "Let me show you the world-famous empty room," I said into the silence, and, before my father could speak, added, "No clothes allowed." Deanna shrugged and began peeling away her outer layers. My girlfriend was a specialist in rising to occasions. I'd found no bluff she couldn't call. As I opened the door Arfy whisked in ahead of us.

"It's almost *midnight*," my father whined.

"Will you bring us some blankets and pillows and stuff?" My rage might have been like the fledgling creature, protruding from John Hurt's bloody carcass, in *Alien*; I numbered among the witnesses struck dumb that it even existed. My father lifted a cookie from a desultory plate that had been set out, possibly many hours ago, and began gnawing. He could as well have chewed his shirtsleeve, or arm.

Was my mother a conspirator, too? All I know is she executed my commands (for they really were commands, of a prodigal who'd proven his force *in absentia*) with robotic precision. She delivered pillows, copious smooth-folded sheets, and the guest bed's duvet to the empty room's door. By this point Deanna and I were concealed naked behind it, having widened the gap only a few inches in order to toss our undergarments onto the pile. Midnight came and went unremarked on either side of that barrier. "Candles," I answered when, as I opened the door to gather in offerings, my mother inquired whether there were more we needed.

"Your parents seem pretty great," Deanna said with superb neutrality, as she lit the first of the joints she'd rolled. We'd switched off the empty room's ugly overhead (a lamp would have bruised my father's concept), and outside the snow, dribbling down through a windless sky, glowed like blue cotton candy in the penumbra of the driveway's single bulb. We fucked twice, quietly but concealing nothing, Deanna's three culminatory outcries rising through the ceiling and floorboards above, Arfy curling meekly onto a pillow in the corner once it was clear no attention was available for her.

Afterwards I crept out. My mother and father had retreated upstairs. Deanna and I used the bathroom and then I collected some Tupperware for future such occasions. I also gathered food, including a Saran-wrapped platter I found in the fridge, full of triangular sandwiches: chicken salad, cream cheese and cucumber, crustless and heavily salt-and-peppered, just the way we liked them. I moved the den's stereo into the empty room too. It wasn't good, but good enough for Deanna's homemade cassettes.

Charlotte came tapping at our window, clued-in by the tread marks in the driveway's snow or the flickering of our candlelight. Wrapping myself in a sheet, I raised the sash, which I'd already cracked to permit circulation of smoky air. Arfy keened delight, nosing at the opened window, and Charlotte waved off whatever friend had delivered her home. Headlights swerved off into the night.

"What time is it, anyway?" I asked her.

Charlotte shrugged. "Four, five, beats me. Is that pee-pee?" She meant the yellow fling-pattern staining the snow behind her. I nodded. "Sick," she said approvingly.

"Climb in."

The empty room, being a *tabula rasa*, bore aspects of total corruptibility, a potential we'd in childish obedience overlooked until now. Our poses, cross-legged

in sheets, around the plate of triangular sandwiches, the ashtray, and the flickering candle, which illuminated the tumble of pillows and duvet like a pink-pale mountain range, evoked a Native American or Haitian Voodoo ritual site. Nothing of this scene would have signified much in a UMass dorm room. Here, revolution.

"What's that?" said Charlotte.

Deanna understood the question. "They're called Echo and the Bunnymen. This is 'Killing Moon,' it's pretty much their best song."

"You got mom's sandwiches? That's *crazy*." Charlotte took the joint from Deanna's hand. Arfy got into her lap.

"It's safe out there, if you want something from your room."

"You guys want to fool around, huh? Dream on, unless you want to make some kind of tent out of these sheets, because *no way* am I leaving here before you."

"You don't have to leave," said Deanna. "We already fooled around."

My sister raised her hand. "Enough about that."

"They're upstairs," I said.

"Well, congratulations on a unique accomplishment," said Charlotte, sardonic emphasis derived from my father's manner, however much she'd have hated to believe it. "They haven't been upstairs at the same time in a year."

"If we keep the music playing I doubt you have to worry about them coming down."

"What are you suggesting?"

I gestured at the empty room, vacuum laboratory of my father's pretenses, suffocating vault of days, bogus conundrum of our childhood. The ingredients for disaster surrounded us, beyond these four walls, on shelves, in attics and garage, hanging in stairwells, magnetized to appliances, a kingdom of bullshit assembled with the lapidary patience of madness, if none of the originality. It was this, I suppose, for which he was fated to be punished: whether with a superabundance of Little Big Books and Danish "Floating Action" Pens, or in planting and cementing in place *an authentic New York City* parking meter at the base of our driveway, or by the onerous emptiness of his empty room, my father had bored us half to death.

"Haven't you ever wondered," I asked my sister then, "how much stuff we could fit in here, if we tried?" [18]

aimee bender
A SLICE OF LEMON CAKE

aimee bender

I don't write novels in an order but just build scenes as they pop up, and then later look at what's happened and see where the storyline goes. This scene was in an earlier version of my 2010 novel The Particular Sadness of Lemon Cake, *where Joseph, the brother of the narrator, Rose, has been hospitalized and is now home from the hospital and at a party. Rose, Joseph, and Joseph's friend, George, form a kind of triangle throughout the book, and I liked taking them out of the homestead and letting them see George's world, his apartment—the three of them at a party doing party-things.*

It never worked with the flow of the book. The pacing couldn't swallow this scene without it feeling like a kind of awkward hiccup, and Rose's admiration for George, which was important to the story, was clear enough without the scene. Joseph's hospitalizations wound up only mentioned in a sentence or two. I had a good time writing it, though, and am glad Black Clock *has provided a place for it.*

In preparation for college, the spring of his senior year, around the same time as the emergence of my mother's affair with Larry, various brown packing boxes that had been captured and hoarded began exiting my brother Joseph's bedroom and lining up in the hall. Rows of them, big and small. He was many months early in terms of packing, so I grew used to navigating my way down the corridor, edging my back and backpack between the walls as the space narrowed. When he did finally leave that September, I strolled through the house, arms stretched out, the hallway wide as a boulevard. We could drive cars through here! I thought.

With this packing, Joe had unexpectedly become a czar of organization: Biology Books, said one box, in thick black pen; Dragon Figurines, on another. His friend George still came over all the time, but instead of science, the two now huddled in Joe's room and pored over the musty contents of drawers, talking about the dorm facilities and debating what to pack/what to leave behind. George, who did not know his father, and whose mother worked double shifts as a nurse for the elderly, didn't

have a whole lot of stuff, and he seemed to get a vicarious thrill from sorting through Joe's. I did not expect this—for some reason, for the two of them, all of college had collapsed into a clutter-busting TV program, and I'd walk past the doorway and see George on a stool, rummaging in a high cabinet, holding up the bent wing of an old birch model airplane: Can we chuck this? he'd say, and across the room, Joseph would nod, vigorously. Toss it! he'd crow. Trashola! The next box that showed up in the hallway said Goodwill on it, in the same thick black pen, and while they were outside on the grass with a tape measure going over the stated dimensions of the college dorm bookshelving, I lifted the box flaps and pulled out what I wanted: a ratty green iguana sweatshirt, a bouncy ball, a red model train caboose. The items themselves didn't interest me so much, but for some reason I just wanted to recirculate the goods in the household. Not like Goodwill would've accepted that box anyway.

George was taller now, with a long stride, long legs in jeans, and his face had moved into proportion with itself, and even if neither one of them would ever admit it, and they gabbed on happily about being roommates, I could feel the expiration date on my brother as a social partner. How could Joseph possibly keep up? At school, I would sit cross-legged with my vending machine lunch, with my friend Eliza under the white skies of a Los Angeles winter, and I'd watch George over the landfilled yellow-grassed quad that split the junior high lunch area from the high school's. He'd be gesturing about something, one hand in the air, the other lightly dusting the shoulder of a girl, and a few feet too far away sat my brother, on a stone bench, listening. The two did not belong in the same picture. The girls, at that stage, seemed slumpy or gawky or angular or sullen, but George had an acute radar for late bloomers, and even that June, when he had a graduation party at his mother's apartment and had invited all these high school friends over, I was stunned by the accuracy of his leanings. He could sniff out beauty like a bloodhound, even in the most hidden corners of a face.

I was invited to that party, but as more of a watchdog than a participant.

That was a notable party, for me. It was where I'd learned a certain ventriloquy. At the time, I was about to finish high school, and he'd just moved into a new apartment off Washington Street in Culver City, post college, because he'd fallen in love with good food and jazz and wanted to go to the Jazz Bakery as often as possible; I had no car so I took a couple busses over and walked the streets in, climbing the outdoor stone stairway to the open door which spilled out sounds of party talk. I didn't know anyone well, so I went in and up to the buffet table, and there, at the rose-engraved silver tray of cheese-

and-wine, I found myself surrounded by what felt like hoards of gorgeous women, faces I recognized from high school but ones that had somehow walked into their looks as if they, the looks, were a room they could not access until age 21, like a physical trust fund that had come due in full. I nodded, hello. No one knew who I was. Here, said one woman with streaming black hair, handing me a nametag, which I promptly put in my pocket. Who used nametags at a birthday party?

    I stood at the edges of the buffet, holding a glass of wine as if I were my mother, and although I felt young and out of place, and the wine bugged me, and the saxophone on the stereo was too loud, and the nametags made it seem like a work conference, I couldn't stop staring at Matilda Gonzales's long nose and how now she looked just like a Modigliani painting, or at the freckled redhead, who I'd watched across the quad for years, and who was wearing chains of gold necklaces around her neck in a way that made me feel like I was inside an important Greek myth. I was, at that time, 17. I had never had sex. I had no college fervor. I busied myself at the table, filling my plate with a glob of dip and an assortment of broken tortilla chips. Parties of any kind were usually hard for me because all social interactions involved food, but this table, set out by George, was a rare heaven; I had ten blissful minutes, leaning against the wall, dipping those chips, closing my eyes and chewing, until one stuck in my throat and I had to take a sip from the vodka punch bowl only to discover that it had been mixed, recognizably, by my brother—that horrible urchin small feeling inside, such a contrast to the beautiful warmth in the spinach-cheese dip which all meant I had to rush to the kitchen sink to spit the mouthful into the drain; Are you okay? asked Ellie Oakley, lounging in the kitchen area, now a dead ringer for Elizabeth Taylor but who, in high school, had seemed so big-eyed she'd reminded me of a fetus. I'm fine, I said, wiping my mouth with a striped dishtowel. Excuse me. I just never liked vodka, I said.

    Aren't you Joseph's kid sister? she asked, peering closer.

    Yes.

    Her eyes were wet, and violet, and looked artificially dyed.

    Is he straight? she asked. She leaned a hip on the edge of the sink, and slurred a little bit. Water glassed her eyes. One red-dipped finger hovered in the air, like she was making a point. I could see her calculating, in her drunkenness, the proximity of Joseph's value to George's, not unlike how a fan will find love in the arms of a star's lackey, if only for a night, all of it an ineffective carnal playing-out of the transitive property of equality.

I don't know, I said. Ask him.

She used the sink faucet to steady herself. I did, she sighed.

And?

He said his twelfth vertebra tilted left, she said, but other than that, he believed so.

She sighed at the thought of it, and rested her head on the counter. It made me smile, what she said. Against my will, even with that bad taste in my mouth. I looked past her, through the boxes of cereal and into the living room area, at my brother, sitting alone on the sofa, reading a book. He had a beer by his side, and a small plate with one cracker and one carefully cut wedge of swiss cheese on it. They were props only. According to years and years of my observations, the beer would grow warm, and the microbes would find that cheese and cracker before Joseph ever did.

At the time of that party he had been home from the hospital for a week. He had disappeared for five days, showing up on the sixth on the floor of his dorm room, wan and starving and bluish and dehydrated. He still looked too skinny, and if you examined his wrist, the circular pressed mark of the hospital wristband was still, faintly, visible. No one knew where he'd been. He refused to say. The doctors found no drugs in his system, and put him on a drip IV, treating him like a ski victim found lost in the mountains after days of search parties and inquiry. Although George had always been welcoming to me, and no doubt would've extended some kind of invitation, I had been asked to this party in particular as a kind of watchdog in case anything happened. The whole week, both Mom and George had spent hours on the phone, or at his door at home, convincing my brother to go to the party, as if that was all he needed, a good party, to reverse things. George, who was usually more tuned into reality, must've done his coaxing speeches out of guilt, because while Joseph was in the hospital, strapped to the IV, wearing a blue paper gown, twining his leg around the table during doctor questionings to steady himself, George had been settling linen napkins in his lap and sipping from crystal goblets of ice water at various lunches with MIT faculty, who were actively courting him for their doctoral program in physics. George had graduated Caltech with high honors; Joseph had still only completed one full semester. By the time of that party, my brother had dropped in and out of school so many times it was impossible to string a transcript together with any coherence and the list of courses added and dropped made a broken bead necklace of A's and C's and W's. If the two roads named George and Joe had been diverging since senior year of high school—since those lunches with George's hand lightly dusting the shoulder of a

girl—the point of true widening was about to happen, where one road can't spy the other anymore, where the distance was such that landscapes and climates changed and the flora of one road could no longer mesh with the other. My mother saw none of this. It's your best friend's birthday! she had pleaded to Joseph's closed door. It'll be fun!

In the kitchen, Ellie lay her head on the counter, and ran her fingers over the rim of a bowl of guacamole. I'm so fucked up, she said.

Her eyelashes were black and long. Ellie Oakley, who had even considered my brother as a viable possibility. I leaned over and tucked her hands under her cheek, making a pillow.

Rest a little, I said.

The rest of the party I spent on the sofa, next to my brother, watching the people, wondering which woman might continue the birthday celebration and stay over. George spent a lot of time talking to Jessie Champaign, a bitchy one whose new pointy haircut announced her cheekbones like a racecar sportscaster. She spit out her words when she spoke. The minute she'd walked in, she strode right up to the couch and asked my brother what on earth was wrong with him. You look AWFUL, she'd said, slipping off her fake fur-lined coat. So do you, mumbled Joe. Jessie was small, in spikey high heels, and she'd stood at the couch edge and wrinkled her nose. Um, no, she'd said, in her tiny silver dress; I don't. And off she went to get a drink. I watched her navigate the bar area with her elbows, the dress hitching up until it barely covered anything and I glared lasers into her back even if she was right on both counts. To compete, via puppetry, I coached a few others who came by to say hi to both of us, the couch of Edelsteins. Go talk to him about his grandfather, I whispered, when I saw the gold-chained redhead cast a longing look in George's direction. He was leaning on a bookcase, rubbing his eyebrow, listening attentively to an enthusiastic chemist. When had he become so handsome? Something about him, about the ease and care of his leaning. The redhead sighed. She had an appealing freckle right under her left lower eyelashes. Ask him about his grandfather's baking soda experiment, I hissed, as she wobbled up in her boots. It's a homerun question, I said.

She approached the bookcase slowly, necklaces rustling. I flung a few crackers off Joseph's plate into the forest of knees.

At eleven on the dot, Joe and I went outside to wait for my mother's car, which ambled up to the apartment building just a few minutes late. Huddles of people outside, smoking, watched as we entered the car, and she hugged us both as we settled

into our seats. Her hair was slightly disheveled in its ponytail, messy at the rubber band, a look I'd come to associate with a visit to Larry. So how was it? she asked, her voice rising lightly.

Fine, I said.

Fine, said Joseph, still reading his book.

Great! said Mom, putting the car into reverse. A few smokers waved from George's apartment steps. Jessie Champaign left in her fake fur coat on the arm of another guy, and her eyes pierced the window as we pulled away.

Are you drunk? Mom asked, almost hopefully.

No, said Joe.

I'm drunk, I said.

Oh, Rose, said Mom, shaking her head, but in the rearview mirror, her eyebrows raised with a hint of approval. I'd said it for her. One regular teenager. Fact was, I was not a bit drunk, in large part because the grapes in the wine were too snotty to me to even finish the glass—the vintner, even in the dim distance, like an unbearable pompous caricature of himself. Mom put on the radio, violins. We drove east on Venice Boulevard, passing furniture warehouses lit up inside, showcasing brown suede couches and brass heron lamps. Under the freeway onramp at Robertson/National. Past the chipping paint stores, then north on La Brea, speckled with rug and vase loft shops with too-witty names that reminded me of Ellie Oakley, who I'd seen last stumbling through George's living room, wearing a nametag that said Take My Keys. After Mom pulled into the driveway, we filed through the front door together and then split off into our various spots like billiard balls; Joe, as of that week, had moved home again, and his bedroom was a spare version of its earlier self. Most of his generic belongings had stayed at Caltech, to be packed up later, or recycled by the dorm advisor, for some other student, someday. Mom put on the teakettle as we settled into bed.

This is where it went, but none of that was in place years earlier, as the brown boxes entered the hallway, and as Joseph and George went through each book and stacked them in groups: To Keep, To Return to the Library, To Use as Kindling. Only later would I view those piles of brown boxes in the hallway as great squares of desperate hope, and only later would it make sense that he'd put them all out so many months too early because the pull to stay was so strong. Perhaps he thought a forceful exit strategy would ensure his departure, a departure maybe he knew, even then, was temporary.

Black Clock BC 18 / 40

susan straight
FOR SALE: BABY NIKES, NEVER WORN

susan straight

In 2009 I was commissioned to write a story for a fine letterpress edition of a book called *For Sale, Baby Shoes, Never Worn,* which would contain six original short works of fiction of six pages each, written by six writers based on those apocryphal six words, often called the world's shortest short story, or the first ever flash fiction, and attributed to Ernest Hemingway.

    Foolscap Press had this singular idea. There were no guidelines or suggestions—just those words, which contained universes imaginable in countless ways to humans. Three women, three men. A famous comedic actor; a journalist; a photographer; writers who lived in Paris, London and California—six people who had nothing in common except words.

    I walked around with those words in my head for weeks. A mantra, a chant, a fearful lamentation that could have been uttered from whenever humans began to wear shoes or trade goods, a lamentation that has survived until now, when baby humans might have no pair of shoes or hundreds. I have three daughters. I have more than one hundred nephews and nieces and young second and third cousins, great-nieces and nephews, and even three great-great nieces.

    That year, drive-by shootings and gang violence were everywhere in Riverside, San Bernardino, Los Angeles, Pomona. Each attack, whether on someone I knew or someone I knew only from a newspaper article, was like a wave that ground us into the hard sand at the bottom of the shallow beach. Have you ever been held under by successive waves on a dangerous day? You struggle up, raise your head gasping above the greenish water, and then you see the next swell and consider giving up and floating down forever.

    One night at the mall with my middle daughter, who needed basketball shoes from Foot Locker, I stood transfixed in front of the smallest sneakers I'd ever seen. Nike Shox, black and red and white, about five inches long.

    I began the story with Baby Nikes. I wrote many drafts over a year. The version published in the letterpress edition is lovely, the oversized book a work of art with a cover

of the palest green shirred fabric, perfect for the wrapping on a baby gift for a parent who doesn't know whether a girl or boy is expected. Each story is illustrated—a drawing of the tiny Nike Shox for mine.

But I had to cut the story by a third, to fit. And that seems a small care, since I didn't eliminate an entire character or trim entire scenes, but I excised many lines of detail. It is such an L.A. story—it couldn't have taken place anywhere but that particular neighborhood in that particular time, and the grandmother, born in Louisiana, and her neighbor, born in Oaxaca, could only exist on that kind of street in historic South Central. Even the texts are of that particular time and place. For that reason I'm glad to have restored lines about the minor characters, the yards and music and conversations. It's like adding back the magenta thread to a piece of tapestry—maybe only I would ever notice, but I do.

Car doors slamming. Just dawn. Albertine saw the faint shadow of bougainvillea on the wall. She made her bed every morning. Every morning. She pulled the yellow-rose-printed sheets tight. If she didn't make the bed when she was a child, Grammere Marie would chase her back inside the house with a fig tree branch stripped of leaves, stinging the backs of Albertine's legs.

Every day. Even Sunday.

More car doors slamming, and voices. The music. Trumpets. Mexican music. Albertine froze.

In the other bedroom, the quilt was smooth. The bed her daughter Cherisse had refused to sleep in last night. The bed Cherisse had slept in all her life until college. And the bassinet was still against the wall. She only had a dresser drawer for Cherisse, back in 1970. But a bassinet this time.

She moved to the dim hallway, listening. Car doors slamming, slamming.

He had left her there. Amina. He had gotten out of the car and slammed the door and left her there. The police said the driver door was closed. Amina would have heard him leave her there in the other seat. If she could still hear.

Voices speaking Spanish. A child calling, *Papi! Papi!*

Josefina's perpetual yard sale, across the street.

Then she heard the drumbeats. Faint. Coming from Central Avenue. Then closer, so loud and boom boom boom that the vibration shook the walls. She put her forehead against the plaster. The dull explosion over and over. The metal of the

car. Pernell would have shot them. He had a rifle. Her heart throbbing against her breastbone. A car with speakers. Boom boom boom.

The drums so loud the plaster trembled. A spooling of words from the deep voice. *Boom boom Girl. Boom boom World.*

The same song as three nights ago, when pounding drums sped past and she hadn't heard anything else. Or she would have run outside.

She might have found them in time.

They sing *Boom boom Girl* and *Boom boom World* and then they shoot.

She lay on the hallway floor. The narrow long rug like a dark red river that had been there for thirty years. She curled herself like a pillbug. Not on her back. Not like a coffin. Like the baby had been curled inside the water of her mother. Her granddaughter. Amina was having a boy. Had he drowned? How did they breathe in the water? When she was pregnant with Cherisse, no one knew anything. She carried a heavy weight of baby, of kicking and feet pushing out the skin near her navel, and all was mysterious. No grainy black and white pictures of something curled inside a silvery space.

Stop, drop and roll, Mama! That's what they said to do. If you're on fire.

Albertine rolled onto her stomach. She had cried for three days. Her eyes burned as if someone had put embers there. Inside the holes. The eye sockets. Cherisse showing her the skeleton in the science book, and then the muscles. Then Cherisse coming home from school saying *Stop, drop and roll,* and collapsing onto the living room rug like her bones had dissolved.

You can put your own fire out, Mama.

By sixth grade, Cherisse had said, *They always say, Your mama the lunch lady.* Her face pulled back like a turtle. *You don't want something?*

What?

You just gon serve the lunch and come home and clean the house?

What you want me to want?

Something.

I want my baby to be happy.

I'm not a baby.

Her eyes were dry and swollen hot. No tears. When you were young, there was more water inside. She hadn't cried like this even when the men showed up on the porch with medals like candy gum and said Pernell Johnson had been killed in Vietnam. She hadn't let herself go hysterical because she was pregnant with

Cherisse, and the old women back in Louisiana used to say, *Cry and cry, that baby water fill up with salt and they drink it. Them tears make a baby sad the rest of they life. They feel you shakin and they scared before they come out in the world.*

But Albertine hadn't been in Louisiana since she was twenty. There was no one here to explain anything. She was sixty now. The last branch on the tree.

When the bullet went into the brain, did the heart forget to beat? Is that what the TV show said? If the bigger heart stopped beating, how long did it take for the baby heart to slow?

Revella would let herself in. At the kitchen door. She had a key. She would find Albertine lying here on the hallway floor like a—

Albertine pushed herself up with her elbow. Hands and knees. In her robe. The muscles in her back complaining like when Amina was little, wanting to play.

I'm too old to play like that, baby.

Mama, you're not that old.

She'd still gotten up every morning and made her bed, told Amina to make her bed, and cooked eggs, grits and coffee before Amina went off to the college.

She was in the first year of the nursing program. She'd met this boy—Jhamal—after a football game. He'd come over a few times—perfect smile, scalp so shorn his hair was like a lace net over his skull. Polite. *He run with them fools?* Albertine asked Amina after that.

No, mama, he's a baller. He's careful. Big universities are looking at him. You see his skin? Like a Dove bar.

But Albertine had heard him from the kitchen. *Why you have to be so fine? I'm not supposed to get caught up, now. But look at you.*

She leaned forward and put her forehead on the rug. Like those men praying five times a day. What would the Lord think? Prostrate. Crawling.

Pernell would shoot them. But he wouldn't even know who to shoot. In Seven Oaks he'd crouch in the canefields when they burned. He'd shoot rabbits, and Albertine would pull off the skins.

She crawled toward the doorway. Her knees. Revella would let herself in. Revella would be wearing her brown velour sweatsuit. She had bought Albertine a black one. She would talk to Albertine again about moving to Fontana, to a condo

near her pastor and her church, where it was safer. She would find Albertine crawling.

Silence. She crawled up the wall and stood, put her palm on the cool plaster. The dark narrow hallway, where Cherisse's fingerprints had been like faint black ladybugs on the white paint where she steadied herself with her hands, coming to the back bedroom when she had a bad dream.

Cherisse had bad dreams forever as a child, the fingerprints at hip level, and then she went to school and fell in love with insects and grew up hard and said things like, *Beetles have more of a moral compass than anyone around here.* Then she went to UCLA and studied entomology and specialized in wasps and never came home though it was only ten miles and there were buses. But during her junior year, when she was twenty, she came home pregnant.

She never said the father's name. She named the baby Amina. Then she went back to UCLA, graduated two years later, and went to Washington, D.C. to work at the Smithsonian, cataloguing insects. Albertine imagined her in wood-paneled rooms with hundreds of drawers, pulling out cases of wasps with their tiny abdomens pierced by pins. But she had no idea what the rooms looked like. The Smithsonian was like a red-brick castle when Amina showed it to her on the computer.

When Albertine saw wasps hovering around the rosebushes in the front yard, so thirsty in August in L.A. that they would land right on the hose, waiting for the right drop on the right leaf, their beautiful elfin faces looked human, their legs dangling like gold chains broken from around someone's throat.

Someone knocked on the kitchen door. "Miss Albertine." A boy. Not him. Not the boy who had left Amina there. "Miss Albertine?"

She made her feet move down the hallway. The chifforobe. The bowfront glass case her Grammere Marie had sent with her to California, when Pernell was being sent to the base near Los Angeles.

The kitchen empty and clean. The casserole dishes washed and stacked up on the counter. Revella had brought gumbo. Dolores had brought string beans and potatoes cooked down with sausage. Josefina had sent a pan of chicken enchiladas.

The face at the window in the kitchen door was Josefina's middle son. Miguel. He'd been about seven when Josefina bought her house ten years ago. He held up a small pink box, his hair brilliant black needles glistening in the sun.

She told him once, *You look like a porcupine, baby.* And he'd said, *What's that? We didn't have no porcupine in Oaxaca.*

"You okay, Miss Albertine?" he said when she opened the door.

"Yes, baby, I'm okay." Her eyes felt like coals.

"From my mom." He put the pink box into her hand, and she nearly dropped it. "I'm sorry." He put it on the counter. The heart-shaped pastries from the Mexican bakery. To apologize for the cars along her curb. The way Josefina did every Sunday.

Albertine looked down the driveway. Josefina's chainlink fence was hung with men's shirts on one side, and baby dresses on the other. Women bent over the card tables along the driveway, holding up men's shoes and asking *how much?*

The baby dresses were like small pink and yellow ballerinas tied to the wire.

Miguel went down the driveway. Albertine's driveway was empty. The Regal had been towed away by the police. She wouldn't look down toward the corner, toward Central Avenue, where the yellow tape had blocked off the street. The corner of the cement step under her foot was chipped off. It was the last thing Pernell had done before he left—he'd been trying to fix a car part, and his hammer hit the step. Cherisse used to put her finger inside the hole until it was smooth, as though a snail had lived there.

She touched the corner of the chifforobe. Inside the top drawer was her life. The deed to the house. The insurance papers from when Pernell had been killed. The medal. The pink slip to the Buick Regal she'd bought in 1978. The one she still drove until three days ago. Burgundy.

The shelves behind the curved glass held Cherisse's diploma from Jefferson High School. The picture of her in cap and gown. And Amina's diploma, too. Jefferson High. Class of 2007. Her hair straightened, flowing into two points from under her cap.

Both of them with Pernell's eyes. Slanted and tilted and black. He looked nearly Chinese himself, and when he came back from the first tour he said, *They got me shootin at dudes look like me. But I try not to get close enough to see their faces.* Back in Seven Oaks, when they were kids, everyone called him Chan.

Cherisse's palm print on a round pink plate, from kindergarten.

And her baby shoes. Bronzed baby shoes.

The second shelf was crowded with useless small things. Three fancy teacups from Revella, two glass ballet dancers someone had given Cherisse long ago, and little plastic things from teachers and students. Birthday cards and graduation cards and a metal plaque from the Science Fair. Cherisse used to refuse to wipe them off, on Saturdays when Albertine made her spend the morning cleaning.

Why you gon make me dust em off and the dust fly up in the air and come right back down in an hour? For reals, Mama.

But this dust was different from the particles of earth Albertine had swept up in her mother's wooden house near the cane fields.

She said, *This my dust. When I was little, somebody else dust flyin round, and this my dust. You wet that rag and get them cups clean.*

When Cherisse wiped off her own bronzed baby shoes, she'd roll her eyes and say, *Clichés collect dust, Mama. All they do.*

But Albertine had first seen bronzed baby shoes when she was nearly a baby herself. In Mr. McQuine's house. Seven Oaks. When she and her mother were called in from the field to help clean for a party. On a shelf built into the wall near the fireplace mantel—three pairs of bronzed baby shoes. The two daughters and one son of Mr. McQuine's mother. The inheritors of the plantation.

Shelf painted white. The room big. A chandelier.

She had been barefoot. She remembered her first neighbors, Revella and the others, saying, *You get that baby some Buster Browns? You go to the shoe store? Get that baby some Buster Browns. So her foot shape right later. You get them shoes with support, so she walk like a queen when she get to be a big girl.*

A black and red heat bloomed in her head. Like a drop of food coloring in a glass of water. Twisting, moving, then threads of hate. She swung open the closet door and got a box. She opened the latch that stuck on the glass front and bent again and again to put the cups and dancers inside. The mug that said her name. The china dolls and the pretty gold-rimmed plates she had bought when she got married.

No need to wrap the figurines in newspaper because she was taking them to Josefina for the tables. Mexican women could have the glass dancers.

She left Seven Oaks for California when Pernell was sent to the base, and when he came back after the first tour of Vietnam he was home for six months. They

bought the house at 39th and Central, and then he went back to the war.

They stood in front of this small house with white plaster like frosting, and red tile roof with half-moon holes like a million dark eyes when Albertine looked up from the green-painted front steps. Pernell said, *Damn, we got a house. A house. Look at this! Two bedrooms and a big old window in the front.*

But you leavin, she said.

I'ma be back here in a hot minute. My job—shoot em. You know. They shoot me and I shoot them. I better be good. Your job—be here when I get back. Cause some them girls don't wait. They find somebody else. Don't go. Don't go.

She didn't.

Even when Cherisse told her to go. Even when Cherisse refused to come back for Amina's birthday parties. The three of them at the W Hotel in Westwood, in the lobby where grass grew in cement planters and the restaurant was lit by tiny lights like fireflies.

Cherisse said that there were fireflies in Washington, D.C., and Amina had asked if it was true, if you caught them in a jar they died, and Cherisse said *Everything dies eventually*, and Amina said *That's when you stick a pin in it to make it important* and Cherisse said *People have no idea how important it is to catalogue the world.*

Amina said, *I want to be a phlebotomist. Cherisse. If you take out the blood and figure out what's wrong with it, and you give people the right drug it gets erased.*

The bottom of the box was full. Her eyes burned. She headed down the hallway for the baby Nikes. But Revella let herself into the kitchen, shouting, "That boy comin across the street. Them Mexicans. I told you, them Mexican boys down the way had to been the ones shot the car. We in a war. I told you, my pastor done found us a condo—"

"Yes," Albertine said, stepping onto the linoleum. "We can go to Fontana."

Revella was silent for once. For a moment. She wore the brown velour. Her hair was freshly pressed, the curls shining like Cherisse's toy. The Slinky.

Then Revella said, "What you doin with that box? You not dressed yet? You sure you okay? When Cherisse comin for the viewing?"

"She called. She's not comin."

Albertine went down the two kitchen steps with the box. She hadn't been outside since the police brought her back. The grass was dry and stiff. She was near the edge of the yard. The lantana bush covered in pink and yellow flowers.

Miguel was sitting in his car across the street, working on the speakers. Josefina was helping an old woman close the trunk of her car. Josefina lifted her hand the way the Indians did in the old movies. But she looked like a tiny African queen. Darker than Albertine or Revella. Her braid a crown. Her housecoat covered with pink orchids. She had seven boys.

The lantana bush smelled sweet and oily. It had been there when they bought the house. There was a picture in the chifforobe drawer. Black and white photo with scalloped edges. Someone had left it behind. A white woman with glasses, pigeon bosom and tight-belted dress, standing on the lawn. "Lucille and Lantana—Our Home 1952."

Pernell laughed, held the photo. *She had to been dead to sell it to us.*

The glint of something in the bush. Albertine put down the box.

A cell phone. Black and heavy and small in her hand. Like a piece of sugar burned to black shine in a pot. She must have cried out, because Josefina ran across the street.

Josefina said something in Spanish to Miguel, and he took the phone. "Dead," he said softly. He waited until a truck passed and then bent inside his car, plugging the phone into something.

Revella said from the driveway, "You don't need no more mess. Come on inside, Albertine."

But Albertine looked down the street. Six houses away, just near the corner of Central. Where there were still jazz clubs when she and Pernell came. Now there was a recycling center, and the Mexican bakery. The yellow crime tape gone. The Regal gone. The asphalt empty.

Miguel said, "It's his phone. The guy."

Josefina took Albertine's arm. They waited for a van playing Mexican music, trumpets swinging. Albertine opened the passenger door and sat down. The bottom of a well—dark seats, and sinking.

Miguel looked up from the phone, deep in concentration, as if from a book. He held it out and she looked at the letters.

"You want me to read them?"

"Jhamal, right? Nobody seen him again?"

Albertine pictured him running, throwing the cell phone into the bush, and passing right by her house, her door, never screaming out that Amina was in the car, bleeding.

She held it and he pushed a button. He moved the lines down and read softly as if from the Bible.

"Yea. Wit this girl."

"No. She aiight. Not the 1. But coo 4 now."

"She came to tha game. I scored 2 TDs.

"Nursin or sum shit like that."

"Sum fools from tha party seen us @7-11. I-ballin me. Where u from & like that."

"Idk. She half sleep."

"jus dropping her off. Ill be over 2 ur place. ttyl."

Miguel looked up. "That's what I heard them say. Where you from?"

The sun moved on the windshield. Cloudy smudges of handprint like ghosts.

"Where were you?"

"Sitting here. The window was open. I was texting this girl. I seen a black Escalade down there. Somebody yelled Where you from? And then they started shootin."

"That's all they say?" Albertine asked.

He nodded. "I ducked down and they went past." His hair was blinding and silver in the sun. "They were black. They yelled something like 60s. The boy had been driving her car. Amina was in the passenger seat, half sleeping because it was about midnight and she was five months pregnant. But he didn't know that yet. She hadn't shown him the shoes.

I bought some little Nike Shox. I didn't want to tell him yet till I knew it was a boy. She had the ultrasound the morning before.

I was asleep. I had the fan on cause I hate hearin all them cars, all them drums.

Brain. Belly. How long did it take for the baby to die?

She had sat there in the car, Amina, as if resting, until the sun came up and a man pushing a shopping cart filled with recyclable cans saw the blood on the window.

She walked past Revella, who was speaking—her mouth open, her red lipstick moving, her arms folded. She went back into the bedroom for the baby Nikes.

Cherisse crying last night on the phone. *Why didn't you move? I told you to move years ago. I would have given you money.*

What did the baby do? She'd spent hours lying in bed seeing him curled in the water.

You're telling me one coffin or two? That's what you're telling me?

The boys. Pernell shot the men in the jungle. But he didn't shoot at men from behind the lantana. Or the bougainvillea. Amina. Amina. Her cheekbones so high, her eyes nearly hidden when she smiled.

Cherisse calling near midnight, Albertine half asleep on the couch. *I can't do it. I can't come down there. I went to the funeral home an hour ago and they wouldn't let me in at first. They said I wasn't family. They said they'd seen the mother and it wasn't me. And when they let me in I saw the other casket. Why couldn't they just leave him with her? He was so small.*

They didn't even see Amina in the car. She was nothing. Nothing. They wanted each other. Every night they hunted each other and wrote numbers on walls. Every wall she passed was covered with numbers. Their hands in the air with fingers curled and numbered like old arthritic hands back in Louisiana.

So that the baby's heart could be stopped by a bullet bigger than his toes.

Revella was talking and talking. Albertine went down the hallway. The bedroom dim and still. Amina's clean clothes stacked in the laundry basket. Smell of cocoa butter lotion from Target. Where they'd bought the bassinet.

Portable rocking bassinet with the toy box base. The screams rose up inside like barks. Barking in her throat like metal sponges.

Look at this, Mama. "Tadpoles Basic Green Moses Basket." *A Moses basket? That's what they call it?*

Albertine picked up the shopping bag from Foot Locker. Inside was a six-pack of sleepers Amina had bought because she couldn't wait, and the shoebox.

She didn't open it. The baby shoes were black and red and white. Gangsterish. But Amina said, *For a little baller. Look at the bottoms.* Red rubbery things like suction cups. *So he can jump!*

She put the bag inside the bassinet. They bought it early because it was on sale. She pushed the whole thing across the floor, bumped the doorway again.

Albertine pushed past Revella in the kitchen, hit her in the knee. Soft velour. Revella shouted, "Albertine, you can't do that."

Down the two steps gently. More cars cruised past Josefina's yard. Tubas and trumpets. Boom boom girl sleeping until dark. Pernell would shoot them, but he wouldn't know who to shoot. Shoot them all. A branch on a tree. She pushed the bassinet across the street.

Past two women pushing strollers, plastic bags tied to the handles like lumpy white fruit. Don't look. She stopped in front of Josefina's feet and kept her head down, crossing back blindly.

But Miguel stopped her on the asphalt. She looked at the lantana flowers. Tiny pink and yellow umbrellas.

"She says you should keep these. She says she seen the other shoes in your cabinet. You should keep these next to the other ones."

Josefina said something else, her hand a tiny dark starfish on Albertine's wrist.

"She says if she sells them, it's like he wasn't ever here."

She handed the box back to Albertine. Nike Shox. *For my baby baller*, Amina said. Like he would have bounced into the air with his very first steps.

brian evenson
THE OPEN CURTAIN

brian evenson

The passages that follow here are the beginning of an earlier version of the third and final section of my novel The Open Curtain (2006). Originally, I'd had the idea that the main character, Rudd, would end up in Northern Mexico, the book culminating in one of the several colonies that Mormons established there when they realized it was impossible for Utah to be granted statehood while polygamy was still being visibly practiced by Mormons in the United States. There, a kind of psychic battle would continue, culminating in a lethal encounter in a series of caves and Rudd's destruction at the hands of his (real or imagined) half-brother Lael. I wrote this section all out, almost 20,000 words in all, and revised it a number of times. I liked parts of it very much, but was never completely satisfied with it. Very gradually, and with increasing despair, I came to feel that not only was it not yet right, it was not something that I could ever tinker into shape. So, after months and months of playing around with it and trying to force it to work, I finally realized I had to let it go and jettisoned it.

This was only one of a number of attempts to get that ending right, but it was the longest, the most revised, and the most sustained. I wrote close to a thousand pages of possible endings before finally stumbling onto the third section as it currently stands, the version with Post-its, which I'm very happy with.

The excerpt that I have given here is a little more than a quarter of that third section, taken from the beginning. It follows Rudd on his trip from Utah into El Paso and over the Mexican border, and is based on notes from a bus trip I took. The beginning, which breaks into a kind of evasive first person, was meant to set up something later in the third section more so than as a metafictional gesture, though of course it's both.

The final quarter or so of section three (not included here) was something that I used, in much different form, for the ending of one of my stories, "Grottor." It belongs there more than it ever did with this story. There are also some pages in the middle of the third section talking about a wall with teeth embedded in it. These pages ended up being important for my story "The Body Politic," which originally appeared in Black Clock 9.

I.

As far as I have been able to ascertain—and at this point my understanding of Rudd grows temporarily dim—he travelled the first few miles on foot. Just as he had done as a boy, he passed the cemetery his father was buried in, his feet beginning to ache as he walked out along State Route 89, along the shoulder where the gravel was fine, almost powdery. Hardly himself, but this time no policeman to pick him up and direct him along his way. It must have taken two, perhaps three, hours to walk to Springville, coming over the hill and down past the drive-in, past the grocery store, the town hall, and then back out of town again, the houses thinning into gardens and then to larger fields. A gradual curve and a run upslope to the four sorry streets of Mapleton, then more fields, only fields for a time. And then, walking or hitching rides as he could, a trudge up into the mountains, perhaps staying for as long as he could on the dirt road that ran beside the river and then scrambling up the hillside to the highway above. Slowly winding up the mountain, turning right and downslope to level ground and past the remnants of Thistle, flooded out several years before when the dam burst: houses still visible at the bottom of the water, the hillside a slide of mud, the bark stripped off the older trees. An old Cadillac smashed athwart a now-dead oak. Past nearby farms and ranches, through Birdseye and Fairview, Mount Pleasant and other misnomers. Then Ephraim—college town, county seat, more turkeys living there than humans (even counting the human dead)—sleeping one night or perhaps two or perhaps none at all in the tall dry grass edging the road's shoulder. Drinking alkaline-heavy water from horsepumps or rainbirds, or from the river when there was a river, or from the bathroom taps of gas stations. Food as he could beg it or fruit stolen from orchards or plain and simple fasting, *The Lord's Gift of Hunger*, as his mother used to call it before she decided she was done being his mother.

It makes a good enough story, explains enough that we can go on. Yet perhaps it happened another way. Perhaps it was plain and easy, with little hardship—picked up almost immediately by a Snow college student just finished with a weekend spent with her boyfriend in Provo, coming back to Ephraim for Monday's classes, alone or with friends, in a white Ford van, in a red Dodge Mustang, fill in the details.

Or perhaps a trucker—though less common on Route 89 than I-5, there were still more than a few, and a few surely willing to risk giving a ride to a young and potentially deranged man.

Or more likely a farmer or a rancher, a series of ranchers or farmers, each one willing to give Rudd a lift down the road to the end of their spread, either for the

temporary company or because they were cautious about letting anyone walk the edge of their land. Perhaps to the end of their acreage or even farther, far enough to find a cup of coffee, if he, Mormon but not Mormon, was drinking coffee by that time. And then more walking, seven dusty miles from Ephraim to Manti.

In Manti, the Mormon temple on the town's edge, but also, in the middle of town, a polygamist splinter group in a downtown storefront, *Church of the Firstborn*, an eagle with widespread wings painted in gold on the window glass. Here, there are scattered memories, like emblems, some of them perhaps even real, gaps between. Knowing Rudd, knowing in particular Rudd's fascination for his self-murdered bigamous father, I can imagine a sojourn for a time in Manti, among the Firstborn, perhaps living closely with them, groomed for participation in their enterprise— though as a rule, they're much keener on recruiting women. He is given a room in the back of someone's house, allowed to sleep in the garage, allowed a few weeks on someone's couch in exchange for helping with the garden or reslatting the shed out back. A job is arranged for him—perhaps shoveling manure at the turkey farms seven miles north, back in Ephraim. He commutes each day with a passel of polygamists in the wooden slat-sided bed of an old Chevy. He is encouraged to stay, a daughter is offered to entice him into the faith and either he accepts and then reneges or never accepts at all. But in any case, he soon gives all up and is moving south again, down toward Mexico, in search of his half-brother.

I could make all that up, generate a life around it, provide *dramatic moments*, show *development*, suggest *change* and by so doing work around to some sort of *epiphany* and ultimately *salvation*, make from the raw material that is Rudd a moral tale that seems relevant and significant. It would be a good story, but it would have nothing to do with the truth. The truth is, Rudd is, for more than a few months, largely absent from himself. He just simply isn't *there*, is only occasionally present to a degree which will engrave itself upon his memory. But for the most part, his memory retains no more than a series of scattered objects, detached from their worlds. Only seldom is there a cohesive instance, a cohesive day. From which one might gather that Rudd is in fact falling apart. When in fact the opposite is the case. He is just beginning to come together again.

I'll tell it like he would want me to do, tell it not too far slant from how the story has been told so far. Which is to say, as if objectively, but cycled through a skull, the supposed neutrality hardly neutral at all, hardly even a conceit. What one sees is not always what is there, but what the skull perceives. Reality is subsidiary to

perception. I will give his bits and pieces, forgo the attempts to postulate between the gaps, offer his version of the world. For who am I to do otherwise?

II.

Consciousness came back to him in fits and starts, a knowledge that he existed coming some time before an awareness of the world around him. He was, he came to realize, in some sort of small terminal, in a small waiting room, the walls of a white plaster streaked with dust. He felt groggy. In one of his hands was a filthy paper sleeve. There was blood on the back of his knuckles and his clothing was rank with sweat. He parted the sleeve to find a bus ticket tucked inside. *Price, UT*, it said, under point of origin, *El Paso, TX* under destination.

He stood and stumbled the perimeter of the waiting room until he found a bathroom. Inside, he regarded his face in the polished tin sheet that served as a mirror, saw a man that looked for all intents and purposes like a bearded version of himself, despite pocks in the tin whorling the face.

He washed the blood off the back of his hands, washed his face as well. The hair on his chin and jaw felt strange. Taking off his shirt, he splashed water onto his chest, his arms, dried himself with paper towels. He blocked the drain with a wadded paper towel, washed his shirt as best he could with the powdered soap from the dispenser. Wringing the shirt out, he flapped it about in the air to dry.

Eventually, he put the damp shirt back on, went back into the waiting room. There was a ticket window in one wall, a middle-aged woman in it, hair dyed a pale yellow. She was reading a paperback, her glasses on a chain.

"Excuse me," he said to her. "Can you tell me, is this Texas?"

"You already asked me that," she said, without looking up. "It's not."

"Could you tell me then, is this Price?"

"You already asked me that too."

He stood looking at her. "I did?" he said.

"A while ago," she said. She tucked her index finger between the pages, folded the book closed around it. She looked at him over the top rim of her glasses, head still bent down. "You don't remember?"

"I don't remember what you told me."

"Look, mister," she said, "first you come buy a ticket off me and then ten minutes later you're back to ask what town this is? When you just bought the damn

ticket? And then ten minutes after that you're back asking the same question all over again? What's wrong with you?"

"So, this is Price, is it?"

"I want you to go sit in your chair," she said, rising from her own chair and bringing her face closer to the glass. "Go back over and sit and wait for the bus to come. I don't want you coming over here again."

He went back to where he had been sitting. There was, he realized, a canvas bag under the seat. Pulling it out, he placed it on the chair next to him. Perhaps it was his, he thought. He looked around to see if anyone was watching him. Nobody was. He unzipped it.

Inside, a pile of clothing he did not recognize as his own. A wristwatch, which he took out and put on his wrist. His driver's license, which he put in his pants pocket. An eelskin wallet, empty, the lining torn out of it. A new road map of Mexico. *I'm going to Mexico, apparently*, Rudd thought. *Lael is there.* At the bottom of the bag, a loose wedding ring, a single solitaire—*Lyndi*, he remembered, *Where's Lyndi?*

Zipping the bag back up, he went to the pay phone, picked up the receiver. He searched his pockets for change, found none. He dialed collect.

"Lyndi," he said, when she accepted charges. "Hi. Why aren't you here?"

"I want you to tell me where you are," said Lyndi.

He looked around at the blank walls of the waiting room. There were no signs. There was a bus now outside, its driver standing beside it, lighting a cigarette. He could hear faintly, he now realized, the throb of its engine through the door.

"Price, I think."

"Price," she said. "Why?"

"I don't know," he said, still looking at the bus. He could not tell where it was going. He looked at his wristwatch but the time didn't seem right to him. He looked at the station clock, above the ticket window, and found that it gave a different time entirely.

"Listen to me, Rudd," she said. "Rudd? Where have you been the last few months?"

"Has it been months?" he said. "That long?"

"There's something I need to ask you," she said. "Something serious. Not over the phone. I need you to come home. Do you think you can do that?"

He did not know what she was talking about. How had it been to be married

to her, he wondered, and why had he left? There was something wrong with him, she was saying, which might be true, but how would she know what and then what to do about it?

Was he still there? she was asking. *Was he?*

"No," he said.

"No?" she said. "No what?"

"I can't come there," he said. He watched the driver finish his cigarette, blunt the butt against the sole of his shoe. He stretched, then climbed up the stairs and into the bus.

"Why not?" said Lyndi.

"I'm out of money."

"Are you calling because you're out of money?" she asked. "Stay there," she said. "I'll send someone to help you."

"Lyndi," he said, staring at the bus. "I have to go. Lael's waiting."

"What?" she said, her voice shrill. "Lael? Rudd, where are you going?"

He let the receiver fall and shouldering the bag went out the waiting room doors, into the blare of sun beyond.

The land was drying up, the soil grown sandy. He pressed his forehead against the bus window, felt at once the air conditioning blowing up alongside the window and the way the glass was heated by the sun outside. He saw two small white crosses to the side of the road, almost hidden in sage. The unfurled tread of a tire, flopped atop the corrugated strip of blacktop meant to wake drivers drifting off the road. Posts topped with white and yellow reflectors, metal, holes all the way up. Mile markers, telephone poles. The corrugated strip gone and replaced by fine gravel a yard wide, soon taken over by weeds. He licked his lips. *Frequent high winds*, a sign read. A running plain wire fence, two barbed top wires. He followed the fence mentally, its regular rhythm, until suddenly it turned a right angle and veered away, uphill.

They stopped at a rest area and he got out, looked at the map, listened to the weather report (hot, dry) coming from a hidden speaker. He went into the bathroom, was confronted by a burnished steel mirror with three bullet holes in it, flies turning on its surface. He heard the bus start outside, hurried to climb aboard, made his way down the aisle, squeezing past a smiling man and back into his seat. They started back up, slowly merging onto the highway.

A small metal silo with the roof punched in, the word *Sioux* on the side. *Fuel 24 Hours*. A tumbledown, abandoned barn. A just harvested field, bare except for circles of uncut grain around a series of telephone poles cutting diagonally across the field. A Volvo, passing on the right, on the shoulder, with two bikes on its roof. A twenty-foot Pace Arrow pulling a Subaru. Tractor-trailers of all kinds. The road creased with drizzle-lines of tar, to fill old cracks. The blur of an empty antifreeze jug, left half-crushed on the roadside. Giant wheeled watering machines, some straight lines of pipe with wheels between, others anchored in the middle to turn an acres-wide circle. Hay covered in billowing white plastic, a ramshackle plank fence, *Next Exit 7 Miles*, a distant radio tower.

He closed his eyes, slowly opening them again to follow the dip and rise of the telephone wires outside. The man in the seat next to him reached out, touched his arm.

"Can I ask what you're looking at?" the man asked.

Rudd squirmed around in his seat. The man was heavy-set and slightly puffy, his hair slicked back, his cheeks full and cherubic. He was wearing a shirt with pearl buttons, the word *Repent* embroidered over one of the pockets.

"Do you want the window?" asked Rudd.

The man shook his head. "Just desert, right?"

Rudd nodded.

The man nodded back, stuck his hand out. It took Rudd a moment to realize the man intended for him to shake it. "Bud," said the man. "Bud Henry."

"Rudd," said Rudd.

"Where are you heading?" Bud asked.

Rudd took out his ticket, looked at it. "It says El Paso."

"El Paso's home," said Budd. "I'm just back from the minister's conference."

It took a minute to register. Rudd nodded, nervously smiled.

"We got drunk on the spirit," Bud volunteered. "We were weaving about feeling His power. He's like electricity."

"I grew up Mormon myself," said Rudd.

The man grinned eagerly, smiled. "We're all God's children, more or less. Do you mind if I ask a question or so, Rod?"

"Umm," said Rudd.

"Rodney, do you have a personal relationship with Jesus Christ our Lord and Savior?"

"Who?"

"If you have to ask, it means the answer is no. Rodney, I want to share something with you."

"No," Rudd said quickly. "I mean, I do have one. I'm just a little hard of hearing."

Bud broke into smiles. "That's good," he said. "That's just beautiful. Will you pray with me, brother?"

"Pray with you?"

The man started to bow his head, reached out for Rudd's hand.

"Come on," the man said. "I can teach you. Don't be shy."

"I'm praying to Jesus right now," Rudd claimed. "I'm always praying to him in my heart. I don't need to pray aloud. My whole life is a prayer."

"Let's shout our thanks to the Lord," said the man, forcibly taking Rudd's hand. "Let's shout it out."

"But I don't want to shout it out," said Rudd, and when the man began with his *Praise Jesus* and his *Holy Jesus* and *Strike me Lord*, Rudd turned to face the window again. His face felt hot and he realized he was sweating. It was like being in Church again, but worse—in Church there was none of this hard sell, no loud shoutings. But like Church there was a script. If you didn't say the lines they wanted you to say, the script went on as if you had said them anyway.

Bud suddenly had his eyes open. "Could you feel it?" he asked. "The power of God coursing through my hand and into you like electricity? My hand's a live wire for God."

Rudd shook his head, trying to extricate his hand.

"That's what God feels like," Bud said. "Praise be to Him."

Rudd shook his hand free, turned away.

"How can you turn away from his goodness?" Bud asked, hurt. "How can you turn your back on God?" The man muttered a few more phrases of exclamation, then said, "God is telling me, Rod, that I should start a bus ministry. That I should right from this minute forward occupy the buses and search out lost souls. God wants you to help."

"I'm sorry," Rudd said. "But—"

"If you can't ride the bus and spread the word you can give support for those who can," said Bud Henry.

"I don't have any money," said Rudd.

"What you give will come back to you tenfold," said Bud. "The wealth goes straight to Jesus in souls. God be my witness."

Somehow Rudd forced himself to stop listening. Eventually the man stood, crossed the aisle, sat on the other side of the bus next to a man wearing a tan Stetson.

"Have you embraced Jesus Christ our Lord?" Rudd heard Bud Henry ask.

An orange moving van on the side of the highway, its emergency signal flashing, a man motionless in front of it, staring at the hood. A plastic bag blown against a fence. The sound of a truck gearing down. A mile marker creased and leaning. The telephone poles no longer simple crosses but like two crosses sharing a common bar. *Valdez for Senate* on a fence, hay baled and scattered through the field behind it. A man in a cowboy hat and a wife beater, carrying a stack of hubcaps under one arm. A dog in the shadow beneath an overpass, tongue lolling. Tire skid marks, shattered glass. A tangle of dead wood. He felt lightheaded from lack of food. A burning field on the roadside, a horse trailer in the middle of a field and surrounded by horses. Sagebrush, some of it dry and dead. Sunflowers, scraggly trees, strange rock formations, unearthly. A boat in the middle of a field. Coming up over a rise and the mountains suddenly rearing up blue to the Southwest. A chipmunk darting across the road and under the tires. Muddy arroyo, *Flowers of Christ Church*, combines, clouds corrugating the sky, billboard for *Alfalfa Cubes*, more mountains now. Two horses standing side to side for the heat, hawks circling overhead. Across the aisle, Bud Henry praying.

At Clines Corners, New Mexico, they stopped for a while, the driver forcing them all out, urging them toward the café. *Does Jesus have any money he can loan me?* Rudd wanted to ask Bud Henry, but Bud stayed beside the man in the Stetson all the way onto the wooden porch, Jesusing him. Rudd followed at a little distance, went through the glass doors and into the vestibule, an incongruent aluminum add-on. He went into the building proper, checked a series of telephone coin-return slots for change, found nothing.

"Sit anywhere," a waitress in a light brown blouse told him. "I'll get to you as soon as I can."

"I don't have any money," Rudd said, softly, but she was already pouring someone's coffee without having heard.

He wandered around the café and then, once people began to look at him, went back outside. He walked along the retro-wooden porch edging the café and the

general store associated with it, down past the gas pumps, around the corner. There was a gas station just around the corner, a little off the road, no cars at it, apparently closed though it looked mostly new. He started down the hill and toward it.

Between the pumps and the station itself were low piles of something that looked like pale dirt or sun-whitened manure, a smell coming off it. He came through the grass and down the hill. The piles seemed to be glistening. The lights were off inside the building. It wasn't until he was within a few feet of the piles that he realized they weren't dirt or manure at all but thousands of pale brown beetles, each pile a wavering and slowly moving mound. He wondered what, if anything, lay beneath. Careful to watch his feet, he picked his way back up the hill.

He awoke to the aching of his stomach, hungry, the vibration of the bus coming through his head from where it rested against the window. From the corner of his eye, he could see a landscape gone slant, a strange and tainted blur of desert. He watched it ooze past.

When they reached the outskirts of El Paso, he sat fully up. "Here it is," he could hear Bud Henry saying in the back. "That's my town!"

They passed a car with a devastated vinyl roof, the torn bits fluttering. A chipped ceramic Rottweiler with real puppies in the front yard of a small house. The yards of the houses were pale dirt or white and red rock, a few grass plots here and there. They passed two tree-like shrubs next to the side of a building, their tops cut flat, the wall above them filthy where the tops used to be.

They pulled in beside the station and Rudd joined the queue to get off. He went into the station long enough to see a woman holding a 3-year-old boy. She was petite with a careful pageboy haircut, penny loafers, wearing jeans and a red-and-white striped shirt, its sleeves carefully rolled up and creased over. She seemed entirely normal except she was wearing gauze all over her face, patches of it stained and sticky and yellow. The child kept reaching for the gauze and she kept gently pushing his hand away. Shocked, Rudd turned about and started out of the station in the first direction he turned. Only later did he realize that he had left his bag on the bus, but by the time he doubled back, the bus was gone.

He found a rescue mission that gave him a coupon he cashed in down the street for thin vegetable soup in a paper cup. He ate greedily at first, until his stomach began to ache in a different way. Sitting down on the edge of the curb, he sipped at the soup

slowly until it was gone. *This will help your body*, the priest had said when he handed him the coupon. *You must let God help your soul.*

"Do you have a coupon for that too?" Rudd had been tempted to ask.

It was hot. He left the cup crumpled on the curb and walked down crowded streets to a small square park bounded by black ironwork, diagonal paths cutting an X through it, as if canceling it out. He followed one path through and then moved along the perimeter to reach the other path, finally coming to rest on a bench beside which lay a man covered in newspaper.

"Which way to the border?" Rudd asked him.

The pile of newspaper didn't answer him. Rudd stayed on the bench regarding it, watching the wind ruffle it slightly. He could see the red of a stocking cap, a pale elbow, the tip of a boot.

"Hey," he said. "I'm asking you a question."

He stood and pushed at the man with the side of his foot, the newspapers spilling away to reveal more newspapers beneath, these ones stained with blood. He pushed again and the newspapers across the face crumpled back to reveal the cap pulled down to cover the eyes and hooked under the nose, the mouth open and the skin around it pulled back tight to reveal a set of yellowed teeth.

He set out south, asked along the way until someone stopped long enough to tell him where to cross the border. The streets before the border were a sort of no-man's land of scattered shops, signs mostly in Spanish, progressive dilapidation, then a canal strung to either side with barbed wire. On the other side, the roads were rutted and sometimes just dirt, the houses of a different character entirely. A wide cement bridge crossed the canal. Northbound, monitoring the traffic coming up from Mexico, was U.S. customs with booths to check cars and a path for pedestrians to follow into a narrow bare room and then out the other side. Going south there was next to nothing for pedestrians, only a little plywood booth at the end of the bridge, an old turnstile in front of it. He watched a group of American businessmen stop at the booth and then pass through the turnstile. He started across the bridge. There was a metal plate and a slot, he saw, in the front portion of the booth. Like a ticket window. He slowed, let a mother and child pass through, watched each of them drop a quarter through the slot. Looking straight ahead, he tried to follow them through, but the turnstile locked up.

He took the few steps back to the booth. Behind wooden bars, the paint flaking off them, was a guard wearing some kind of uniform. People were going around Rudd, dropping the money through the slot and sliding through the turnstile. "What?" Rudd said.

The guard pulled himself out of his chair, pointed to a yellowed paper taped outside the window.

"Twenty-five cents," he said, accent thick, too loud. "One quarter."

"I already put in a quarter," Rudd said.

"You lying," he said. "Go home."

"I don't have a quarter."

The guard brought his face close to the bars. He looked right and left, still taking money as it passed through the slot, putting it into a bucket beside him. "What you got," the guard asked.

"Nothing," Rudd said.

"You got something."

Rudd reached into his pockets, pulled them inside out, stood back so the man could see how empty they were.

"You watch," the guard said, reaching out to grab his wrist.

"That's worth a lot more than a quarter."

"I don't give no change. You want to go through, no?"

Rudd took the watch from his wrist, examined it, shook his head.

"Hokay, hokay," the guard said. "Just give the *pila eléctrica*."

"The what?"

"*Batería*. You know, all closed in the watch. Makes to go."

"The battery."

The guard nodded impatiently. "Go way and take it out and push it just as a coin."

Rudd walked back to the edge of the booth and squatted, turning the band inside out to expose the watchback. He split one of his thumbnails trying to pry the back off, finally succeed in working the back free with the edge of his front teeth. He held the metal disk in his mouth a moment, spat it into his hand.

Inside, the watch was a mess of circuits, the battery a smooth circle with a cross stamped on the back of it. He knocked the watch against his palm until the battery popped out. Holding it between his lips, he put the watch together again, slipped it over his wrist. He looked at the face. 2:43. At the window, he slid the

battery through the slot. The guard picked it up, held it to one eye, then motioned him through.

He clicked through the turnstile, took the last few steps on the bridge and then into the town, past a policeman standing with his arms crossed. He moved on and into the street. He walked down a little, past taximen grouped at the first corner, calling him and smiling, one holding a tattered advertisement for *Girls Girls Girls—XXX—Se Hable Ingles—She speak English*. "We go?" he said, pushing the paper toward Rudd's face. He shook his head, kept walking.

The street itself was dirty, strewn with garbage, the asphalt of a rough grade and irregular, cracked, stained in places with a white chemical residue of some sort. He went past t-shirt shops, souvenir shops, a bar, a window hung with bled and plucked chickens, their severed heads scattered on the floor below them, around a drain. More English signs in those few streets than in the streets just to the American side of the border. He crossed to the other side of the street, looked through a doorway at what seemed a nearly deserted indoor market, kept on.

He avoided the taximen at the corner, fewer than the first corner, more paunched, more eager and swaggering in their attempts for his attentions. "Taxi? Taxi?" one kept saying, following him up the street until he was forced to duck into the nearest open door, which proved a bar.

Señor? said the bartender. There were fans spinning dimly near the ceiling, above the lights, pushing smoke around. A few of the other patrons looked up briefly, went back to their drinks. Through the glass door behind him, Rudd could see the taximan standing, smoking a cigarette.

"Beer," Rudd said. "*Cerveza.*"

The bartender nodded. "Beer," he said. He had turned to take a glass from the runners when Rudd realized he hadn't any money. He looked at his watch, 2:43, something was wrong. He considered trying to draw the bartender's attention again, but instead moved quickly for the door.

He opened the door, thought he heard a shout from behind him, from the bartender. He walked quickly past the taximan who was already crushing his cigarette out against the side of the building and calling "My friend, my friend," the d's at the word's end hardly vocalized.

It is important, he told himself, *not to look back.*

He stepped off the curb, wound around a taxicab, slapped its body loudly to keep it from backing over him. A policeman at the next corner pushed himself off the

wall, stared at him. Rudd looked down, kept on. He came to the edge of a gallery, a sign with a crude picture of a bus beside it, an American couple waiting beside it, speaking loudly in English.

A block ahead, the street ended in a building of some sort. He turned down the mid-block alley, followed it in past piles of moldering newspapers and glossies as asphalt gave way to dirt. The wall was stained with blood. He passed an open peeling door through which he saw three fat men playing cards. He walked on through a scattering of broken glass and eggshells. He heard a voice call out behind him. He did not turn around, walked faster through dirt-caked garbage, along a cinderblock fence spread with flat spiderwebs or perhaps just cobwebs.

"*Amigo*," he heard. "My fren'."

He came out of the alley onto a larger street, looked about as people stepped around him, then followed the street up, the road winding roughly south.

"Stop," said the voice behind him, a subtle "e" breathed before the "s": *Estop*. The voice was closer now. "*Amigo, por favor.*"

Feeling safer on the larger street, he broke his stride, looked behind him. It was a boy a little younger than himself, who broke into a smile when he saw Rudd turn.

"Yes, yes," he said, pronouncing the "y" as "dj." But then, when Rudd turned away and kept walking, he said, as if in great despair, "No, my friend, no!"

Rudd kept up the hill, the voice slowly gaining on him until it was just over his shoulder. He stopped suddenly, spun around.

"What do you want?" Rudd asked.

The boy lifted his hands, shook his head. "*Amigo!*" he said cheerily and too loud. Then pointed to himself.

"I don't have any money," said Rudd as the hill leveled out. "No *dinero*," he said, turning his pockets inside out and shaking them. "You won't get anything off me."

The boy's face returned to a pained expression, a look of disgust. Rudd looked at his watch. 2:43.

"*No lo necesito*," the boy said.

"What does that mean?" asked Rudd.

The boy took hold of Rudd's shirt, tugged at it. "*Ven, ven,*" he said.

Rudd shook the hand off, kept walking, faster now. The boy kept following. "Leave me alone!" Rudd shouted.

The boy smiled, showing nearly all of his teeth. "*Amigo!*" he said. "My fren'."

He crossed the top of the hill, the road turning to dirt and splitting in two, each curving through clumps of houses, the boy's breath in his ear.

"To where you go?" asked the boy.

"South," Rudd said. He shook him off, starting down one of the paths, the dirt crumbling a little under his feet. There was a squeal behind him and he turned to see the boy coming quickly at him, a short knife in the boy's hand and sliding toward his throat, the boy's face shadowing over, darkness already on its way.

geoff nicholson
THE LOST NICHOLSONS

geoff nicholson

The first magazine ever to accept a piece of my fiction was Bananas, an English "literary tabloid" founded by the novelist Emma Tennant, and in it she published work by the likes of J.G. Ballard, Angela Carter, Heathcote Williams and Harold Pinter, all of whom I idolized. There was nowhere I'd rather have been published.

I submitted a story titled "Troy Carter Pulls It Off," a genre-bending, noirish, "speculative fiction" pastiche, and soon got a letter back, though not from Emma Tennant herself, saying the story had been accepted for publication. Yes, this was so long ago that editors still communicated by letter.

I didn't know it at the time but things recently had changed at Bananas. Tennant had sold the magazine to a woman named Abigail Mozley who, according to later rumor, bought it because she wanted to sleep with J.G. Ballard. Cynics argued that if you wanted to sleep with J.G. Ballard all you had to do was buy a single copy of Bananas, but this was, of course, a very cheap shot.

On the day of publication I went to the bookshop of London's Institute of Contemporary Arts, one of the few places I knew that sold Bananas, and I bought a copy of "my" issue, hot off the press. I sat on the grass across the street, thumbed though the magazine; and my story wasn't there. I was confused, and bitterly disappointed, but somehow not entirely surprised. It had seemed too good to be true.

A few days later another letter came, this time from Mozley, explaining that she was new to this whole editing and publishing game, and she'd miscalculated the pagination. She had too much material and so my story and a couple of others had been left out. The tone was casual and unapologetic, there certainly was no suggestion that my story would appear in a later issue, and it didn't. I'm sure a different author would have tracked down the editor, berated and denounced her, but I knew it wouldn't have done me any good, and somehow I intuited that this was how things went for writers in the world of literary magazines. If you couldn't handle the rejection, you were in the wrong game.

Before I began to write this piece, I was absolutely sure I had a copy of "Troy Carter Pulls It Off" somewhere in the Nicholson Archive (i.e. in one of the boxes of files

in the junk room), but long and increasingly desperate searches have failed to find it. My memory of the story is now patchy. I know it takes place entirely in the office of Troy Carter, who is a counter-cultural detective-cum-secret agent type (the resemblance to Jerry Cornelius might just possibly have been considered an homage).

A femme fatale arrives and reports that her husband, named John America, has gone missing. She shows Carter a Polaroid of a man on a beach, wearing stars and stripes swimming trunks. "This is my husband," she says. "No, no," says Carter, because that's the kind of guy he is, "this is just a photograph of your husband." The interview goes on longer than most would want, until Carter accepts the case, and the last line runs, "And so Troy Carter went off to look for America."

The story now seems as lost as any piece of Nicholson is ever likely to be. I'm not saying this is necessarily a bad thing.

After the (quote, unquote) success of my novel Bleeding London, *I found myself living in New York with a new girlfriend and the foundations of a brand new life. Naturally I spent most of my time feeling adrift, alienated and utterly lost.*

I had lived in London for more than twenty years, and Bleeding London *utilized all my experience and knowledge of the city's eccentricities and dark corners. Inevitably I had no such knowledge of New York, though I was eager to acquire some, and of course I had to justify my existence as a writer, so I began a novel titled* Wasting New York, *featuring a hero who had moved to New York from London and spent most of his time feeling adrift, alienated and utterly lost. I didn't want to make the hero a writer so I made him a photographer, which in retrospect I think was a poor idea and a way of frustrating the reader: Verbal descriptions of photographs are never enough.*

Still, the notion was that, as a photographer, the hero had a reason to explore the streets of New York, just as I was doing, mostly Brooklyn and Manhattan. I was intrigued by the grid system, the numbered and lettered streets and avenues, something unknown in Britain. I lived in Park Slope at the corner of Seventh and Seventh. The grid seemed to be imposing order on a city that might otherwise be utter chaos, though occasionally I wondered if the rigidity of structure somehow encouraged certain citizens to express their own chaotic natures. This seemed like promising material, something that had long been a "recurring theme" in my writing.

The final component of the novel was alcohol. In New York I'd discovered a taste for the martini, a drink not unknown in England but not easy to find, and regarded there

as a fancy and highfalutin thing, really only available in places that called themselves cocktail bars. (Things have changed a little since then, but not a whole lot.) The idea that you could go into any New York neighborhood bar and not be laughed at when you ordered one seemed to me the height of American metropolitan sophistication. The fact that the martini also had the capacity to knock me sideways and transform both my consciousness and the world was part of the attraction too.

Well, how would a writer combine these elements into a novel that anybody would actually want to read? I have absolutely no idea. My agent liked the book, and he was not a man who told lies about these things, but he just couldn't find any publisher on either side of the Atlantic who showed any interest in it. Sometimes you just have to let it go.

I haven't dared reread the whole novel. There's a lot of disagreeable sex (by turns chaotic and programmatic), and a Paul Austerish subplot: characters pursuing characters who are themselves pursuing other characters, which today doesn't seem a very good idea even when Auster does it. But I did look again at the first chapter and it really doesn't strike me as so terrible. It reads like the promising opening of a novel—just not the one I wrote nor ever now intend to.

New York: Beauty, Order, Convenience

Perhaps somebody had told Jack about the summers in New York. Perhaps they'd described the wet heat, the sodden horse blanket of humidity that crushed you on the streets, perhaps they'd mentioned its weight, its density, its capacity to provoke crippling enervation. Perhaps they had. People had given him a lot of advice before he came to New York from London, and most of it he'd instantly forgotten, so yes, just possibly somebody had mentioned the heat. But he's absolutely damn sure nobody had ever told him about the apocalyptic storms that broke right on five thirty, as the streets were filling with the rush hour, when the sky turned grey as rat fur, and the lightning exploded and the thunder broke, not just rattling the plate glass windows in the stores and offices, but seeming to shake the girders and the cast iron buildings, the very paving slabs under your feet. And then the rain would power down in sheets and cables of water that sent people running for cover, diving into subway entrances, fighting for cabs, or as in his own case, slouching into the nearest anonymous corner bar.

He's pretty sure he hasn't been here before but he can't be absolutely certain.

After a while they all start to look alike; a long dark thin room, a tin ceiling, some wood paneling that may not be quite as cheap as it looks, then raked rows of backlit liquor bottles, like a miniature glass skyline. It's cooler here than in the street, but not much; a couple of overhead fans churn the air languidly. He looks in the mirror behind the bar and sees his own reflection. He thinks he looks OK. He's not stupid enough to think he looks like a native, like one of the locals, but at least he has the sense that he doesn't look completely, ridiculously out of place, that he doesn't look like a rube or a hick, or worst of all—like a tourist; and that's important to him, that's the whole point; assimilation, blending in.

People have told him he could do more with his Englishness in this city, make it work for him, convince people that he's something special, something engagingly alien: witty, sarcastic, well-bred, a bit of an aristocrat. He's seen other Englishmen performing that act, but he finds it downright offensive. He wouldn't demean himself that way. That's not what he's here for.

He plants himself on a bar stool and after a professionally considered delay, the barman pads over to ask what he's drinking. The barman is a tough, wiry old guy; someone you wouldn't want to tangle with, but a man who breaks up fights rather than starts them. There's something worn and deflated about his heavy, white face, although a set of improbably smooth, gleaming false teeth shines out through a narrow crescent of a mouth. This is a man who laughs a lot, though not necessarily at the same things you do.

"A gin martini," Jack says.

The barman says, "What kind of gin?"

"Whatever," says Jack.

"Olives?"

"Sure."

"Anything else I should know?"

"Make it the way you always make it."

The barman nods. He respects a drinker who lets him do things his own way. He respects a man who respects him. Jack watches carefully as the martini gets made. It's not a matter of keeping an eye on things, of looking to find fault, it's more that he likes to watch the infinite, minute variations; if and how the barman chills the glass, how much or how little vermouth, how long it gets shaken for and in what time signature. There must be some bartender somewhere in New York who stirs rather than shakes, but Jack has yet to meet him.

When he first arrived in New York Jack decided he'd be a drinker of Manhattans; whisky, vermouth, bitters and a maraschino cherry. It seemed appropriate, it seemed like the only possibility, a way of engaging thoroughly with the city. But then he decided that maybe it was too glib, too obvious, and that in fact it was only the name that was appropriate, not the drink itself. The whisky was OK because it was strong and fierce, and the bitters seemed to fit well enough, and maybe the vermouth was more or less OK given the Italian influence in New York. But the cherry? No, that didn't work at all. New York just wasn't a maraschino kind of a place. And anyway, he found the whisky disagreed with him, made him sick, left him with mean, wretched hangovers. So he has made the martini his drink of choice; the silver bullet, a gigantic slug of cold gin with the merest hint of vermouth and dilution; something to drive away the summer.

As he works, the barman tells an old joke. "So these two guys are walking down the street and they see two dogs doing it doggie style on somebody's lawn, and the first guy says, 'My wife never lets me do it to her like that,' and his friend says, 'You should give her a couple of martinis. After that she'll do anything.' So the guy says he'll give it a try. Next time they meet up the friend asks, 'So, did the martinis work?' and the guy says, 'Yeah, but you were way off on your numbers. I had to give her three martinis before she'd even get naked on the lawn'."

Jack smiles thinly. He's heard it before. He's heard them all. That's what it's like when you're involved in some serious martini research. The barman looks a little disappointed at the lack of reaction as he places the glass on the paper napkin in front of Jack. The drink sits there looking chilled and metallic and infinitely promising, condensation misting the sides of the conical chalice, liquid right up to the very rim, forming a meniscus, so it has to be lifted carefully and seriously if it's not to be slopped and spilled. You can't be slapdash, you can't just knock it back, however much you might want to.

Jack likes these moments of sobriety and clarity, the moment before it all starts. He sits there, a man content with rituals that are profoundly though not uniquely his own; the glass, the alcohol, the olive, the raw transforming rush as the coldness of the gin kicks in, makes the world cooler and more blurred and reassuringly distant. There are those who find solace in the bottom of a glass, but not Jack. He finds it in the top, in that first icy, liquid blast.

Sometimes he thinks it was a simple matter of geography that made him come to New York, the way the streets are laid out, the grid system, the "Commissioners'

Plan" of 1811, the imposition of streets and avenues without regard to topology, designed—if you believe what Commissioners tell you—to bring "beauty, order and convenience" to the city. These are not three words that he'd once have thought of using to describe New York, but now he sees how it makes sense, and this is also what his bar hopping and martini drinking will bring him.

He has been measuring out the city, not in coffee spoons but in martini glasses. There has been nothing too systematic about it, and he knows that his measurements exist on no agreed or easily explicable scale. He is not a completist. He has no need to go to every bar, to every district. He won't be heading up to Harlem to see how the brothers do things. He won't be going up to the two hundreds in some mistaken belief that the difficulty of the journey somehow indicates the importance of the quest, and yet he's certainly been around. He has drunk martinis all over the place, in sports bars and theme bars, in dives and Irish taverns, in neighborhood bars and fancy watering holes, in Alphabet City and Hell's Kitchen and Tribeca and Gramercy Park.

He is exploring the limits of the city, and also of the drink, and no doubt of himself. He likes the martini because it is so simple, so specific, yet not incapable of variation. Dry or drier, clean or dirty, the Black Dog, the Gibson. And yet the beast remains the same: you're still drinking a martini. These are variations within the form, not *of* the form. But once you start adding white chocolate liqueur or Benedictine or green Chartreuse you no longer have a martini at all…you have…well if you have to have it spelled out you'll never get it at all.

Some of the martinis he's consumed on his travels have not been good—too warm or too watery—but most have been just fine in that they've been cold and strong and got the job done, and some have even been great, imbued with that extra something, whatever it is; but they could always have been better. So what's he looking for? Perfection? The perfect martini? Well, he'd definitely settle for that.

That's why he didn't instruct the barman. You can't tell the guy how to make the perfect martini, because then it becomes a question of how well he can follow instructions. He has to be able to do it by himself, by instinct. Perfection has to just happen.

He has trained himself to sit at the bar, a thing he never did back in England. At home he sought out corner tables, places where he could have his back to the wall, where the room played out like a diorama, but here he's learned to be a barfly and it suits him. At first he needed props and shields; a book or a newspaper, since a man alone at a bar is a target for other drinkers, for those who want to talk, to confess, to

start an argument. But these days he doesn't worry. He can talk or not talk. He can deal with what comes along. He can defend himself if he needs to, but mostly he doesn't feel the need.

The barman is talking again. "Hear about the woman who complained, 'After three martinis my husband turns into a disgusting animal, and after four I pass out altogether'?"

Jack again feigns amusement, and hears a clap of laughter from a woman sitting a couple of stools away from him. He's not sure if she was there all along or whether she's a new arrival. He hears her say to the barman, "Vodka. Rocks." Once he wouldn't have believed that anybody would ever say anything so terse, so cinematic. He'd have thought they must be quoting or sending themselves up. But no, in New York this is how people really talk. They call each other "buddy." They say, "Take it easy." They say, "I'm outta here." It still sounds strange to him, but no longer entirely improbable. It's a vernacular he understands, even if he'd feel uncomfortable using it.

He looks at her. She's short and pale and skinny and not old; very New York. Her clothes are dark and loose over her body. The lips and eyes are dark too, the hands are long and capable-looking. They fidget with her glass, her sun specs, they touch a packet of cigarettes she has in front of her, although she isn't smoking. She looks tough, and self-sufficient, but in New York that means nothing. It's how you're supposed to look in this city, especially if you're a woman drinking alone in a bar.

He looks and he does that thing that he doesn't want to do, that men can't stop themselves doing to women, however correct they want to be; assessing, judging, deciding if she's attractive, if she's up to his standards. He thinks it's good to have standards, but he still wishes he didn't do this. So he clocks that she's young enough, attractive enough. But enough for what?

"Hey, I like your t-shirt," he says.

He's not lying. It's mostly black but it has a chessboard on it in white, the pieces in position like a chess puzzle.

"Thanks," she says, without enthusiasm. Her voice is deep, sharp, lightly smoked.

"Well," Jack says, "I suppose Manhattan's a bit like a chessboard, isn't it? You know, the way the streets meet at right angles, cut the city up into blocks?"

"Yeah right," she says, the familiar double-positive, "except for the West Village or the Financial District or Tribeca or Chinatown or Inwood. And around the edges you got Roosevelt Drive, Henry Hudson Parkway, East River Drive, and they're

continuous and they curve. And Broadway of course, that sucker just goes wherever it likes. And New York blocks aren't square, they're rectangular. But sure, apart from that, yeah, Manhattan's a lot like a chessboard."

She empties her glass in two unconsidered swallows. His own glass is empty now too. He orders himself another martini. It seems a little early in the game to buy her one. Time for another joke from the barman. As he mixes the drink he asks, "Why's a martini like a woman's breast?"

Jack knows the answer, of course, but he says, "Tell me."

"Because three's too many and one's not enough."

The barman gives a canine laugh and the woman looks up. With a controlled indignation she says, "As a member of the mastectomy community, I find that remark deeply offensive."

Jack can't tell if she's serious, and neither can the bartender. Is she drunk? Is she trying to embarrass them? Is she really a member of the mastectomy community? Is there any such thing? Does she really mean to imply that she's had one, or two, mastectomies?

"No offense," the barman says. "Just a joke."

And Jack can see the barman's having the same thoughts. Is this woman drowning her sorrows for her missing breast or breasts? In which case, are those prosthetics pushing out the front of her chessboard black shirt? Either way the barman feels a need to make amends.

"Have a drink on the house," he says.

She nods, acquiesces, not quite graciously, points her finger at Jack's glass, indicating that she'll have what he's having.

The barman does his stuff again, a little less meticulously this time, Jack notices, and as he hands over the drink he says to the woman, "Why's a martini like a testicle? Think about it. Same answer. Same joke. OK?"

She gives a half-strength smile, then takes up the martini glass and puts it to her mouth and swigs the drink recklessly. Outside it's just about stopped raining. The sidewalks are steaming. People have decided it's time to make a move. Jack looks out, checks his watch. It's still early and he still has nowhere to go.

The barman asks the woman how her martini is and she says, "Just about perfect." But Jack can tell she doesn't mean it.

I've heard people talk about novels that "write themselves." I would certainly like to be the "author" of one of those, even if I don't believe there's really any such thing, but sure, some novels are easier to write than others. In my own case they get harder as I get older. It would be nice to think this was something to do with having increasingly high standards.

I have a novel coming out in 2014. Depending on how you do the calculation it's been somewhere between six and nine years in the making. The title is The City Under the Skin, *though it's been called a lot of other things along the way. Creatively the writing has been arduous, frustrating and painful. On the business end there has been a new agent, a new publisher, and two new editors, one of whom quit the company in the middle of the editing process (not my fault, honest).*

If you're looking for an easy description, I suppose the novel is a "literary thriller." Literature I'm pretty comfortable with; the thrills were harder to get right. Endless rewrites and new drafts were required, often changing the basic clockwork of the novel so that characters did things for plausible reasons, not simply to satisfy the clockwork. Consequently characters came and went, sometimes fusing with others, regularly changing name, age, gender and ethnicity. And of course many plotlines, scenes and sometimes whole sections were ditched along the way, simply because they didn't "work."

However, one section that everybody agreed did work was the one below: A group of geeky urban explorers take our heroine on a voyage through the city's underworld. It was a good idea. We all liked Alastair and Sachin, we loved Dimitri, and we were pretty keen on the iron maidens as a plot device. I just couldn't find a way to fit them all in with the rest of the novel. They too hit the cutting room floor: darlings that had to be killed. The novel certainly makes more sense in their absence, but even so, I miss them.

Nerds Is Us

They were nerds. Lindy Vargas saw this, decided this, from a couple of blocks away. They were waiting for her in the appointed place at the appointed hour, "dusk" (their terminology and insistence) at the corner of Hope Street and Tenth, on the edge of downtown, on a patch of unpaved waste ground that was doing temporary service as a parking lot.

There were three of them—she'd been expecting more—three awkward young guys, standing in a loose huddle, backs to the world, all bad posture, bad skin, bad hair, with something embarrassed yet arrogant in their body language. Two were

wearing camouflage, another was in what looked like a Second World War flying suit complete with goggles, and they were all wearing what might be considered utility belts. One of the two in camouflage was lanky to the point of chemical imbalance, and carried a vast backpack, various tools, ropes and bungee cords strapped across his body, and atop it all a red miner's helmet with a big light on the front. This, she knew, was Dimitri, her contact, her guide, the second in command, and also in a vague manner of speaking, in some way that she was already regretting, her date.

Lindy had met Dimitri online. How else does anybody ever meet anybody? She'd been trawling for information rather than social connection but when she saw on his profile that his main interest was "urban exploration" she emailed him, "Tell me more," and he replied, "Y'know, creative trespass—penetrating forbidden zones—psychogeography—investigating abandoned structures—factories, asylums, silos, secret facilities, underground lacunae, vaults, bomb shelters, bunkers, ghost stations. Founding member of OWL. Good guys. Sometimes we take guests. Wanna come?" Her reply, "You bet."

It wasn't that easy however. Only after a series of further emails that seemed designed to test her faith, resolve and possibly gullibility, was she at last about to meet up with Dimitri and his big city spelunkers, and suddenly this seemed an utterly doomed and frankly juvenile enterprise. She didn't even know what OWL stood for: Dimitri omitted, declined to tell her. As an acronym it seemed oddly feeble. She tried guessing what the letters might stand for, but it seemed pointless, and maybe they didn't stand for anything at all, maybe it was just a way of saying they were wise and nocturnal. Anyway, it was all seeming totally ridiculous now, and Dimitri, who'd come over as droll and flirtatious online, now seemed to be just a callow, self-conscious doofus. Still, worse was to come. There was a coded exchange to be negotiated.

They saw her, pretended not to, intensified their boyish chatter. Now, as directed and specified, she had to establish her bona fides. She thought she might have trouble keeping a straight face. She walked up to the group, their glances shot off in all directions to avoid eye contact, and she addressed Dimitri, "I'm looking for Utopia Street."

She knew she'd receive one of two possible replies. If he said, "Well, you don't want to start from here," then it was all off: That was a signal that it was time to abort. Frankly she didn't expect it. Why would they be hanging about on the street corner if they wanted to abort the expedition?

The other answer, the one she got was, "Aren't we all?" which meant the coast was clear, that it was time for her to deliver her next line, "Why? Is it so hard to find?"

She'd been given a list of possible answers, and she'd just about memorized what she was supposed to respond in each case, but there were gaps in her knowledge, and when Dimitri said, "It's even harder to lose," she was relieved because this was another good answer, the easy one, and it required her to say nothing whatsoever. Things were going well. Dimitri looked her up and down, though there seemed to be something less than coded about this, and then he produced a pack of cigarettes, "Here, have you tried this brand?"

"No," she said deliberately, "I haven't tried that brand. Won't it stunt my growth?"

"The world will stunt your growth."

He smiled shyly; maybe he found this absurd too. He said, "My name's Dimitri," which of course she already knew, but hold on, this was still part of the code. And then she said, "I'm Lindy Vargas," and then he had to say, "You don't look like a Lindy Vargas," and she said, "What does a Lindy Vargas look like?" and OK, that was it, thank God, the last line, the signal that she was in. Even so, it wasn't as if anything like normal relations then ensued.

"This is Sachin," said Dimitri, and introduced a short, greasy-haired, greasy-skinned young guy wearing an Iron Maiden t-shirt under his camouflage jacket, though not a garish, graphic one showing Eddie the Head in a state of zombie decomposition, but a simple design with just the band's name stretched across his boy boobs.

"Nice to, to meet you," Sachin said.

"And this is Alastair. He's our fearless leader."

Well yes, Alastair did look like the genetic prize of the team, though these things were comparative. He was the wearer of the flying suit and goggles, of average build, regular of feature, only a little chinless. He nodded his head in a way that was less a greeting than a show of supercilious tolerance, and said, "We're going to have to blindfold you."

"Why?" said Lindy.

She feared just for a moment that this might be some hideous initiation rite, or worse, that she'd find herself later, in some veiled and vicious part of the city, in an alley, naked and violated by nerds, and who would have sympathy, who would say that she could have expected anything else?

"I'm not going to end up naked and violated in some alley, am I?" she said.

The guys looked genuinely shocked at the suggestion; hurt too.

"We're just being careful," said Dimitri. "We don't know you. You could be an infiltrator, an investigative reporter, a cop. We're prepared to trust you but only to a limited extent."

"But I have to trust you completely?"

"If you don't trust us then why did you come?"

She had to shrug that one away.

"Also, it's fun blindfolding girls," said Sachin.

"Shut up Sachin," said Dimitri, and Sachin shut up and descended into damp, suppressed sniggering.

"OK, so blindfold me already."

With some embarrassment and awkwardness the boys put a blindfold on her; actually a thick woolen scarf, folded over three times to form a scratchy, hairy pad that covered her eyes, her nose, and most of her mouth. She breathed as best she could. They spun her round a few times, not to the point of dizziness but enough that she could no longer tell north from south from east from west, couldn't tell Tenth from Hope. And then someone, Dimitri she guessed, took her limply by the arm and they began walking; not very fast and not very far, but she was surprised how hard it was to judge distance when there were no visual clues; hard to gauge the shape of the route too. She knew she wasn't being led in a straight line but it was hard to tell how far she was straying from the straight and narrow.

And then there were stairs, a downward flight of twenty-two steps—she counted them—and as she descended she became aware of a rising coldness and the smell of dilute ammonia and maybe spoiled meat, and also aware of a thick roaring sound that grew louder with each step. She thought at first that it sounded like water, as if she were entering the mouth of a gigantic seashell, but then it seemed more like traffic or machines. And suddenly there was a boom, something muted and muffled, a sound from deep inside the earth.

"What's that?" she said.

"Just an explosion," said Alastair.

"What?"

"They're blasting tunnels for the new subway line," Dimitri explained. "You hear it a lot down here. It's nothing to worry about."

Lindy hoped she could believe that.

"And I still say we should get our hands on some of those explosives," said

Alastair, and it sounded like he was reviving an old argument, one that Dimitri and Sachin didn't want to repeat, at least not here and now.

They were at the bottom of the stairs, on level, wet ground, the soles of Lindy Vargas's boots slipped, and then someone pulled the scarf off her, and she saw she was in a deep place, not precisely subterranean since there was an opening overhead with a grating: Velvety evening light filtered down through a mesh of bars and barbed wire. She was in a circular concrete space, like a deep bear pit, perhaps part of a storm drain, perhaps something more specialized. Around her on all sides were tunnel mouths, nondescript, arched, not wide, each leading into undefined and indistinguishable varieties of receding darkness.

"Pick a tunnel," said Dimitri. "Any tunnel."

She didn't really pick, just nodded at the one directly in front of her.

"Good choice," said Dimitri, but she assumed he'd have said that whichever she'd picked.

He switched on his helmet lamp and the other guys produced powerful flashlights from belts and backpacks. Lindy was acutely aware that they didn't offer her one. They started walking.

"Welcome to my world," said Alastair, as though addressing a large and distant audience. "Welcome to the city that never sleeps very well, the big mandrake, *la ville hallucinaire*. I know what you're thinking. You're asking yourself, why do we do it? Why do we explore these dark, dangerous, potentially lethal places?"

Lindy Vargas wasn't really thinking that, but she sensed that he really did want to explain himself, that he had a prepared speech, perhaps a mission statement.

"We're not just here for self-gratification," said Alastair. "We're here because we want to do good. Suppose somebody gets lost down here, suppose little Timmy wanders into the void, tumbles down a manhole, becomes disoriented and hysterical, then we sweep into action, we go in and find the kid, bring him out to a grateful and admiring world, though of course we won't stand there lapping up the admiration; we'll keep our anonymity. We'll be gone before they know it."

"You know, like the Lone Ranger," Dimitri added, and Lindy was pleased that he didn't wholly share Alastair's humorless subterranean worldview.

Alastair had said all this as they progressed through a grim, low-ceilinged stretch of tunnel. Perhaps a bit of patter was necessary to disguise the dullness of the first part of the journey.

"Or put it another way," said Alastair, "suppose terrorists have planted

something somewhere under the city and they want a cool billion or they'll blow it up, or even if they don't want money, if they're just bent on suicidal destruction, nihilists, a death cult, well you know, who are they going to call?"

"You?"

"Yes. Well no, not directly, because they don't even know we exist and they definitely don't have our phone number, which is how we like it, so we'd have to call them. And we would. Offering our services."

"Don't they have their own people?"

As she said this she was aware she didn't know who "they" were and she felt equally sketchy about Alastair's notion of "we." Was it just the three of them, or were there others; fellow travelers, reservists, sleeper cells? The guys emitted a group laugh; knowing, superior, just this side of creepy.

"They don't have a clue what's going on down here," said Dimitri. "They don't even have maps."

"They don't?"

"Nobody has maps."

"Not even you?"

Dimitri looked at her with cool, yet admiring suspicion: She was asking all the right questions.

"It depends what you mean by a map," Alastair said. "There's nothing drawn or set down, nothing you could fold up and put in your pocket. But we know our way around. We've got the knowledge. Mental maps. In here." He pointed a long finger toward his own forehead, then waved it around more generally, to concede that his fellow conspirators shared at least some of it.

"And when the worst happens," said Dimitri, "it'll be really good to know our way around down here."

"What's the worst that can happen?" Lindy Vargas asked disingenuously.

"We don't know that yet. But if we need to, we can withdraw, sink into the ground, hide out down here for years if necessary."

It seemed to Lindy that this was just stunted, post-apocalyptic, post-adolescent, survivalist fantasy, some curious hybridization of *Journey to the Center of the Earth, Phantom of the Opera, Terminator,* and no doubt myriad other nerd-based sources that she'd never heard of. Of course she didn't say that aloud. She didn't want to alienate these lunatics, not while she was down here with them, while they were leading her God knows where.

She noticed a series of scars running along the walls of the tunnel, deep horizontal gouges, as though something solid and metallic, perhaps a piece of machinery barely narrow enough to get through the tunnel, had been dragged this way. The marks continued for a few hundred yards, stopped, and were replaced by a horizontal line of spray-painted arrows, each perhaps six feet long, pointing onward and forward, in a variety of colors—silver, white, yellow, sky blue—colors that repeated though not in any predictable sequence.

"See," said Dimitri, "we're not the only people who come down here."

"You mean you didn't paint these?"

Dimitri shot her a desiccating look.

"We hate graffiti," said Alastair. "If we ever found anybody down here spraying graffiti, well, well…."

"We don't know what we'd do," Dimitri finished the sentence for him, then said to Lindy, "Hey, we're about to come to a good part."

They turned a corner and the tunnel changed direction, ran away in a long, broad curve. The boys shone their flashlights along the wall, revealing more graffiti, though they didn't seem to disapprove of these so much. They were more like cave paintings, petroglyphs, Aboriginal art. There were no arrows here but there were crosses, some resembling plus signs, some like x's, some Christian or Celtic, Maltese and iron. There were squares, circles, triangles, hexagrams; sometimes one inside another. There were swastikas and a bull's eye, a rising sun, half moons, stars, hearts, crescents, a lightning flash, a skull and crossbones; far more than she could quickly identify or would subsequently be able to remember.

"In general," Alastair started again, "we don't really believe in climaxes, in photo opportunities, perfect viewpoints. We're not sightseers. The journey is the destination. The road to heaven is heaven. But since you're a newbie down here, we understand that you might need a journey's end."

"Might I?" said Lindy Vargas.

Alastair wasn't wrong. She accepted that padding about in damp, dim light, in tunnels, looking at wall art, or whatever the hell it was, didn't really constitute a great night out. So yes, she would like to see some wonder, some "highlight" that made it all worthwhile; but she wasn't getting her hopes up.

"Here, around this corner. You might want to take a few deep breaths, though not too deep, there are some noxious things down here."

She realized they were standing near a deep, apse-shaped concrete alcove.

It had been invisible because the boys had been assiduously pointing their flashlights away from it. Now, in an unexpected display of coordination, they fused their light beams together. In the unsteady, dappled spray of light she saw, what, she wasn't sure, something human-sized and human-shaped, standing upright, but not human. At first she thought it might be a garden statue, then a robot, then a mummy, maybe a life-size Russian doll.

Dimitri approached the thing, a man about to demonstrate a piece of equipment. The thing was indeed human-shaped, a container; a person or body could have fit easily inside, as if it might be a vertically arranged sarcophagus, though more barrel-shaped, and it looked Germanic rather than Egyptian, made of wood with metal bands and fittings.

Dimitri fiddled with a latch on the front, and the thing opened up. It had hinged panels that separated like two doors, to reveal the body-sized cavity inside. Lindy Vargas was glad there was nothing in there, that it hadn't opened onto something fleshy or rotting or skeletal, but she saw that the inside was not absolutely empty. Spikes and blades clustered in various parts of the interior, mounted on its inner surfaces. If a human body were inside this thing and the doors closed, the spikes would impale the body, slash it open, aiming specifically for the eyes, throat and genitals.

"You know what this is, now?" Dimitri asked.

"Yes," said Lindy Vargas cautiously. "Isn't it a, what do you call it?" Then she looked at Sachin, "Is it an iron maiden?"

"Very good," said Dimitri. "An iron maiden is exactly what it is."

Sachin preened. His chest puffed inside his t-shirt.

"What?" said Lindy Vargas. "You guys dragged this thing down here for some role playing?"

Alastair was, or pretended to be, offended.

"Of course we didn't," he said. "We found it here, exactly as it is. The world's scary enough without us having to introduce props."

She was glad he said that, glad that this wasn't some elaborate and facetious Grand Guignol designed to impress and scare girls.

"But it *is* a prop, isn't it?" she said with more certainty than she felt. "It isn't a genuine medieval torture antique, is it? It's from a chamber of horrors or a magic show or something, right?"

"Well," said Dimitri, "we can't vouch for its provenance, but an iron maiden is what an iron maiden does. We haven't tried it out, if that's what you mean."

Lindy Vargas moved closer, pressed a fingertip against one of the internal spikes. Yes, it was sharp and solid enough, and it didn't fold or retract the way she'd expect a magic prop would, but that might have been all part of the illusion. Perhaps there was a hidden button or trigger that made them fold.

"Those strange, dark stains in there, they're probably not blood," said Alastair. "But we're not sure. The fact is, we don't know what it is. We don't know who brought it here or why or when. And we're not sure that it matters. It's a mystery. We like mysteries. Not all mysteries need to be solved."

"OK," said Lindy Vargas. "You got me. It's not a bad journey's end."

"It's not quite the end," said Dimitri.

The flashlights dispersed a little, carved a bigger circle of light and moved to the right so that Lindy now saw what had been in the shadows all along, another device, similar but much smaller, another iron maiden but this one was child-sized. She wanted to laugh. This was so horrible, so crass. There was something so simple and grotesque about the simultaneous torture of mother and child; that's how she saw it, though she wasn't sure why. It could just as easily have been father and child, uncle and niece, grandfather and granddaughter, man and dwarf (the iron munchkin), though none of this would make it much better.

She shuddered and then, despite willing herself not to, she began to weep. It wasn't loud or dramatic, but it was more than enough to throw the guys into agonies of embarrassment. This was worse than they could ever have imagined.

Alastair wasn't any better prepared to handle it than the other two, but at least, as the leader, he could say, "OK, we go back now." And then in a stage whisper to Dimitri, "I told you this was a very, very bad idea."

janet fitch
A SHRINE FOR UNBELIEVERS

janet fitch

My *2006 novel* Paint It Black—*set in the punk Eighties in Los Angeles—began as a three-voiced book: art model and rocker Josie Tyrell, troubled art-student Michael— then called Mitch—Faraday, and his mother Meredith, a concert pianist, daughter of a Viennese composer. As the book evolved it became Josie's story alone, beginning with Michael's suicide, but in the original version the book moved backwards and forwards in time, and section II let Mitch speak for himself. At this early stage, the novel was called* A Shrine for Unbelievers.

Mitch Faraday sat in the student infirmary next to Ulricke, the German night nurse, watching her knit. Exhaustion was what was written on his chart, exhaustion was what they always wrote at Hahvad, whether it was suicide, overdose, assault or theft or speaking in tongues. Exhaustion of life's possibility before the age of consent. He hadn't slept for a week this time. Sat up with Ulricke all night as she twisted yarn between her chubby fingers like Fate, twisting and impaling the slender strand, chaining soft grayness into a net to catch falling souls. Ricke, blessed among women. Rocking in her whitewashed chair to the rhythm of a heartbeat. Mitch wished he could crawl into her plump lap and let her rock him, maybe he could sleep then, and trust the darkness, but he kept seeing the peas in the dining hall that were too many different colors; he had been reading Nabokov, the story about the Siamese Twins, and the peas and the stench of cooking and a boy talking about a girl he'd slept with who had a third nipple, the boy's yellow teeth, suddenly he couldn't bear it anymore. Ricke was the only human being left.

Her son Max had been killed last year in a car accident. Sixteen years old, he had just started driving. *Had been.* It seemed impossible that such a thing could happen, the way a person could be here, have such wonderful ideas, that forward impulse called life, and then *had been.* Mitch had spent much of his career at Hahvad hiding in the infirmary, had gotten to know Max quite well. *Exhaustion,* read the

notes to his professors, excusing the unfinished papers, the missed deadlines, the examinations unprepared. He'd liked Max, Max was funny, he could look at people and tell you what animal they were. For example, his mother was a hamster, and the girl in the purple room, the botched suicide, was a badger. Mitch's History of Consciousness professor, C.H.R. Lewis, was a wildebeest.

"So what am I?" Mitch had asked.

"No way," Max said. "You'll be pissed."

"Promise," Mitch said.

"Siamese cat," Max said.

Mitch laughed, embarrassed, but instantly seeing himself in Max's eyes. *Siamese cat.* Of course he was. Staring quizzically, slightly cross-eyed, from the white damask couch, wondering about life out the window.

Ricke rocked and knit, she'd been a child in Germany during the war, she remembered the bombs, and hiding in shelters, and eating bread baked with sawdust when the wheat ran out. Her parents were probably Nazis, but what right had he to question her, she was his only link, the only human being with an ounce of tenderness in this godforsaken place, this machine for grinding the mind into smaller and smaller chunks, until it passed through the sieve and emerged with a diploma. Sawdust. *We are the hollow men, headpiece filled with straw.* Dazzling the world with our vacancy.

He was cold. He was always cold in Cambridge. The snow fell down out the window, like a silence imposed; *shh*, it said, *shhh and don't tell.* It was his third year at Hahvad, and he would never get used to the cold; it moved through your body as if skin had not yet been invented, it curled up in your bones and rattled them like an Arctic Milt Jackson playing the skeletal vibes. He could never get warm here. He dreamed of a California under skies of electric blue, fields of yellow mustard and circling hawks golden in the sun. He begged his mother, his father, each year to let him come home, go to UCLA, but the name Hahvad was sweeter than any son, Isaac sacrificed to Lord Crimson.

Ricke would never have sacrificed Max to the maw of Hahvad, thrown him to the Moloch of class narcissism. He sketched her, plump and blonde, with her rimless glasses, it was the only thing he could do with his hands now. If only the fates were so kind with their yarn, their needles clicking, if only they were so kind. He could weep every time she touched his hair, asked if there was anything she could do. He couldn't go to class anymore, what did Derrida and Malraux have to do with anything, words,

he had changed his major a third time and still, meaning faded like ink in sunlight, there was no substance anywhere, no beauty. The other students' petty enthusiasms, their gross competitiveness, spotty faces and the skim of acid on top of the coffee, the colors of the peas, Nabokov and the twins—and why was it so cold? Though they'd been giving him Vitamin B shots, it didn't do a damn bit of good. He shivered in the Hudson's Bay blanket he wore wrapped around him like a Manhassett.

"College isn't everything," Ulricke said, purling his fate. "You should take the year off. Go lie on a beach. Hitchhike through Europe. Life is short."

"I can't," Mitch said. "My parents won't let me." Hahvad. He could never explain to his father about the peas, and how his roommate Thomas cut his fingernails onto the floor so he had to walk on the clippings, and how the sense bled out of his essays and they died as he wrote them, and about Valentina. Her fur hat tickling his cheek. He thought about all the others here at the infirmary. All the same, sons and daughters of privilege. Like so many priceless vases with hidden, intrinsic flaws, which gave way when you tried to fill them. The girls starving themselves to death, searching for perfection. Boys opening up their veins, looking for truth in the red red blood. He was just so cold. He had been saving the sleeping pills Ricke gave him, and took them all at once on a snowy March evening. He felt bad doing it, she had just lost Max last year, but she could knit herself another son. Thomas had come that morning to tell him Valentina was marrying the gnu from History of Consciousness. He had to stop the cold.

He spent the rest of the spring lying by the pool in a patch of sun at his mother's house in L.A., wrapped in a blanket, listening to the distant drone of a gardener's leaf blower and the voluble mockingbirds, the honey smell of the jasmine, studying the irregular geometries of blue between the branches of the old oak, like a puzzle he should know the answer to. It would be on the test.

Finally, his mother told him she couldn't have it anymore, he would have to do something or go back to Westwood, where he had been placed as a teenager *for your own good*, to weed the director's flowerbed, sit in group therapy, eat the mismatched peas. Be raped in his bed by his coke addict roommate.

"You have to do something," she said. "I don't care what it is, just as long as you go."

Faced with a return to Westwood, he roused himself. His mother had brochures, she had done her research. He leafed through the clippings she dumped

in his lap, calendars, three-fold mailers. Tree People, Friends of the River, the Sierra Club. String quartets brokered through the Chamber Music society. Writing classes at UCLA. New Hope Home for the Aged visitors program. Nurse's helper at Children's Hospital. He had to laugh. Exactly what a depressed person should do. Help Others. Appreciate Nature. Delve into the Arts. He could tell she'd broken out her Parents of Troubled Children handbook. She was good at this. Taking care of her flawed child, turning his cracks to the wall. Just don't turn around, no one will see.

So that afternoon, Meredith drove him down dilapidated Alvarado Blvd. to the formal modern colonnade of the art college, and stood watching as he registered for life drawing, watercolor, and the Artist's Book. *Art therapy.* He'd rolled down his window on the way home, and she'd rolled it back up again from the driver's panel, shocked that he might allow some street person to reach in, to touch them.

The airy life drawing studio, third row, left-hand seat proved a surprising refuge, even if only a precarious one. He liked the way the light fell on the models when he sat on the left, it fell obliquely, slicing the form rather than sculpting it. He was in a cubistic mood, dislocated, he wanted to break things apart and put them together in absurd ways. Today there had been the young man, Fred, who owned a great deal of black body hair, his penis long and thick, framed in that mass of black curls like a slug in moss. His joints were pronounced and angular, as if every bone in his body had been broken and badly reset. It was this quality Mitch accented in his charcoal renderings, the aftermath of torture.

He sketched Margie, a fiery red-haired woman with a belly scored by stretch marks. He had never before seen a body which had given birth, not directly, not presented simply and as a matter of fact. His mother was never nude, always discreetly veiled in nightgowns which only revealed her outlines, embarrassingly rich when she leaned over to kiss him goodnight. The way she smelled and her breasts spilled out toward him, a deluge of flesh.

It was not Margie's squarish breasts which interested him, her huge pale nipples, or her red pubic wisps. It was her belly that fascinated him, shriveled with stretch marks from pregnancies. He loved her easy way with it, easy and self-assured, as if the body was there for use, not for stylization. He liked her without knowing any more about her than her name, imagined the children who rode inside, how many might there have been. She had given life, right there, right there on the body was the proof. He wondered if Meredith had such scars from his birth. He shuddered to

think of it, and yet, wished she had the courage of this woman, to show her belly, to say, in effect, yes, *I am a woman who bore children, my useful body. I am not untouched by life, by time.* Meredith never aged. When they traveled, she liked to pretend he was her lover and not her son, having coffee in a café in the late-morning sun, reading *Le Figaro*, plucking a feather from his hair.

The model's children—there had to have been several—had stretched and luxuriated in the generosity of her belly, left their red welts, and she wore them without shame. How odd to carry life in your body like that. He would be afraid, he had to admit. Like an alien in one of those horrible movies, which grew inside the hapless crewmember until it broke out, all membranous and writhing, claws and teeth. Women were so brave—even Meredith, who had been knocked out the whole time.

The model moved to the next pose. The longer poses were hard on the older models, he could see how she put her hand to her back, arched to break the tension. He felt sorry for her that at her age, at least thirty, she was doing this for a living. He wished he could just give her some money, but he had learned early in life that no one appreciated being the object of a rich boy's pity.

There were other models—a large black man, soft, smiling, dreadlocked. Mitch was fascinated by the softness of that male form. Herb. And the muscular woman with monumental feet, Debby. He loved those feet. He would have loved to sculpt them in marble, like a Juno in a ruined temple, nothing left but the feet. But today was a lucky day. His favorite model had arrived.

She stepped behind the screen to disrobe, then emerged in her skin. Small and slight, light as a daydream, a tremendous, thoughtless grace about her as she walked barefoot across the small posing stage and climbed onto the stool. He had never seen such a beautiful girl—certainly not at Hahvad. Her hair was bleached platinum blonde, it looked like she cut it herself, the roots and pubic hair by contrast were dark, the large eyes glossy dark. At first, the hair put him off, the blatant falsity of it, but now he was used to it, he decided he liked it very much, it seemed carefree and humorous rather than grotesque, and enhanced the dark eyes. He sketched her fine collarbones, the delicate architecture of her ribs, her legs, so tenderly.

Sometimes she watched the artists, sometimes closed her eyes. She seemed to be humming. He wondered what she was thinking, sitting up there nude in a room of fifteen clothed people. He wondered if she was cold. He wondered if she was hungry.

She looked so young, *farouche, dikii* in the Russian. She didn't seem like a student, there was no curiosity in her eyes, only a simple expectancy. He imagined that for once, here was a girl who was what she appeared to be, nothing behind the mask, there was no mask.

After class he hesitated. He wished he could meet her, talk to her, but he wasn't the kind of boy who went up to girls and introduced himself. It seemed pushy, like *of course you want to know me.* He didn't believe in that. He thought that if people were meant to meet, they would. He believed in a hidden current generating reality, and if it carried you to another person, then it was supposed to happen. If not, there was no sense in trying.

When she came back out from behind the screen where she dressed, her outfit made him smile, a thrift store dress and red cowboy boots. He wanted to tell her how she made him feel, her spine like a string of matched pearls, her unselfconsciousness, but then she was leaving with her purse over her shoulder, and he knew he would not follow her out; *failure of will in a character*, he knew from some long ago writing class, was a serious fault. If he was a character, he would never be a protagonist, only a minor character, the neighbor, a passerby, someone seen on the street. *An attendant lord, one that will do, to swell a progress, start a scene or two.*

He took his sketchbook and walked out past a cluster of other students. Some of them even said goodbye to him, but they lived in some other world, where things happened, where people had lives. Sometimes he tried to talk to them, but it never got beyond a single exchange, a ritual, he was no good at small talk. *Hi, how ya doing?* He never knew what to say. *Fine*, you were supposed to say. But he rebelled at *fine*. He rebelled at rituals. He wanted to know people, down to the very bottom of their souls.

Once, the girl with the diamond-shaped eyeglasses had asked him to come with them, they were all going out for coffee. He wanted to, but then he imagined what it would be like, sitting around with these people, listening to them spout off their ill-considered ideas but unable to correct them, or if he did, that silence falling over the conversation as it did in his seminars at Hahvad. His timing was off in human relations, he never was able to fall into that easy give and take. He made people uneasy. They tried, they smiled, they asked him about himself, but he always said too much or not enough and definitely the wrong thing. He shook his head and said no.

He walked home all the way up from MacArthur Park, taking the hilly residential streets, passing people working on their cars or practicing drums in their

open garages, children riding tricycles on narrow driveways, garage doors open to tightly packed storage, the houses rising up steeply above or dropping down sharply below garage level. It was July, the hot sun coming down, but still cold in the shade. He wore a tweed jacket brown and green, he was still cold, he had never really gotten warm.

He wasn't athletic, but he loved to walk. He could walk ten, twenty miles at a stretch. He did not drive. It was one of his touchstones. Unlike every other redblooded Southern Californian teen, he did not wait breathlessly until he was fifteen and a half and could get his driver's permit. He did not sign up for driver's training in high school. His father offered him lessons from a former racecar driver. Though he would have liked to meet a former racecar driver, he didn't want to learn to drive. He liked taking the bus. He liked to see the people, their faces, hear their conversations. His father bought him a BMW sports car. That was his father's idea of young manhood's fondest desire. A hot sports car to get all the babes.

There was a cooling breeze, stroking the fronds of the palm trees overhead like a comb though a girl's long hair. He picked a tiny lantana blossom, twenty tiny red and orange four-petaled flowers bundled into a single bloom like a Victorian nosegay. It smelled of dust and old shoes, but it was pretty. He stuck it in his buttonhole and smiled at himself, imagining the son his father would have liked to have had, who drove a Beemer and got all the babes. That son played tennis, had a gang of friends who drank orange juice spiked with vodka and carried Trojans in their wallets, laughed at girls they slept with, called them sluts and hogs behind their backs. He knew which sons his father wanted.

His father never got over him hating the car. It wasn't even just the car, it was the whole driving experience, the way you had to pay attention, look through the frame of the windscreen, the radio blathering on, all the people cut off from all the other people in their little boxes. The car wasn't an extension of the person, the person became part of the machine, and he didn't want to be that. He was on strike. He protested. He gave Bartleby's refusal, but of course, his father had never read Bartleby. He couldn't understand Mitch's protest of the television/microwave/two Mercedes life. His father owned a fiber optics company, he had about as much self-awareness as the number four greyhound at a dog race.

Mitch tried to explain it to his father once, in a good moment, during his second scotch. You had a window with Richard Faraday, the Second Scotch Window.

The first wasn't enough, and the third was too much. Mitch explained to his bronzed, tucked and toned silver-haired father, "It's the fixity of the car, don't you see? The politics of transportation."

"All transportation has politics," his father said, gazing out the plate windows of his Newport Beach house, his eyes following the dance of the sailboats as they left the marina, white sails slicing the blue. "You try negotiating with teamsters sometime."

"No, not labor politics," Mitch said. *You idiot*, he thought. "No, politics like physically implied in the structure of the car. You're driving, or you're the passenger, or you're in the back seat, see? The driver's the dictator, the great fascist God—"

"This is an Oedipal thing again?" Richard said.

"It's just a metaphor," Mitch said. He wasn't about to discuss old Siggy F. with Richard Faraday, god forbid.

Chrissie clicked into the room on high-heeled sandals. "Is this like a father-son thing?" She sat down next to his father, one leg tucked under her, ruffled his father's cropped silver hair. She was about twenty-five, small and tan in a white t-shirt and jeans, her blonde hair long and streaked, giving her a palomino effect. She was well-meaning but she loved his father, therefore she was useless as an independent entity.

"Don't talk down to me, matey," Richard said, brushing her off unconsciously without even tossing her a glance. "I know what a fucking metaphor is."

Of course, it wasn't a metaphor but the thing itself. Mitch tried to lower his voice—his father was exceptionally cruel when his voice rose into pre-pubescent registers. "So you're either the Almighty Driver, or else you're the passenger, the Mute Witness. Like, 'shut up, who's driving here?'" It was what his father always said to Chrissie, whenever they went anywhere.

Chrissie concealed a smile, straightening a stack of big books on the coffee table Mitch was sure neither of them had ever opened. *Leonardo. Treasures of the Prado. The Pre-Columbians.*

The ice chimed in his father's glass like music. "Well, that is the truth. Only one person can drive the vehicle at a time, and that's the person wears the pants, either metaphorically or in fact."

It was hopeless, and yet, Mitch wanted him to understand why. What was so distasteful about the red Beemer.

"Oh for Pete's sake," Chrissie said. "Mitch, give it up. He'll never get it."

"What don't I get?" his father snapped at her, and held out his glass. Chrissie

got up and took it to the bar, added new ice, splashed on another two fingers of scotch. His father watched to be sure the ritual was performed correctly, then turned back to Mitch. "I'm going to say it plain and simple, Mitchy, my boy. In this life, the man drives. That's the bottom line. The man drives. You want to be a man, drive the car."

"But I don't. That's what I'm trying to say," Mitch said. "The politics are blatant. Chrissie's just as good a driver as you—"

"Crap," his father said.

"Oh, honestly." Chrissie gave his father the scotch, and instead of sitting back down next to him on the white leather Italian couch, she plopped discouragedly into a plump armchair.

Mitch knew he would be beaten but he needed to go on. He needed his father to understand this if he never understood anything else. "She drives beautifully. But if the Man is around, then she's demoted to Mute Witness." He could feel the tears forming, squeezing his neck. It was the story of their lives. God, the Mute Witness and the Hostage. "And the child sits in back. Children and old people, who don't even get to witness. Who don't even know where they're being taken."

His father had started his third scotch, and his color was up. "So what's the point here? You're giving me a headache."

Now Mitch didn't even know anymore what he was trying to say, he had forgotten, he just knew that his father was losing interest and his red face infuriated him, his Waterford tumbler and his air of unquestioning domination. He had to make his point, if only he could remember... "I'd rather take the bus than inhabit any of those roles, don't you see? On the bus there are sights, real people. People who can't avoid life. Not like us in our Mercedes with the air conditioner going—"

"Each and every one of them would sell his own mother for a Mercedes," his father said. "Who are you kidding."

Just then, the maid came in with a tray of hot hors d'oeuvres, a new maid, he wondered what happened to Evangelina. The woman's eyes flickered, trying not to hear what they were fighting about. Mitch was embarrassed, but his father, who was getting crocked, turned to address her. "He wants to let life touch him. Most of us work our asses off so life will touch us a little less, but my son, the genius, wants to let life punch him in the mouth. Can you believe this?" The woman looked frightened, offering them all some of the cheese puffs she'd made, his father's favorite. "You want

to let life touch you?" Richard said, putting a cheese puff in his mouth. "I'll let life touch you. I'll boot you out onto the freeway some sunny Sunday, and you can see what it feels like to have life run over you like a sixteen-wheeler. You won't last an hour out there, pretty boy. So no more of this crap. You're going to learn to drive that car and that's that. You're a man, and that's what the man does. He drives."

Mitch opened his mouth to say more, but the tears came out, he knew his voice had climbed to the danger level—how could he tell his father he didn't want to be a man, not in the way his father meant, he wanted to be a person, he wanted his father to love him, to understand how he was dying, suffocating.

"Think about girls," his father continued, not one to back off once he had the advantage. "What girl worth a crap would be willing to take the bus on a date, tell me that buddy. Would you, Chrissie? Even if you had the squirmies for old Mitch here, would you go out with him if you had to take the bus? Sit at some filthy bus stop with some homeless guy drooling on you to go out for a hot night on the town?"

Chrissie smiled and shrugged her shoulders apologetically.

"Whaddya say to that, pretty boy Floyd. The market has spoken."

Mitch sat with his head in his hands. Somewhere, there was a girl who wouldn't care. He had to believe that. If he didn't believe that, all was lost.

"You're going to drive that thing, and that's that," his father told him, and planted the keys on the glass tabletop with a drunken whack.

The next day Mitch took the Beemer out and drove it into a parked Lexus two doors down, left it there with the keys in the ignition and his father's information on the Lexus's windshield.

Now, walking home, he crossed Sunset and climbed up into the neighborhood with a view of the reservoir, the great pines rustling overhead, past vacant lots filled with fennel and lupine and walking cliff asters. The little starry flowers on the gangly stems. He stopped to touch one of the innocent blooms. This is reality, he said to himself. This starry flower in his hand. The world behind the world, a tiny rent in the illusion. Somehow it reminded him of the model with the big eyes and the bleached hair. Wildflower.

In front of another house grew donkey tails and fuchsias with their ruffled skirts, like girls in party dresses, organdy and lace. Crossing a polished floor. Cotillion. He was taken there at his mother's bizarre insistence, to try to remedy what she saw as his painful shyness, when it was something else entirely. Twelve-year-old girls in

organdy and lace, their hair fiercely gleaming, the pinkness of their scalps, the little gloved hands in his. The way they stepped without grace or rhythm across the dance floor at the Wilshire Ebell. Pamela Bausch, her white neck, little pearls nestled in the hollow of her throat. He could still see that hollow, the string of pearls looping inside the delicate indentation. He wanted to slide his tongue along the pearls, along the bones and into the secret dip. If only she could have known his passion for her, it would have burnt her to cinders. But all she saw, of course, could have seen, was the gawky twelve-year-old bookish boy so odd he didn't even attend school. He was opaque, a shard from an ancient civilization turned up in a field under the plow, she didn't know the first thing about him and he couldn't begin to explain.

"Faggot," she whispered as she changed partners.

He walked along Coronado Street, densely foliaged, sun-warmed summer jasmine hanging over fences, exuding clouds of impossible sweetness into the air, roseformed succulents clustering along driveways, boys shooting baskets in a driveway with a concentration and intensity as if the losing players would be sacrificed as they had been on the ball courts of Chichen Itza. If only they were. Ka-thunk, ka-thunk.

If only he had been born into a truer place and time. He might have been a Phoenician oarsman, bringing the precious purple dye across the sea to trade in Thebes, the wind in his face. Or a scribe in Alexandria, in the shadow of the great Library, pressing stylus into wax. He could have been an archer in the Queen's army in Palmyra, living in barracks with his comrades, or a craftsman of some kind, a tanner in 15th century Firenze or a goldsmith in Spain under the Moors. He might have kept an inn in Elizabethan England, where the bawdy life overcame even death, tempered by poetry and sweet William of Avon. Europe in the Enlightenment, even the early days of the 20th century. Anywhere but at the butt end of the battered 20th century in the banality of ersatz America.

The climb to his mother's house up the winding streets of Los Feliz finally warmed him, but once he passed through the gates, the yard was surrounded with old trees and again it was cold. He climbed to his room and lay down under the covers of his narrow bed, thinking again of the model with her deerlike dark eyes, her fine bones. The beauty mark on her pubis. He thought about that mark, the neat triangle of her dark pubic hair, a fairy girl but also flesh, how light she would feel in his arms.

Distant traffic and the breeze in the pittosporums wound its way into his fantasy of her. He knew she was different, a girl he could love, not just from afar, but

absolutely. He could be a man with her, he could mean something. He had never found a girl at Hahvad he felt anything like this for, they were all so terrifyingly opinionated and brilliant, sure of themselves, or else shy and analytical. He had come close a couple of times, in this or that dorm room, the sitting next to, the embarrassed looks, hands rubbing up and down his skin, kneading his thighs, the pleading note in the voice. All that wanting. It revolted him, frightened him. He had wanted them so much at a distance, but when they were right there, kissing him, he could not remember what made him desire them. He was nineteen and a virgin. He had wondered if he was queer. He forced himself to look at other boys in his house in the shower room, in case he had missed some sign of desire, but he found the thought of kissing Don Bell or Raymond Swadler, good-looking boys, still left him cold, their spotty asses and crude jokes.

He shuddered to remember the way he brushed off the girls, Naomi Sperling, Heather Vail. He blanched at his own cowardice. He was attracted to their intellect, their wit, their directness, they became friends easily. Naomi wrote to him in Greek. Silvia Cardenas had already finished her first novel, boys were falling all over themselves to walk her from class to class, hear her talk about Neruda and Lorca and Borges.

But he failed when they came too close. It was as if he was a creature who dwelled underground, and they cast too much light. He needed a flickering girl, a shy, fairy girl, who was not her ideas but the thing itself, something of beauty, someone with whom he might pass through the veil of illusion to the true world, not someone with a mind like a scalpel, which she used like an 18th century anatomist, dissecting the dead body, trying to find the soul.

True, he missed Naomi's brilliance, Heather's cynical wit. When he called Silvia, she hung up. He called a few more times, but could never keep her on the line long enough to apologize. He went to see her at the house she was sharing off Brattle Street. She came to the door, wearing a dirty sweater, her hair all lank and stringy. It was snowing, he remembered. It was always snowing. And she said, "Do I know you?"

"Are you joking?" Mitch said. "It's me, Mitch."

"You're a dead man. I see you in the halls, I see a dead man, walking around. You're dead, Mitch. Go somewhere and lie down, won't you?"

In a strange way, he was dead. Girls picked him out from the other boys, drawn to his eyes like Irish fog or his helplessness, his hands, they took him home,

made him herb tea or rubbed his back, they chanted love but he was a ghost, not a man at all, just as his father always said.

He sighed, turned on his back. But with the little model he could be a man, he knew it. Now there was sun, and the girl with her shy charm, the naked delicacy of her bones, did she ever eat? Well he would feed her, he should have thought of that, stop on the way to class, pick up something rare and yet substantial, tantalizing but simple. And books, he could give her Blake, or Malory, he could find a copy of Walter Scott, *Lady of the Lake*. He would make offerings, light candles, perform prostrations, he would prove himself worthy of notice. *All in green went my love riding.*

All in green, the mayfly's transparent wings in his brief summer dance, he could not help but touch himself; seeing her on a rock like the White Rock girl in a picture he found in a magazine and tacked on his wall, gazing into a stream. And he in green with pointed ears, a rustic pipe from which he made exquisite melodies. And she followed him into the forest green, deeper and deeper, until she reached his mossy bower. [18]

Black Clock

diana wagman
BIG SHOES

When I told my agent I was writing a book about clowns, her eyes rolled back in her head. Nobody likes clowns. People are afraid of clowns. Clowns just aren't interesting. I disagreed. I went to the Clown Convention in Las Vegas (at Circus Circus of course). I did a ride-along with a birthday party clown. I took clowning classes. Every clown I met, from the Homeland Security officer to the Leisure World Top Banana, was fascinating to me. Four hundred sixty-seven pages later I had a clown tale. I'd added a magician and a contortionist. I thought it was swell.

My agent had a different opinion. As a matter of fact it was such a different opinion, she didn't want to be my agent anymore. We parted company and I put the clowns in a bottom drawer. Eventually they morphed into my latest novel, The Care and Feeding of Exotic Pets. *The only clown has less than a page of story time. I still love them, my clowns. One day I will write the Great American Clown Novel.*

Coulrophobia is the fear of clowns.

I looked at the children sitting in a semi circle around me. They were not afraid. Their small 9-year-old faces were free of worry, free of blemishes, free of any interest in me at all. They were utterly, totally bored. My orange ringlets, round red nose, and blue painted-on eyelashes were not enough. Nothing I had done so far had worked. I scratched my head, purposely making my wig move back and forth on my forehead. No response. I did a pratfall as I went over to my carpetbag, giving them a good glimpse of my polka-dot bloomers. Two boys offered a lukewarm titter. The birthday girl, Alice, was talking to her friend. Her outfit probably cost more money than I would make all weekend.

A tall boy, older than the rest, had been a pain in my ass for the entire party. He asked my bra size, speculated on the zits underneath my whiteface, and asked if I was a friend of John Wayne Gacy. Then he proceeded to tell the other kids the story of John Wayne Gacy the clown, and the twenty-six dismembered little boys found in his

basement. I had to break character to shut him up. While I dug desperately through my carpetbag of tricks, he stood up, yawned, and then wandered off. I was glad to see him go.

This should have been Freaky Freddy's party but he had never shown. He was an okay clown who did a robot and stand-up comedian kind of thing. Older and more sophisticated kids usually liked his act, but he smoked too much pot and since his boyfriend had left him, his reliability had been suffering. Sheila, the CEO of Clown Town, had called me at the last minute to substitute. It was my third party of the day. I was beat, but I needed the money and goddamn it, I was going to make these rich kids laugh no matter what. I cajoled the birthday girl to come up next to me. She stood up, but then she crossed her arms and looked me up and down with contempt. I was trained to deal with a child's fear, but elementary school cynicism was much, much harder. I grabbed a Happy Birthday crown out of my bag and presented it to her with a ridiculous curtsey. She rolled her eyes, but reached for it. It leapt away from her. She gasped. A reaction, praise the lord. Her friends giggled. She reached again and again the crown jumped out of her hand. It was an old trick, bought for eight bucks at the magic shop, but I did it well. I grinned. Alice was smiling as she tried again and again. Her friends began to laugh and yell suggestions.

Best of all, Alice's mother, Gail, was finally looking happy. This party meant a lot to her, I could tell. Maybe it was the first birthday after the divorce. There wasn't a dad to be seen, no grinning guy standing in the corner taking photos or in the other room watching a basketball game. Gail wasn't wearing a ring. I felt the swell of single mother solidarity. Lacy, my 11-year-old daughter, was at her dad's for the weekend.

Jason came running back into the room. "There's another clown!"

Freddy, I thought, he's not getting paid for this.

"He's in the pool!" Jason continued. "He's in the pool with all his clothes on."

How stoned could Freddy be? I shook my head. "He must've thought this was a swimming party," I said to the kids.

Gail turned to me. Her eyes were wide and terrified. Maybe it was just Freddy's fake hair clogging up the filter that scared her, but she looked stricken.

Spermophobia is the fear of germs.

"Everybody stay here," I said as I handed the birthday girl a bag of balloons. "Magic balloons. Bet you can't blow them up."

Obediently, Alice began handing them out.

I went to Gail. "Which way?"

She plucked at my clown sleeve and led me out. She looked over her shoulder at me. Her hair was long and auburn with a blonde streak in the front. Her nose was aquiline. She reminded me of Lassie, the way she looked and the way she pulled at me, wanting me to do something she could not articulate. Please, Timmy, please.

"It's okay." I resisted the impulse to pat her head.

We walked through the expensively rustic Southwestern-style living room and out to the grassy backyard where tastefully decorated tables were set up for cake eating later. There was a slope to a lower level and a six-foot-tall redwood fence.

"This way," Gail panted.

"I'm right behind you."

The Beverly Hills sunshine was hazy and hot. My huge shoes slapped against the flagstone walk. I followed Gail down the steps and through the gate. There was the swimming pool. Enormous. Blue. Inviting. Or it would have been except that floating in it, face down, was Freaky Freddy.

Hydrophobia is the fear of water. Piscinophobia is the fear of swimming pools.

What the hell? "Freddy," I said aloud as if he was taking a dip. "Freddy!" His neon green hair undulated around his head. His silver lab coat floated on either side like some bizarre kind of water wings. Did he fall in? Didn't he know how to swim? Was he drunk? My confusion tumbled in after him, splashed beside him. Then I realized the red clouds in the water were not his face paint washing away, but his blood.

"Oh my God," Gail wailed. "Oh, oh, oh. Is he dead?"

A chorus of exclamations went up behind me. The kids had followed us after all.

"Dead?"

"Really?"

"Did he drown?

"Let me see!"

I stepped between the body and the kids. "Dial 911," I said to Gail. She was staring at Freddy. I elbowed her. "Do it."

She nodded blankly and pulled her cell phone from her pocket. I tried to herd the kids back into the house. They didn't want to go. My painted smile and pink polka dots were nowhere near as interesting as death. They broke away from me, kept running back to the fence, to the gate, circling the swimming pool. I appealed to Gail but she had the phone to her ear and her eyes on Freddy.

"The pool was supposed to be off limits," she whispered.

As if Freddy had been a wayward birthday party guest.

Finally, the Mexican housekeeper came out and gathered the kids. She refused to take any of their crap, but just as they were trooping back inside, we heard the sirens.

"The police!" Jason shouted. "Cool!"

He took off again for the front yard and the others followed, leaving the housekeeper with her hands on her hips. Flipping privileged kids. I guess cops and ambulances were a novelty to them—as opposed to the kids in my neighborhood. It was the seventy-two-inch TV in the den and the three different birthday cakes that would have stopped my daughter cold.

The paramedics used a pole with a hook on the end to pull Freddy out of the water. They flopped him poolside and he sounded like a wet towel slapping bare skin.

They must do this a lot, I thought, often enough to carry a special tool.

Freddy did not look good. His face paint had worn off in the water leaving his bloated skin yellow as an old bruise. His fingers were swollen until his hands looked like flippers. His mouth hung open, round and moist. His bloodshot eyes bulged. Only forty dead minutes in the water and he was surprisingly fish-like.

I turned away.

Thanatophobia is the fear of death.

The homicide detective sighed as he opened his pad. He was short and bald and African-American. The sun reflected off his caramel-colored head. A beautiful color, I thought, and so smooth, without a single wrinkle.

He looked at me. "I'm Detective Miller. Can I ask you a few questions?"

I wanted to correct him, 'may I,' but I only said, "Of course."

"Are you a friend?"

I glanced down at my costume, then back at Detective Miller. "We worked together."

"For Clown Town?" He didn't crack a smile.

"I'm the Mayor. Freddy was Chief Engineer and Rocket Scientist."

Miller raised his eyebrows.

"We all have titles," I told him. "It was Sheila's idea. She's the CEO, Captain of Entertainment Occurrences."

"Sheila who?"

"Sheila Sherwood." I gave him the address and phone number of Clown Town,

a one-room office over a bakery. "I didn't know Freddy very well," I volunteered, "but I know he just broke up with Rick, his boyfriend. He was really depressed about it."

"You think it was suicide?"

"I don't know."

"I do." The detective closed his book. "He was murdered. Shot in the stomach."

"By whom?"

"Do you know the address of this ex-boyfriend?"

"I actually never met him."

Gail was plucking at my sleeve again. I turned to her.

"Please?" she said. "What do I do?"

"I would definitely drain the pool. Call the pool guy."

"No." She gestured back over her shoulder. "About the children."

"You left them out front?"

"The police are out there."

I sighed. "Call their parents to come get them. I'll stay and play some games or something until they're all picked up." Those kids? I thought again. "No," I said. "I think it's time for television."

Her eyes filled with tears of relief. "Thank you so much."

"Call Jason's mother first. Right away."

She hurried inside. Detective Miller took my name and phone number and gave me his card. I watched them load Freddy onto the stretcher. I said a little silent goodbye to him. Then I headed back through the house to the front yard. Gail had been right; the police were babysitting the children. The kids were gathered around a young officer. He was showing them his nightstick.

"Hey Alice," I walked over to her, "want to try for that crown again?"

She ignored me. They all ignored me. It was over for me. I nudged the handsome cop with the stick. "Oh, man, this is a bummer. Now all the kids will want a dead clown at their party."

He didn't even smile.

It was dark by the time I finally left the mansion and headed across town to my bungalow in the hood. I counted the stars through my car windshield. Nine. Ten. Eleven. I closed my eyes and wished.

Starlight. Starbright. Eleventh star I see tonight.

I never wish on the first star. By the time it appears in the Los Angeles dusk, I know its wishes are used up. Starting on the East Coast and all the way across the

country, people have wished on the night's first star. Therefore I count and then wish on the eleventh star I see. Eleven is my favorite number.

Of course, in L.A., between the smog and the light pollution and the marine layer of haze, eleven stars are not always visible. That just makes it doubly lucky when I actually can make that wish.

Starlight. Starbright. Eleventh star I see tonight. I wish I may, I wish I might, have the wish I wish tonight. I wished that no one else anywhere would ever be murdered. I wished for no more bloody swimming pools, homicide detectives, bloated bodies. I shivered in the car and wished again and again for Lacy to always be safe. Even—or especially—with her father. Then I wished for my little house to be empty and secure when I arrived.

I was almost home. I had a blind date that night. I'd been excited about it earlier but Freddy's murder had definitely dampened my enthusiasm for an unknown man. I was out of milk and I very badly needed a cup of coffee.

There is a Code of Conduct for clowns. We are not supposed to drink, smoke, swear, or flip the bird at another driver in our costumes. We are supposed to stay in character. I am Wiggly Winnie, Mayor of Clown Town. I am sweet and mostly silent. I am clumsy and self-deprecating. I believe in this code. It is an integral part of clowning but I excused myself that night. Normally, I would not have stopped for milk in my alter ego, but then normally, clowns don't show up dead in swimming pools.

I parked at the mini-market two blocks from my house. The new owner, an Asian man, had recently painted the building purple. I wondered if it was a color that had some religious or lucky significance. I slipped my giant shoes back on—I can't drive in my size 16s—and went in.

The owner was behind the counter watching a small black and white television tuned to a Chinese station. He saw me but was too polite to acknowledge my outfit. I went to the back to the refrigerator case. Most of the case was filled with six-packs of beer and malt liquor; milk was not his best seller.

Four boys, *cholos*, came in with shaved heads, baggy khakis, and tight white wife-beaters. They were young and fit, their tattoos like blueberry stains on their smooth skin. They jostled each other. I saw one slip a package of peanut butter crackers in his pants. They looked at me. Their leader, taller than the others and angrily handsome, nodded at me.

"Hey, Clowny."

I nodded back, pint of milk in hand.

"I got some balls you can juggle," one of the other boys said and giggled.

I smiled, laughed a little, thinking it best to acknowledge him, and walked to the counter. They discussed beer, chose their six-pack and came up behind me.

"No beer." The owner shook his head at the boys. "No ID, no beer."

The leader's face grew tight and small. His posse got quiet.

"No beer," the owner said again.

"Yes, beer."

"No."

The boy beside me reached for something in his pocket. I saw his hand with H-A-T-E tattooed across the knuckles.

"I'll buy it," I said.

Everyone looked at me.

"I really feel like a beer tonight. I sure am thirsty." I gave an exaggerated clown wink to the boys. "I am parched, like a dying clown in the desert."

They laughed. The owner relaxed. "Yes. You can buy beer."

I bought the beer and the milk. I walked out and the boys followed me. They were not much older than the kids at the birthday party. They were not old enough to buy beer, but old enough to hurt someone for a six-pack. I handed them the bag. One of them offered me some money.

"No thanks," I said. "Have fun."

The leader reached in the bag and took out my milk. I would have forgotten it.

"Thank you," I said.

Thank you for not killing that man in front of me.

I got back in my car. I waited until they drove away before I started my car. I forgot to take my shoes off and my foot slipped off the clutch and I stalled. Only then did the tears slide down my face and my hands begin to tremble. All of a sudden going home in the dark scared me.

Nyctophobia is the fear of the dark.

I pulled off my red pigtailed wig. I tried to wipe off my makeup with my hands. A car drove by and I hid my painted face. I had to call Sheila. I took out my cell phone and dialed.

Sheila picked up on the first ring and coughed into the phone, her familiar, clotted cough. Then she spoke, "Clown Town." More coughing, deep and wet, and her hoarse voice again, "If you lived here, you'd be calling home."

"Hey, Sheila."

"Oh, Jesus, Winnie. Poor old fucking Freddy."

"You heard?"

"This place was crawling with cops." She grunted and tried to clear the phlegm from her throat. "I said that once in a film. With tears in my eyes. Fifty fucking years ago."

I could hear her breath wheezing through her damaged lungs.

"Fucking Freaky Freddy," she said again. I listened to her take a long drag on her cigarette. I heard her exhale. And cough horribly again into the phone. "Don't worry. I'll pay you double for the death gig."

"Have the cops figured anything out?"

Sheila croaked, which for her was a laugh. "They don't care about some drug-buying clown. He owed a zillion people money. He was late and unreliable and an asshole. Hell, I wanted to shoot him myself half the time."

"Is there someone who can work for me tomorrow?"

"Jesus Christ, Winnie."

"After Freddy, I mean—"

"Mighty late notice, wouldn't you say? What time is your first party?"

"Not until two o'clock. What about Phunny Phil?"

"Booked."

"Cuddly Cathy?"

"Tomorrow's Sunday. Fucking Cuddly Christian Cathy." Sheila snorted, inducing a small fit of coughing. "Don't you give up on me." Sheila's husky voice grew deeper. "Not because of Freddy. Don't let one bad clown ruin the whole carload."

I didn't feel like laughing.

There was a pause and then Sheila said, "Wiggly Winnie, you're my favorite."

"You say that to all the clowns."

"Actually, I don't. You actually bring fucking joy to children everywhere."

Cherophobia is the fear of joy.

"Okay," I said. "Okay. I'll work tomorrow. But I'm wearing a flak jacket under my pinafore."

"Aw, Wiggles, who would want to hurt you?"

I listened to her croak and cough and smoke and cough again as I said goodbye. Plenty of people, I wanted to tell her as I pulled away from the curb and drove the two blocks to my tiny, empty house. Plenty of people hate clowns in general, and me in particular.

Black Clock

michael ventura
TO NAME AND BE NAMED: ELIA KAZAN AND HUAC APRIL 14, 1952

michael ventura

When Greil Marcus was editing 2009's A New Literary History of America, *he asked me to contribute a piece about Elia Kazan's testimony before the House UnAmerican Activities Committee in 1952.*

My word limit was two thousand. Marcus and the superb film historian David Thomson were my editors.

My first submission was five thousand words. Very unprofessional. I'd been carried away by the material.

Marcus and Thomson were gentle about my unprofessionalism, but firm: The word limit was two thousand.

I kicked, but I cut it—not down to two thousand words, however.

Marcus and Thomson cut it more and cut it very well. I was pleased with the result. Sometimes I need a boss.

Their edited version is a better read, but my original and somewhat clunky draft gives a fuller picture of Kazan and of his troubled era.

"Anybody who informs on people is doing something disturbing and even disgusting. It doesn't sit well on anyone's conscience. But at the time I felt a certain way, and I think it has to be judged from the perspective of 1952."
— Elia Kazan to Jeff Young, 1971

On New Year's Day 1952—two weeks before Elia Kazan's first testimony before the House UnAmerican Activities Committee—*The New York Times* ran this headline on page nine: THREE CAMPS TO JAIL SPIES ARE PLANNED IN WEST. In the body of the story the flashy word "spies" was discarded for a more inclusive usage: The camps were intended for "subversive elements of the population."

These camps and their purpose are largely forgotten in discussions of what we now call "the McCarthy Era," named for its prime instigator, the "Red-baiting" Republican senator from Wisconsin, Joseph McCarthy (1908-1957). The camps

go unmentioned in Elia Kazan's autobiography, *A Life,* and Richard Schickel's *Elia Kazan: A Biography*, though both books discuss the McCarthy period at length. Victor S. Navasky's *Naming Names,* widely recognized as a classic on the era, mentions the camps only three times, briefly, with no elaboration. It is fruitless to speculate why commentators across the political spectrum share this particular case of historical amnesia, but if, as Kazan suggests, we are to judge his or anyone's testimony to the House UnAmerican Activities Committee "from the perspective of 1952," we need to remember that in 1952 existence of ready-and-waiting internment camps was common knowledge, especially to those considered "subversive elements of the population."

The Emergency Detention Act was first proposed by self-described liberal senators, all Democrats, as reported in the *New York Times* on September 6, 1950, under the headline, BILL WOULD PERMIT REDS INTERNMENT. Specifically the proposed law would "subject known Communists and others liable to become subversive to concentration camp commitments.... [They] could be interned…[by] a declaration of an internal security emergency by the President and Congress." On September 19, a front-page report in the *Times* elaborated that "Communists and others reasonably suspect would be interned summarily;" the proposed bill aimed "particularly at Communist fellow-travelers," and, the *Times* emphasized, "detentions would be prompt." The camps were passed into law (over President Truman's veto) on September 24, 1950, as Title II of the McCarran "Anti-Communist Law." A *Times* editorial the next day praised the camps as a "strengthening feature" of the McCarran Act that allowed for "summary arrest and detention of probable spies and saboteurs." These "probable" people, so the *Times* reported on October 1, were on "the Attorney General's list, based on secret information, and on no hearings."

Although the *Times* periodically reported on the camps during the next several years, only in the first instance did it use the frightening phrase "concentration camp." Still, its language was fearful enough: "subversive elements," "others *liable* to become subversive," "*reasonably* suspect," "fellow-travelers," "*probable*" spies, their identity determined on "secret information" and "no hearings"—usages both vague and inclusive that clearly meant the camps were intended for anyone the government thought fit to intern during an "emergency" the government was free to define and declare. This was more than enough to make anyone of dissenting opinions nervous if not terrified, especially while the Korean War still raged and the United States and the Soviet Union threatened each other almost daily.

This fearful atmosphere was regularly reinforced by official declaration. For instance, on April 28, 1951, the *Times* quoted FBI director J. Edgar Hoover to the effect that "there were 43,217 Communist Party members in the United States—more than half of them in New York State and most of those in New York City…the government [is] ready to arrest 14,000 of the dangerous Reds on a moment's notice."

On January 13, 1952, the day before Elia Kazan's first HUAC testimony, the *Times* reported that "the Justice Department refused again to disclose the purpose of five prison camps authorized by Congress for handling subversives…. As many as 15,000 persons are believed ticketed for immediate seizure."

Justice's refusal was inexplicable. The purpose of the camps had been detailed on the congressional record and, as we've seen, widely reported. That the camps were a real threat was not in question. It had been just seven years since the release of Japanese-Americans from similar camps, where they'd been deprived of liberty and property—without due process and having broken no laws—for the duration of the Second World War; in fact, as had also been reported, several of the camps that housed these Japanese-Americans had been restored to accommodate the Emergency Detention Act. The camps were the backdrop for anyone having anything to do with "the Committee," as HUAC was universally referred to at the time.

Enter Elia Kazan.

On January 14, 1952, the *New York Times*' front-page headlines included U.N. STUDY PREDICTS WIDER PROSPERITY and REARMING SAPS SCHOOL GAINS AS ROLLS AND COSTS SOAR. British philosopher Bertrand Russell's book, *New Hopes for a Changing World*, was advertised and reviewed. The sports section reported that catcher Roy Campanella, the National League's Most Valuable Player of 1951, re-signed with the Dodgers for a yearlong contract estimated at $25,000. Page two carried, as it did every day, official reports of the fighting in Korea. Such was the news when Elia Kazan met with the Committee in executive (that is, private) session.

Kazan had been in the Communist Party during 1934-36 when working with the Group Theatre, an experimental coalition of artists that produced such radical plays as Clifford Odets' *Waiting for Lefty* and *Awake and Sing!*, works that expressed the problems and aspirations of many during the Depression. After the Second World War, Kazan and Lee Strasberg founded the Actors Studio, while Kazan established

himself as America's premier stage director with era-defining works like Tennessee Williams' *A Streetcar Named Desire* and Arthur Miller's *Death of a Salesman*. Among his films, *Pinky* (1949) was Hollywood's most frank portrayal to date of race prejudice in the South; anti-Semitism was the theme of *Gentleman's Agreement,* which won 1947's Academy Award for Best Picture; and Kazan's film version of *A Streetcar Named Desire* made a star of Marlon Brando. *Viva Zapata!*, again starring Brando, dealt sympathetically but unsparingly with the paradoxes of revolutionary movements; it would be released just weeks after his January 14 testimony. Kazan was, in short, one of the most visible and important American artists of his day and the most prominent yet subpoenaed by HUAC.

What the Committee demanded in its interrogations was that a person confess their own radical activities and "name names"—that is, give the committee the names of anyone else taking part in such activities. Actors and directors who refused to name names were unofficially but efficiently blacklisted from working in their professions, as were those named. In addition, "uncooperative witnesses" and anyone named by cooperative witnesses could assume that they were now on the government's lists of the "reasonably suspect" for whom the Emergency Detention Act was designed.

Many artists whom Kazan had directed were already blacklisted, either through being named or for failing to cooperate—most notably, John Garfield, Sam Jaffe and Anne Revere of *Gentleman's Agreement*; Lee J. Cobb of *Death of a Salesman*; Zero Mostel of *Panic in the Streets*; and Kim Hunter of *A Streetcar Named Desire*. Kazan well knew what was at stake.

And he no doubt had followed the testimonies and fortunes of other artists questioned by the Committee. Actors Gary Cooper, Ronald Reagan and Robert Taylor cooperated cheerfully and enthusiastically. Larry Parks, briefly a star for his lead role in *The Jolson Story,* again and again begged during his testimony not to be forced to name names; again and again he gave in and named, bitterly protesting and pitifully ashamed as he did so. The writer Ring Lardner, Jr., refused to name anyone and was forcibly removed from the stand for criticizing the Committee. His protest earned him time in jail. The author of *The Maltese Falcon* and *The Thin Man*, Dashiell Hammett, wouldn't name names and was also jailed.

Lee J. Cobb refused for two years to appear before HUAC, and his treatment, as told to Victor Navasky, vividly portrays the life of those blacklisted: "When the facilities of the government of the United States are drawn on an individual it can be terrifying. The blacklist is just the opening gambit—being deprived of work. Your

passport is confiscated. That's minor. But not being able to move about without being tailed is something else. After a certain point it grows to implied as well as articulated threats, and people succumb. My wife did, and she was institutionalized." Finally Cobb went before the Committee and named twenty people. "I was pretty much worn down. I had no money. I couldn't borrow. I had the expenses of taking care of my children. Why am I subjecting my loved ones to this…? I decided it wasn't worth dying for, and if this gesture ["friendly" testimony] was the way of getting out of the penitentiary I'd do it. I had to be employable again."

Some, like blacklisted screen and TV writer Roy Huggins, gave in because they were terrified of what Huggins called "the Concentration Camp bill." Huggins, whose credits would later include such popular programs as *The Rockford Files,* told Navasky, "So there I was with the possibility of being hustled into a concentration camp while having several people completely dependent upon me. I considered the possibility of being a hero and I couldn't quite make it…. Who the hell is going to take care of two small children, a mother, and a wife, all of whom are totally dependent upon me?"

For his January 14 testimony Elia Kazan was determined, as he later wrote in *A Life,* that "I wouldn't hide anything that concerned me, I wouldn't 'take the Fifth,' but I would not, under any pressure, name others. That would be shameful; it wasn't an alternative worth considering."

That's exactly what he did, frankly admitting his Communist Party activities during his Group Theatre days but refusing to name anyone. He also told HUAC, truthfully, that he'd left the Party after about a year and a half, disgusted and disillusioned by its methods, and that, though decidedly liberal in his views, he'd had nothing whatsoever to do with Communism since. "I concluded," he wrote in *A Life,* "that what these fellows were conducting was a degradation ceremony, in which the act of informing was more important than the information conveyed. I didn't doubt they knew all the names they were asking for…! [They] were making the most of their political opportunity, scoring points for their careers because of the publicity their investigative position brought them—all at the cost of people's lives and careers. I bitterly resented them."

Lee J. Cobb held out under great pressure for two years. Some went to jail, some fought off their accusers in court successfully or not, and others endured the blacklist

indefinitely. (Zero Mostel wasn't seen on the big screen again until 1966.) Elia Kazan held out for not quite two months.

As he reports in *A Life,* all the pressure Kazan experienced was from his wife Molly and his Hollywood producers, Darryl Zanuck and Bud Leighton. He told Leighton, "The men they're waiting for me to name were once good friends." Leighton replied, "I don't care how good friends they were; there is nothing else you can do now." Nothing else, that is, if he wanted to continue to direct films.

And Kazan, "when I thought about it," agreed with Molly that "it was the duty of the government to investigate the Communist movement in our country. I couldn't behave as if my old 'comrades' didn't exist and didn't have an active political program." The severe consequences of his first testimony caused him to question, "What the hell am I giving all this up for? To defend a secrecy I didn't think right and to defend people who'd already been named or soon would be by someone else? I said I'd hated Communists for many years and didn't feel right about giving up my career to defend them…" Kazan requested a second session with the Committee and was granted it on April 10, 1952.

That morning the *New York Times* reported KOREA BATTLE TOLL OF U.S. NOW 107,134. The front page glared forth protests from Congress and the steel industry at President Truman's seizure of steel mills during the current strike. Among lesser stories, a ban on jaywalking was urged for New York City. *Singin' in the Rain* was playing at Radio City Music Hall while neighborhood theaters featured *When Worlds Collide* and the Abbott & Costello comedy *Jack and the Beanstalk.* Blacklisted in Hollywood but not in New York, John Garfield and Lee J. Cobb were giving "stunning performances" in a 52nd Street revival of the Clifford Odets play *Golden Boy* (a fact Cobb neglected to tell Navasky).

Kazan's April 10 testimony was a model of cooperation. He named every name he could remember, telling the Committee, "The American people need the facts and all the facts about all aspects of Communism in order to deal with it wisely and effectively. It is my obligation as a citizen to tell everything that I know." He apologized for repeating "former testimony, but I wanted to make as complete an over-all picture as my fallible memory allows." He listed his artistic achievements, making an emphatic case that none were Communist in any way, shape or form. Kazan concluded his April 10 testimony with, "I will be glad to do anything to help—anything you consider necessary or valuable."

Afterwards in his diary, quoted in *A Life,* he wrote: "Miserably depressed. Can't get my mind off it. I know I've done something wrong. Still convinced I would have done something wrong if I'd done the opposite. I spend every minute making rationalizations for my act.... Molly keeps looking at me. Why?"

People like Lee J. Cobb and Roy Huggins were later tacitly forgiven by the artistic community for cooperating with HUAC because they openly admitted their reasons were deprivation and terror and that they would be forever ashamed of betraying others. As for Elia Kazan—even after his death many have yet to forgive him. Because he was the most important American artist to name names, some believe that had Kazan defied the Committee the duration of the blacklist period would have been shortened. There is no evidence to support that notion; the blacklist remained in force for years after Senator Joe McCarthy himself was discredited and disgraced. Most commentators agree with Kazan that the depth and longevity of the anger directed against him was because he stated boldly, and for most of his life, that naming names to the Committee, however distasteful to him personally, was the right thing to do.

The day after Kazan's supposedly private testimony, the Committee released its contents to the world. The day after that, on April 12, 1952, Kazan did something unprecedented. He bought space in the *New York Times* to publish "A Statement—by Elia Kazan." Kazan tells us in *A Life* that "A Statement" was urged and then written by his wife Molly. "She locked herself in her study and I heard the typewriter, pages being ripped out impatiently, the carriage jammed back to its start position, then more typing." Kazan agreed with what she wrote and signed it. "A Statement" reads, in part:

> *In the past weeks intolerable rumors about my political position have been circulated in New York and Hollywood. I want to make my stand clear:*
>
> *I believe that Communist activities confront the people of this country with an unprecedented and exceptionally tough problem. That is, how to protect ourselves from a dangerous and alien conspiracy and still keep the free, open, healthy way of life that gives us self-respect.*
>
> *I believe that the American people can solve this problem wisely only if they have the facts about Communism. All the facts.*

> *Now, I believe that any American who is in possession of such facts has the obligation to make them known, either to the public or to the appropriate Government agency.*
>
> *...*
>
> *The question will be asked why I did not tell this story sooner. I was held back, primarily, by concern for the reputations and employment of people who may, like myself, have left the party many years ago.*
>
> *I was also held back by a piece of specious reasoning that has silenced many liberals. It goes like this: "You may hate the Communists, but you must not attack or expose them, because if you do you are attacking the right to hold unpopular opinions and you are joining the people who attack civil liberties."*
>
> *I have thought soberly about this. It is, simply, a lie.*
>
> *Secrecy serves the Communists. At the other pole, it serves those who are interested in silencing liberal voices. The employment of a lot of good liberals is threatened because they have allowed themselves to become associated with or silenced by the Communists.*
>
> *Liberals must speak out.*
>
> *...*
>
> *The motion pictures I have made and the plays I have chosen to direct represent my convictions.*
>
> *I expect to continue to make the same kinds of pictures and to direct the same kinds of plays.*
>
> *Elia Kazan*

Two months before, naming names had been "shameful"; now it was Kazan's duty as a citizen. He made his stand and stood by it.

Two assumptions need examining at this point.

The first is Kazan's assumptions that the Committee already knew the names it wanted to hear and that the hearings were public rituals of submission and nothing more—a belief that many who condemn HUAC share. But this assumption is based on no evidence. The complete records of the Committee have never been made public (and may no longer exist). An argument against Kazan's assumption is that many were not blacklisted *until* they were named to the Committee. What is

without doubt is that after people were named, and after their names were released by the Committee to the press, they were on *all* the lists.

Secondly, the assumption of many who condemn Kazan was that he was simply selling out his former colleagues in order to continue working and making money. He was accused of signing a $500,000 film contract the day after he testified. Kazan, on the other hand, says his director's salary was cut in half after his testimony (though that would still leave him far better paid than most Americans in 1952). In fact, neither Kazan, his biographer, nor his detractors have produced contractual evidence of Kazan's finances. Kazan's statements on his employment situation are contradictory. He told Jeff Young in 1971, "I didn't need a job in Hollywood. The blacklist did not extend to Broadway and I was at the top of my theater career." But he wrote in *A Life*, "I began to measure the weight of what I was giving up, my career in films, which I was surrendering for a cause I didn't believe in. It seemed insane. What was I if not a filmmaker?"

What is consistent is Kazan's oft-stated "hatred" (his word) of Communism and his feeling that it would have been "insane" to give up his career for something he didn't believe in. He told Jeff Young, "What I really thought, looking at it in the biggest sense, was that what I did was the better of two mean alternatives." He also told Young, "Maybe I did wrong, probably did. But I really didn't do it for any reason other than that I thought it was right." It is impossible for history to know whether this was his true feeling or whether it was what he had to tell himself to live with what he'd done. What's likely is that he believed it when he said it.

Kazan said to Jeff Young in 1971 that his HUAC testimony "has to be judged from the perspective of 1952." In 1972, he told NBC's Edwin Newman, "It was part of a thing that has to be understood in terms of that time." Again, in 1974, he said to Michel Ciment, "I think that when it's discussed now, it's discussed without relation to the period during which it took place."

In the context of 1952, then, the business of Kazan's April 10 testimony was to name names, and the relevance of "A Statement" rests on those he named and what they did.

In addition to several Communist Party functionaries of the mid-1930s—who, in the context of *that* time, were breaking no laws—the people Kazan named were eight actors and writers of The Group Theatre. "I was assigned [by the Party]

to a 'unit' composed of those party members who were, like myself, members of The Group Theatre acting company." Their mission was to take control of The Group and direct its agenda—again, an activity that broke no laws. Kazan said that in large part his unit failed its mission. How the Soviet threat of 1952 was alleviated by exposing "all the facts" of a bohemian theater's infighting of two decades before, neither HUAC nor Kazan ever explained.

To put Kazan's argument and testimony in close-up focus, consider unit member and Group Theatre actress Phoebe Brand. When naming her Kazan added, "I was instrumental in bringing her into the Party."

Recruiting a new Party member was necessarily a secretive, intimate process and a significant episode in Kazan's life as a Communist—significant enough to be mentioned to the Committee. But Phoebe Brand goes unmentioned in *A Life* and in all of Kazan's published interviews—even when, in *A Life,* he lists Group actors who later became teachers and "helped actors become artists;" Brand, too, became an influential teacher, but she's not on Kazan's list. Kazan's biographer Richard Schickel mentions Brand only in passing as one of the Group's "famously reliable character actors." Schickel ignores Kazan's recruitment of Brand and never interviewed Brand nor anyone else named by Kazan.

Phoebe Brand is worthy of mention in both their works because hers was more than a walk-on part in theatrical history. When she died in 2004 at the age of ninety-six, she rated an obituary in the *New York Times,* the *Boston Globe,* the *Los Angeles Times,* and the *Washington Post*—all but the *Post's* were fairly extensive. The Group's founder, Harold Clurman, in his memoir *The Fervent Years* (1961), recalls in passing her passionate and perhaps naive devotion to his theater. Wendy Smith's *Real Life Drama—The Group Theatre and America* (1990) records that as an actress Brand had "sizzle" and was "funny and sexy." Smith describes her as sometimes "tough-minded," sometimes "shy and introspective," "one of the Group's most politically committed members…. She saw people going through garbage cans…walking coatless in the middle of January. 'You wanted to take your coat off and give it to them, it was really so painful,' [Brand said]." Her "good looks…garnered her several movie offers, [but Brand] was notably vehement in her scorn for Hollywood." One would think a dangerous Communist would desire the visibility and power that might come with Hollywood stardom, but Brand went to Hollywood only after the Group disbanded and her husband, Morris Carnovsky (also named by Kazan), found work there. Even then, she didn't opt for the movies nor did she leave her sense of social justice

behind her on the East Coast. The *Los Angeles Times* told how she "once helped close a Hollywood delicatessen after the owner refused to serve a black actor. Brand, Carnovsky, and about 100 other protestors set up a picket line outside the store." Phoebe Brand acted in theater until being blacklisted after Kazan's testimony, at which point she became an acting teacher. In the 1960s, she was a founding member of Theatre in the Street, directing free plays in New York City and helping to begin the careers of actors like Billy Dee Williams and Raul Julia. Articulate and active into old age, the *Boston Globe* reported that "she taught private lessons to small groups of students in her home," teaching her last class a week before her death in her hospital room.

When one looks closely at Phoebe Brand, Morris Carnovsky and other artists named by Kazan, the eagerness of the Committee to know their names and the grandiosity of Kazan's "A Statement" become, in the context of 1952, almost farcical were it not for the very real danger those named were now subject to. Swiftly blacklisted, they were also, as the *New York Times* phrased it, "ticketed for immediate seizure." The Emergency Detention Act would never be employed, but no one could know that in 1952.

Well into the Fifties, the camps remained in the news to remind America's Phoebe Brands of the peril they might be subject to. In 1955, *New York Times* reporter Luther A. Huston toured three of the camps. On December 27, in a long article that included photographs, he reported that "there is nothing at any of the camps to suggest the 'concentration camps' that horrified the free world in World War II." He reassured his readers that "in the absence of evidence to the contrary and in the light of experience of American methods, the presumption must be that these camps would be humanely conducted, according to civilized rules and procedures."

One hopes that Phoebe Brand's reaction included at least some soft acidic laughter.

Works of art stand by themselves, apart from their creators, and Elia Kazan's importance as an artist is not diminished by his behavior as a man—behavior for which he himself, after "A Statement," made no further exalted claims. As he told Jeff Young, "My name is ambivalence now." He had stated that liberals should tell "all the facts," but not, as it turned out, *all* liberals—not his best friend, Clifford Odets. Kazan writes in *A Life*: "The sad fact is that what was possible for me hurt Clifford mortally. He was never the

same after he testified. He gave away his identity when he did that; he was no longer the rebel hero.... I believe he should have remained defiant, maintaining his treasured identity, and survived as his best self. He was to die before he died." To say that Odets should have maintained his identity rather than expose the Communist menace is to gut the righteous logic of Kazan's own statement. Kazan, typically, made no apology for the contradiction. "My name is ambivalence now."

Critics across the political spectrum often, and for better or worse, judge Elia Kazan's films in the light of his HUAC testimony, but they may be seeing both more and less than is on the screen. With its themes of personal and political betrayal, *Viva Zapata!* was completed months before Kazan met with the Committee. *On the Waterfront,* in which "ratting" is justified under specific circumstances, was a project Kazan had been working on intermittently for years before he testified. His experience with HUAC no doubt focused the film's theme, as did his choice of a screenwriter, another friendly witness, Budd Schulberg; but *On the Waterfront's* basic story was what Kazan had intended from his first interest in the project. *A Face in the Crowd,* also brilliantly written by Schulberg, concerns itself with another level of betrayal entirely—the betrayal of society by the media it has created. In Kazan's pictures, betrayal and rebellion aren't more or less important than in most American melodrama. Rather their power rests on Kazan's ability to inspire brilliant performances and his superb sense of pictorial movement.

Kazan's own favorite film, and his most personal, was 1963's *America America,* based on the journey of the uncle who brought Kazan's family from Turkey to the United States. In its most intense and intimate exchange, the protagonist, Stavros, "is driven to tell [his fiancée] the truth," Kazan said to Jeff Young. That truth is, "Don't trust me." Admitted Kazan, "He's saying he knows himself. That's the deepest, truest line I ever wrote."

Kazan's final statement about his HUAC testimony appears on page 685 of *A Life*. The book goes on for another 140 pages, but Kazan never retracts or modifies what he wrote on page 685, and he would never again mention, for print, his experience as a namer of names.

When his wife Molly died, Kazan received a letter of condolence from Tony Kraber, a Group actor whom he'd named on April 10, 1952.

michael ventura

As I was thinking about this chapter and looking over notes and letters, I happened on Tony Kraber's letter.... Then, a short week ago, I had a dream that surprised me. Tony was glad to see me and I was happy to be with him.... We were in the simplest harmony, it felt fine.... Then I woke and I knew it was in the middle of the night...and I thought what a terrible thing I'd done: not in the political aspect of it, because maybe that was correct; but it didn't matter now, correct or not; all that mattered was the human side of things. I said to myself, "You hurt another human being, a friend of yours, and his family, and no 'political aspect' matters two shits."...I felt that no political cause was worth hurting any human being for. What good deeds were stimulated by what I'd done? What villains exposed? How is the world better for what I did? It had just been a game of power and influence, and I'd been taken in and twisted from my true self. I'd fallen for something I shouldn't have, no matter how hard the pressure or how sound my reasons.... As for why I'd done it, I couldn't look at that anymore.

Then I woke all the way and had breakfast. I knew the past was past and there was nothing I could do about it. [18]

Black Clock

greil marcus
SHAPE OF THINGS TO COME

greil marcus

I wrote The Shape of Things to Come—Prophecy and the American Voice, which was published in 2006, out of a long-standing obsession with the notion of prophecy in American speech. It was an obsession with the way that the Biblical epic of a people's covenant with God, and its inevitable betrayal, and the emergence of prophets who threaten the people with damnation for their apostasy while at the same time calling the people back to their original declaration of trust and fealty, underlay the American story—but with a crucial difference. As the people of Israel understood it, and as their prophets defined it, by breaking a covenant with God they had betrayed God, and he would punish them. In America, beginning even with the Puritans who saw themselves as God's chosen people carrying his word and carrying out his mission, the covenant that people made was with themselves—themselves and, as one of the founding documents in American prophecy put it, "our posterity." In the words of John Winthrop in 1630, the Puritans were devoting themselves to the founding of a community, which would symbolize a nation and the world in which they would live as "members of the same body"—a physical, not merely a moral or political body, so that if one member was diseased, all would suffer, and all would work to heal the afflicted so that the body would not die. With the Declaration of Independence and the Constitution, which Sarah Vowell has called "the greatest two-sided hit single ever made," the commitment was to the undefined but patently limitless promises of life, liberty, and the pursuit of happiness, and the insistence that "all men are created equal." Whatever that meant—and the discussion and the battle over whatever that meant, along with whatever the other words meant—would define the story America had to tell the world and itself. Ultimately, it meant that judgment could no longer be passed off on God. It meant that a people would have to judge themselves. If ruin were to be the result of their betrayal, it would be a ruin they would make and bring upon themselves.

That these promises, from Winthrop to Jefferson, were so deep and so broad that their betrayal was inevitable—that, as with the affirmation of slavery in the Constitution, the betrayal was inseparable from the promise—became, at least in the story I tried to tell, the engine of American history, and prophets emerged to threaten the people with ruin and to call them back to fulfill the promises they had made. That

was because, by accepting that one was a member of the body that came to call itself the United States of America, one made all the promises at the root of its founding one's own, and accepted the burden that if he or she betrayed those promises, then he or she in turn threatened the republic and put its body—the body of its idea, and the real, breathing body of its community—at risk. All Americans took on the burden of judging the country, and thus of judging themselves as members of its body.

The greatest of the prophets who emerged were, at least through the Civil War, religious and political: Garrison, Douglass, Lincoln, and many more. But after Lincoln—either because his Second Inaugural Address took the story as far as it could go, at least in words, or because his assassination erased the damnation he threatened and enshrined the community of love he held out as its escape—prophetic speech disappeared from political speech. It wandered in its own wilderness, but the impulse— the insight that the speech needed to be spoken, that the threats had to be made, and the insistence on betrayal was the only way to give the promise weight and body— did not disappear. As politicians abandoned it and forgot the language, the impulse migrated into art. That's to say that it was taken up by solitary individuals compelled by their fate as members of a spectral community, intrigued and fascinated, sometimes morbidly fascinated, by the drama of promise and betrayal as the essence of American life, and of their lives as American artists.

One of those artists, it seemed to me, was Laurie Anderson. Throughout her career and throughout her life as a public speaker—but especially after the terrorist attacks of 2001, which I saw as the most symbolic and thus the most successful and complete attack on America as a body and idea in American history—she had edged toward that role. So early in my book, I brought her onto its stage…and ultimately took her off it. Frances Coady, my editor at Farrar, Straus and Giroux and the best, most far-seeing and near-sighted editor I've ever worked with—she could see the whole arc of a book even before, to the author, it had one, while at the same time noticing redundant phrases appearing a hundred pages apart—thought it wasn't as strong as the material that preceded and followed it. She argued that compared to the artists who in our time took on the prophetic role, the role of judges, and whose work made up the body of the book— Philip Roth, Bill Pullman, David Lynch, Sheryl Lee, Corin Tucker, David Thomas and Allen Ginsberg—Anderson was circling the question but not really asking it, not really dramatizing it. I agreed, and I wanted to get on with it. I wanted to get to the story I thought I had to tell. Any reader can judge if we were right.

For a single body to stand in for all others—for a single citizen to claim to speak for all others, to tell their story, to link theirs to hers or his to theirs—a kind of play is needed. Scope is needed: The actor, whether a president delivering an historic address, a novelist writing a book, a filmmaker making a movie, or a singer shaping a song, has to do more than offer an artifact. He or she has to build a stage, attract an audience, and get those who show up to sit still. Or tear down the stage, or push the actors off it and take their places in turn. Or realize, when the play is over, that the ground has been pulled out from under their feet.

The play, with all of its actors, writers, directors, stagehands, promoters, and however many might make up its audience, can still be traced back to the first speaker. Speech comes out of the body, but no matter how dead the speaker may be, the body remains an historical fact, proof that whatever imagining has issued from it was grounded in a lived life. In other words, no matter how the speech may go into the air, live in the air or dissolve in it, you can trace the speech back to the event that is made when the words are first spoken, even if that event takes place only in your own mind as you listen, as you imagine the event the speech calls for—and that grounding allows one to see the events that take place as the speech echoes through years to come. It's a loop—a sliding event you can see enacted in, say, the locked-room detective story of Abraham Lincoln's seven-minute March 4, 1865 hit broadside "With Malice Toward None," with the nation still the room and the speech still the key, or in the career of a pop song of just slightly longer length, Laurie Anderson's eight-minute, twenty-one-second "O Superman," appearing in 1981, then circling forward twenty years, then doubling back again and again, the song gathering to itself fragments of other attempts to tell the story she was telling, their whole history.

Someone Once Said
In 1981, Anderson was thirty-four, a former Egyptologist from Chicago and a ten-year veteran of the insular, self-referential New York City performance-art milieu. She played around with a violin and a vocoder, an instrument that allowed her to speak as male or female, young or old, still or echoing; she performed as a trickster. And though various Anderson pieces appeared on obscure new-music anthologies over those years, it wasn't until the spring of the first year of Ronald Reagan's presidency that she released a record of her own: the seven-inch single "O Superman (For Massenet)"/"Walk the Dog," drawn from her then-uncompleted multi-hour performance piece *United States:*

Transportation, Politics, Money and Love. Issued on the tiny New York independent label One Ten, "O Superman" was Anderson's first real venture into a new art space—the market, the pop process, the democratic audience.

The 5,000 copies One Ten originally pressed slowly began to appear in more adventurous record stores and on a few nonprofit FM stations. The record played mostly at night, when the line between dreaming and waking is thinnest—and it's just that line that "O Superman," it seemed, was meant to dissolve.

The record found its way to the late John Peel, the eclectic BBC disc jockey whose anarchic show was beamed across Britain four days a week. "O Superman" went on his playlist, and within weeks it was the most talked about record in the land. Even Capital Radio, London's closest equivalent to an American Top 40 station, was playing it, though there was hardly a copy to be had anywhere in the U.K.—or, by this time, in the U.S. The London independent label Rough Trade picked up some of One Ten's second pressing, another 5,000; that went fast, and Anderson entered the U.K. independent singles charts. Anderson cut a deal with Warner Bros., and by mid-October, just a fortnight after her new label shipped 125,000 copies of the disc, "O Superman" was number two on the British pop charts. It never had anything like that kind of success at home. In the United States, the record made itself felt slowly, over the years, over the decades.

In the fall of 1981, Anderson began to perform the song in public. I saw her at a place called Market Street Cinema in San Francisco—the debut production for a 1,200-seat converted movie theater. It was an interesting bill: Anderson plus William Burroughs and the downtown New York poet John Giorno. The place was jammed. The previous day (when the Warner Bros. signing was only a rumor), I heard people in three different record stores asking rather desperately for "O Superman"—no luck.

Anderson took the stage in a black satin jacket, black shirt, black tie, black pants, her eyes made up to look like those of an emissary from the Village of the Damned, her hair chopped and spiked into a punk do. She immediately defused the expectations of the crowd with a bit of rambling, deadpan patter. She mimed with a neon violin and set a few tapes rolling to no apparent purpose. Having broken the context of high artistic seriousness that had greeted her, she faded into "O Superman."

Nothing else Anderson did that night came close. Much of her work—combining performed music, recorded sound effects, props, movement, talk, and

projected images—fell somewhere between noodling and academic deconstruction. On record, even "O Superman" is at first impressive partly for its commitment to craft and appealing partly because of its seemingly blithe toying with sound and myth. But on stage, I found myself writing at the time, reviewing the concert, it felt like an act of prophecy.

What that might mean is what this book is about. That night, more than twenty years ago, that thought was a stab in the dark, but it was the dark the song itself had summoned up.

Playing a tinny Farfisa organ, filtering and electronically distorting her voice against a never-flagging tape loop of "ah…ah…ah," the interjections seemingly timed to a cricket's chirp, Anderson set comedy against fear: Here, the object of deconstruction was the United States itself.

"O Superman" begins with the then-new leave-a-message instructions of an answering machine. Mom checks in ("Are you coming home?"), and then an anonymous voice: the voice, you come to think soon enough, of the nation's future, or its fortune-teller. But it's also a stalker's voice.

"Well, you don't know me," the creamy voice says, at once spectral and a body in itself, physical, untouchable, "but I know you"—Anderson suddenly lifts and curls the last four words out of speech and into music, bringing you into a conversation that a moment before you were merely overhearing—"And I've got a message / To give to you / Here come the planes…"

The last word was drawn out electronically, giving you time to think about it, to form an image. In San Francisco there was time even to helplessly glance up at the ceiling, with the sudden sense that planes were about to come through the roof. The word carried over into the next verse, and the voice goes on, not pressing any harder, but letting you feel how implacable it was from the beginning: "So you'd better get ready / Ready to go / You can come as you are / But pay as you go."

It's a good joke, but by this point only that anonymous voice can afford a laugh. The voice creates the feeling that one has incurred a debt without knowing it, and that one must now make the debt good. The piece is absolutely terrifying. With a prim little lilt, the voice turns playful, or sadistic: "They're American planes / Made in America / Smoking—or Non-Smoking."

The woman whose machine has picked up the call now picks up the phone itself, but the voice continues with its riddles as if there's been no interruption, as if it's

still speaking to a recorder: "Neither snow nor rain / Nor gloom of night / Shall stay these couriers / From the swift completion / Of their appointed rounds." The voice is gentle, ageless, magically summoning a shared American memory of old catchphrases, old certainties—in this case, the motto running across the face of post offices all over the country—but these couriers, you knew in 1981, were not delivering the mail. There isn't a note, a tone, a word, an inflection that is out of place, that doesn't have its purpose in advancing the awful, revelatory mood of the piece—in moments you can almost see Anderson crouching behind a line, see her back off from a line even as she delivers it.

The song drifts away. The voice departs, and the woman is left to make her peace with its echo, to make sense of it. She gives a speech, or a sermon:

> *When love is gone*
> *There's always justice*
> *And when justice is gone*
> *There's always force*
> *And when force is gone*
> *There's always Mom (Hi, Mom!)*

"*So hold me now,*" the singer commands with a voice from deep in the chest, but still it's as if the command is coming from far away, from someone else, from a judge. As the music begins to sweep up the singer, to make a whirlpool, "all round and round in one vortex," the singer wraps her own arms around herself, as if she is her own mother, her own nation: "Your petrochemical arms…your electronic arms… your military arms."

Was "O Superman" as finished a vision of America as it seemed to be, as complete, as final? Could Anderson's vision, a vision that felt like a visitation, turning Anderson into a creature more abstract than corporeal, stand up to itself, or would the song dissolve in its own precision, revealing Anderson as nothing more than a body, just another would-be pop star trumpeting her hit? Were we to hear "O Superman" on the radio every day, as, in 1981, the British were hearing it, I thought then, were we to hear it as we were waking up, driving a car, without warning, without intent, we would find out how strong the piece really was.

We found out. In a manner almost too literal to think about, as if the song had been a plan of action, it was put into play. It was one thing to imagine what the planes in Anderson's quiet but still melodramatic "Here come the planes" were; it was something else to be told, and not by the singer. By definition, to see a vision be made literal, no matter how lovely the vision, would be a kind of horror; when it happened with "O Superman," the song became impossible to play, even in your head. It had been twenty years. The song was impossible to play; at the same time, it was impossible not to hear it as if you had never heard it before.

On September 19, 2001, a week and a day after the terrorist attacks that had symbolically leveled her city, killed its citizens, killed the firefighters of her own downtown neighborhood, Anderson took the stage at Town Hall in New York City for the first of two scheduled concerts. She had been in Chicago when Muslim terrorists flew planes into the World Trade Center. The Town Hall promoter contacted her to say that people were calling to ask if the shows would still take place. "It was a very unique feeling to be talking and singing about something that was happening that—very second," Anderson said in the fall of 2004, when an interviewer asked if indeed she had considered canceling the performances. "No, I didn't hesitate about doing that…. The work that I've done, a lot of it is about that anyway. It's about fear; it's about death. It's about the present, and so—those things almost get *ignored*, when they're presented as songs. 'You don't realize this is a whole *death album*'—everybody's going, 'Well, that guitar line is so cool,' and you're going, '*Don't you know what this is about?*' And so when something like that happens, it's, *wow*. It's actually about—tonight."

Greeted by loud applause and cheers, she began with a chiming theme, and then a homily: "We want to dedicate our music tonight to the great opportunity we all have to begin to truly understand the events of the last few days, and to act upon them with courage and compassion as we make our plans to live in a completely new world." Anderson delivered her lines in the same preciously measured tones she uses for the various commentaries that she intersperses between songs, or the talking that takes place in the songs—drippingly ironic, even smirking riddles, banal observations that level the unsettling puzzles of the songs themselves, odd stories that always seem to stop just short of a punchline. This night, there was no smirk in her introduction, the irony was meant to be gone, but nevertheless, those measured tones called it back: the cloud of irony that surrounds Anderson's work, the cloud

that one familiar with her performance brings to it, if only to have it dissolved by a song capable of dissolving it, and so the homily turned into a performance of distance, and it was cold. In this manner:

> *We want to dedicate our music tonight*
> *To the great opportunity*
> *We all have*
> *To begin to truly understand*
> *The events of the past few days*
> *And to act upon them*
> *With courage*
> *And with compassion*
> *As we make our plans*
> *To live in a completely new world*

There was a whispery shudder in the word "plans," and a glow in "new world"; otherwise, the words were placed on a surface that was completely flat, so flat that halfway through the lines, the theme playing behind Anderson had begun to sound horribly bland, incapable of communicating or eliciting any feeling at all.

Anderson went into her show, and, with expert orchestration and perfect timing, playing violin and organ, accompanied by bass, concertina, drums, electronic percussion, sampled sounds, and taped vocals, made her way through seventeen songs. As you listen to the recording made that night, you can be momentarily caught up in the particular off-mood of any particular piece—the way Anderson creates a situation in which the mood that situation would produce, or the mood one would bring to it (the situation of a walk down the street, a bad dream, finding oneself alone in a foreign country), is skewed, so that whatever is familiar produces a sense of unfamiliarity, so that your own street becomes a foreign country. But that night, the country was more familiar than it had ever been, and so the expertness and perfect timing, producing that sense of dislocation, were all wrong. It was only in the most florid moments—the lovely rise of "Here they come, here they come" in the beginning of "Strange Angels," held for as long as Anderson could hold the words without benefit of one of her distortion effects, each word, for an instant, a body complete in itself, capable of

representing or enclosing anything—that the lack of corporeality in the performance itself, from song to song, was escaped. Almost everything seemed to be taking place in the air, as if there were no ground on which to light.

Near the end of the night, Anderson reached "O Superman." You can imagine that she had succeeded in making those present forget it, and that that was what she meant to do: to set them up, a bait-and-switch. As if lulling through brilliance, making a play in which the presence of a riddle was so satisfying there was no need to try and solve it, she was ready to kill off all the characters and clear the stage, to lower a screen, turn on a projector, and run *The Big Sleep*—the kind of intrigue in which, as Raymond Chandler defined the hard-boiled American detective story as opposed to the English puzzle mystery, the writer "gave murder back to people that commit it for reasons, not just to provide a corpse."

There is, in any concert, a thrill when the performer strikes up the hit. It's not simply a matter of confirmation: now we're going to get what we came for. It's an inchoate sense that everything the hit contains—the performer's whole career and everything you have invested in it, every time you heard the song before and all the times you will hear it in the future—will as never before take shape as an event, as an unexperienced, unrepeatable occurrence that will, for the first time, reveal what the song truly is. *This* time suddenly feels like the first time and the last time, and you feel on the verge of seizing what the song is actually about, what it says—and there is a sense that, now, the song in action will leave the world to which it is addressed actually different, more heroic or unacceptable, more real or less so.

As Anderson made her way through "O Superman," edging into it, the song itself constructed to make you feel in a tactile, moment-to-moment manner the progress of a person from outdoors, on a nice day, walking into her building, climbing her stairs, opening her door, entering her apartment, closing the door, putting down her bags and purse, turning on her answering machine, it became clear that the song was her "Gimmie Shelter," her "Anarchy in the U.K.," her "Sugar, Sugar": It's the end of the world, and it's catchy. It was always fearsome; it was always cute. But now, instead of looking into the future and sensing a drama and a fate the country had always contained within itself, the song was looking back at a future that had already taken place.

Who, *what* wrote "Here come the planes / They're American planes / Made in America / Smoking, or Non-Smoking"—and how did Anderson find it in herself

to say those lines after it had been revealed that "Smoking" was the answer the song had contained all along? As Anderson performed that night in New York City, eight days after men from elsewhere made her vision of America come true, she gave a great patriotic address, with, scattered through the audience, the dead: Allen Ginsberg, performing pieces of "Wichita Vortex Sutra" in Kansas as he wrote them, Martin Luther King, John Winthrop, Lincoln himself.

But not even Anderson could know, that night, where the song was going, or how the country was still catching up with it, with others now following the song's plan, over the next years leaving one set of planes to history and moving on with another, leaving the person whose own picture this had once been a mere citizen, part of the crowd, or less than that, a spectator of her own vision, which was now not a vision at all, but a credo, not hers by choice but as an American fact. It wasn't two years later, in Oakland, California, that Lindsey Buckingham would introduce Fleetwood Mac's "Peacekeeper," a song that communicated as night thoughts on the second Iraq war, with lines that no longer needed an author, or wanted one: "Someone once said, 'When love is gone, there's always justice, and when justice is gone, there's always force.'" [18]

david l. ulin
LABYRINTH

david l. ulin

I wrote Labyrinth *on something of a dare. A friend had taken on the role of editorial director for a small imprint specializing in novellas, with emerging English readers as an audience. The idea was to publish stories that would be both challenging and accessible, at a length of around 10,000 words. My friend sent me a couple of books he'd already issued: small paperbacks, slender, elegantly designed. I've always been a sucker for novellas, for the amorphous middle ground of them: more expansive than a story, yet readable in one extended riff. They were substantial but, in their own way, elusive also: what Stephen King once characterized as "an anarchy-ridden literary banana republic… apt to make even the most stout-hearted writer of fiction shake and shiver in his boots."*

Of course, that was the thing: I wasn't *a writer of fiction, and I hadn't been for many years. In my twenties and early thirties, I'd made attempts at novels; I had published stories in journals and magazines. Over the last decade and a half, however, my output had dwindled—three or four stories, including one I'd written for an anthology I'd edited, which had got me thinking about fiction again. Writing a small book seemed not-so-daunting, and I had a story I wanted to play with, based on something that had happened in San Francisco a few years before.*

All that is part of Labyrinth. *It's an interior narrative: one man, locked in his head, as he spends an afternoon and evening wandering a city where he used to live. Nothing happens—my favorite fiction is that in which nothing happens—and yet, I hope, everything does. "Then I used to wander in the streets," Albert Camus observes in* The Fall. *"They wander now too, I know! They wander, pretending to hasten toward the tired wife, the forbidding home…. Ah, mon ami, do you know what the solitary creature is like as he wanders in big cities…?"*

As to how to write for emerging readers, the answer is—I didn't know. I just wrote: long sentences, long paragraphs, stream of consciousness. Then we edited it to make a book. The edits kept the flavor of the inquiry, the sense of someone lost in the middle of his life and no longer sure which way to turn. I liked that, as I liked the idea of engaging with those readers, of helping make a space for them. And yet, there was also stuff that

I regretted losing: lines, transitions, a bit of navel-gazing, mostly—which is a strategy I shamelessly employ. In a world where narrative often seems right on the surface, what else can fiction offer but the deep dive, the vertical plunge, the explication of consciousness, of every moment, as the inextricable and complicated knot it is?

"The past is never dead. It's not even past." —William Faulkner

On a plain

He was thinking, as the waters of the Bay rose up outside the airplane window in those last translucent moments before the landing gear touched the tarmac, of a scene he had witnessed through another window, at a garden party a few months before. It had been a Sunday afternoon, warm in Los Angeles, one of those dry November days that shimmer up like mirages, the air sere and desert dusky, light as thin and hollow as a watercolor wash. He had been in the kitchen, drinking a beer, talking to someone, he couldn't remember, when he noticed Annie's friend Sylvie pushing her 6-year-old son on a swing set in the yard. Sylvie would push and the kid would giggle, and then she'd spread her arms in an exaggerated X, like a scarecrow in a field. Sylvie was thin like that, just sticks and skin, face a collage of protuberances arranged beneath a corona of lank brown hair. Through the window, he could see how she clenched her fists, the tilt of her head, the forward angle of her hips, and if he'd been outside, he knew, he would be able to hear her also, a little bit frantic and excited at once. Sylvie had just had a double mastectomy; she'd been diagnosed, over the summer, with a particularly fast-moving breast cancer, and was now, as the saying goes, *fighting for her life*. The first time he'd ever heard that phrase, he'd been 6 himself, driving around Long Beach with his father on the morning after Robert Kennedy was shot. *Senator Kennedy is fighting for his life*, the radio kept saying, and he'd imagined the wounded man lying on a stretcher, fists balled and swinging, as if he were duking it out with death. Thinking about that, he glanced again at Sylvie's hands, so small and bony they looked like walnuts. They didn't appear strong enough to battle their way through the fading autumn light.

And yet, this was precisely what Sylvie was doing, fighting the good fight, standing up for as long as she could. She was out in the yard, with her kid, really *with* him, as if whatever connection she might make here would leave a trace of

something—solace? sustenance?—that would linger, for a while anyway, after she was gone. Annie hated it when he thought like this, as if the outcome were inevitable; and yet, what Annie didn't understand was that he didn't begrudge the effort: not Sylvie's or anyone's. That it was futile only made it more necessary, this small and insufficient attempt to *be here now*. It was all she could do, which was, of course, the lesson he was trying to learn also: to find a way, finally, to get clear of all the noise. Maybe if you could inhabit the moment, one moment, fully enough, all that other stuff would fade, leaving only the paleness of the sunlight and the image of a mother and a son, in the instant before time betrayed them, playing together in the yard.

The plane touched down with a series of skidding bumps, then the brakes kicked in and he was pushed forward in his seat. Outside forces, all these outside forces. The older he got, the more he felt...*buffeted* the word was, as if he were a jet himself, caught in turbulence, tossed from side to side. He didn't know why Sylvie had come into his mind—her issues were not his issues; he was not dying (except, of course, in the way that we are all dying, *he who is not busy being born is busy dying*), and it had been years since he had pushed a child on a swing. Yet he could feel the restlessness, the rootlessness, the idea that time was not his friend any longer (another illusion: that it had ever been). This was intensified by the proximity of San Francisco, towers glittering across the Bay. In its way, it had been his first city, streets a labyrinth of memory. He had lived there the year after high school, and the experience still rose up to remind him of...what? His long-lost possibilities? No, although possibility was part of it, the notion that, in this one brief window, he might have done anything. He had been 18, on his own for the first time, living in a studio apartment in the Haight. All along, he'd known he would not be staying, that when the year was up, he would go to college, and yet, this only had the heightening effect of a ticking clock. He remembered taking the Number 7 bus up Market Street, memorizing the storefronts, buildings stark against the sky like jagged teeth. Before or since, he'd never paid such attention to anything, and thirty years later, he could still be stopped by the right cast of white Pacific light, the scent of eucalyptus, the angle of a terra cotta doorway—all those details and sensations, sense memories of the city, in which the moment was equally present and always, always out of reach.

Finally, the plane pulled up to the gate and cut its engines, and he made his way into the Oakland Airport. He was here for the night: an afternoon meeting and then back home tomorrow, and as he trudged through the terminal, he texted Annie to let her know he'd arrived. It was late morning, and in Los Angeles, she was at work,

teaching toddlers in the library until it was time to get Sadie at school. Jonah would come home later on the city bus, a high school student already, big and bearded, not so much younger than he himself had been when he'd come to the Bay Area. He stepped onto the sidewalk, momentarily stilled by the crisp clarity of the air. It felt… he didn't know, *redolent*, but the more he tried to think of what, the more it eluded him. It was like memory—attempt to pin it down and it slipped from your grasp. The only way to deal with it was sidelong, in a series of glances, as if unsure of what you were looking for.

city City CITY

Yes…redolent. He could feel it as he walked up Powell Street from the BART station, bag across his shoulder like a sling. He was looking for the easiest way to navigate Nob Hill, but there was no good option, so he took a left on Post and went to Taylor, where he humped a ragged passage up the slope. The hotel was on Taylor and California, catty-corner from Grace Cathedral, which squatted, gray-white and hulking, like a model built for God. He loved the Cathedral, loved its stolid air of reassurance, as if the universe were knowable, distinct. That had never been his experience, but he couldn't help drawing solace from it, as if, were you to believe in something hard enough, you might will it into being true. The first time he'd set foot inside had been when he lived here, to attend services with his friends Jack and Brooke after a July 4th car wreck on Highway 101. Even then, it had seemed strange, out of kilter, since none of them were what you'd call believers; the faith they had was in their own invented mix of magical thinking and serendipity. Still, wasn't that why they had come to the Cathedral on that summer Sunday, their belief that San Francisco was a magical landscape, and that their survival, in a car that had first rolled and then crumpled in on itself like a recycled can, had expressed a message sent from the heart of the universe to them? He could never see the Cathedral without thinking of that moment, the three of them so young, Brooke in a skirt, Jack and him in clean jeans and collared shirts, sighing in relief at the fact that they were here at all. If he had thought about it, he would have understood how out-of-place he was, but then, that had been the point, hadn't it: to break with the expected, to step outside the narrative, to create not the world that had been imagined for him but the one he had imagined for himself?

And yet, what was this world he had imagined? In truth, he couldn't say. He hadn't come here to make a real break, but instead to *take a break*. Maybe this was

why that time, or its memory, tugged at him—not because of what it said about his possibilities, but because the whole thing had been an illusion, a story he liked to tell himself. He could see how he looked at 18, long-haired, wearing jeans and a Guatemalan pullover (the same kind Jonah now wore when he went to Venice Beach with his high school friends), wandering the streets of San Francisco like a mendicant, all those endless loops, those meandering spirals, as if he could burn himself into the city through the soles of his feet. Maybe what had made it so intense had been his understanding that it was temporary, that here, for a year anyway, *time had stopped*, an idyll before real life kicked back in. Maybe that was why he had been so present, maybe that was why he had paid attention, because he had known all along that it wasn't going to last. Briefly, the image of Sylvie, out in the yard with her 6-year-old, flickered across the inside of his eyes. *Be here now*, he found himself thinking, *be here now*.

There it was, he thought, as he turned into the lobby of the hotel, up the short flight of marble steps, one, two, three, to the reception desk, the central irony of his adult life: that of all the ideas he had ever tried on, all the people he had ever thought about, the whole thing turned on...Ram Dass? Even as a teenager, he'd never taken him seriously, and yet here he was, thinking and rethinking his most famous phrase as if it were a mantra. *Strange*, he thought, *strange what sticks and strange what doesn't*, as he verified the reservation, let the clerk swipe his credit card for incidentals, received his key card and got directions to his room.

Upstairs, he threw his bag on the bed and opened the shades, looked out at the city spread before him in a tableau. His window faced east, towards the Embarcadero—although he couldn't see it, could barely glimpse a sliver of the Bay Bridge, angling beyond the foot of California Street like an iron web. He watched a cable car chuff up the hill, stopping next to the Fairmont, tourists climbing on and off like animated figures in their multi-colored clothes. Not real, not quite real, as if seeing it from a distance left him at an unbridgeable remove. He stood at the window for a long moment, trying to imagine his way into the scene. It would have been nothing to go downstairs, walk into the brilliant noontime, and yet he couldn't bring himself to move. Instead, he turned and unpacked his laptop, tapped into the wireless network of the hotel. *Another window*, he thought, *another kind of window*, as he checked his email, confirming his meeting, the time and place. It was a formality, this meeting, a loose face-to-face without much at stake, the sort of thing that could have been done over Skype or even the telephone, except for the vague factor of good will. But that was okay, he was happy to be in San Francisco—or, at least, he thought he was.

Secret history

The truth was, he was in San Francisco in pursuit of history, the secret history of his trip. Such a history had, if that were even possible, been kick-started by Facebook, which he'd joined with the belief that it would let him keep watch over his children, who seemed to live within its pages, wandering the endless weave of cyberspace as he'd once walked this city's streets. And that was how it was initially, before the algorithms started churning, rendering connections, digital data sifted and served. He watched Jonah and Sadie from a distance, *lurking*, a word that caught the flavor of it precisely, as if he were looking around the side of a virtual wall. Then the friend requests drifted in: colleagues and co-workers, other parents, serendipitous contacts, and, at last, a slow trickle of old friends. The first of those were oddly thrilling, like postcards from another world. He would log on and, boom, there they would be: the images, smaller than stamps, of people he had known in high school, their features tauter, slacker, or more deeply rendered, two-dimensional reference points for the effects of time. He routinely accepted the requests, even when he didn't care about the person—and here was another secret, that he almost never cared, that it almost never mattered to him who materialized, since it was more the *act* of materializing that intrigued him, the insistence of these echoes to assert themselves. He'd read, a few months earlier, a column in the paper about how Facebook was effacing memory, enabling the past to infect the present, with consequences that we couldn't know. How could we move on if everyone we'd ever met was all of a sudden able to find us? How could we reinvent ourselves? He wasn't sure about that; the fact that someone existed as a name and photograph didn't mean much, especially if you didn't interact with them. And anyway, his willingness to accept friend requests notwithstanding, they were almost always from the wrong people: not, say, Brooke or Jack, with whom he'd kept in touch, but rather the kid who'd sat behind him in homeroom, or the one who traded notes with him in math class, peripheral then and, now, peripheral again.

But then Alex had shown up as a friend request, and something in him had felt a pull. It had been decades since he'd last seen her, since he'd had her in his mind, high school girlfriend for half a second, a few frenzied gropes in dark bedrooms, a sense of dissatisfaction on both sides. Still, there were moments that lingered, which was more than he could say for most people. He remembered one afternoon in Berkeley, not long after the accident, listening to *Emotional Rescue* in a sorority house where she was living for the summer, lying on a common room couch while she tinkled at a piano... or was that something he had read? No, don't do that, it was real enough: more real,

even, for its echoes. Of course, he and Alex had long since broken up by then, which only rendered the whole thing more affecting. For here was the thing about it: that they had liked each other, that their brief interlude of dating had been a tunnel from which they had to emerge to become *friends*, and once she reappeared, all these years later, fuller of face and body but still the same, apparently, he kept thinking of these moments, hallmarks of an earlier incarnation, a different life, one he thought of now, when at all, with a bittersweet awareness of loss.

Alex was looking for something, that was certain, although he was relieved to understand that it was not romantic, since this did not, had never really, had much to do with what they were. No, it was something else, a quiet discontent obvious from her first message, which hinted at the usual middle-aged troubles: family complications, job dissatisfactions, the burden of raising teenage kids. *I'm a better parent from a distance*, she wrote about her older daughter, away at school now, the same age they had been when they'd last seen each other, and he was reminded of Jonah, two years from college and counting every minute, by turns talkative and diffident, protective if not of the details then of the depths of his experience. Like son, like father, he realized when he wrote her back, offering the merest summary of the personal—*married to Annie (for 20 years), two kids (Jonah, 17; Sadie, 13), been living in Los Angeles since 1991*—before shifting to work, and the trip, *this trip*, that he was planning to the Bay Area, where, it turned out, she still lived. They discussed details, traded messages like semaphores, like, what was that old cliché? *Ships in the night*. Yes, ships, he chuckled grimly, like the Titanic and the Carpathia, and as he cycled through the Facebook messages, he kept imagining the past as a giant iceberg, ready to break him if he came too close. Maybe there *was* something to that piece he'd read; maybe the past, virtual or otherwise, was a territory best left alone. But that was the challenge, wasn't it, of both living at this moment and at this time of life? Anyway, if Alex was looking for something, he was, he realized, looking, also—which is why, when she suggested it, he didn't hesitate for half a second before agreeing to meet for a drink.

Down in the hole

Lately, he had been at a loss for words. Not in the sense of having nothing to add to the conversation, but in the sense of having nothing to say. He would find himself—at work, at home, in line for the movies—overwhelmed by something like pure feeling, except that it wasn't pure, at least not in any way he could put his finger on. There was

no clarity, no direction, just a wave of...*distance* was the only way he could put it, as if he were in exile from his life. He would look around, struck by a sense of absolute isolation, unable to get outside himself. He had tried explaining this to Annie, but how could he describe the particular nature of the experience when he wasn't even sure what it felt like, when everything—a slant of light, the angle of a corner—could disconnect him, as if he had been cut adrift in the present with no reference points? Wherever he went, things looked familiar, but he was having trouble putting them together, uncovering a logic, a story he could tell. He was, in other words, having trouble making sense of it, even if he remained unsure, exactly, of what *it* was.

In any case, he didn't expect he'd say much at the meeting...if he were to say anything at all. A little after four o'clock, he went downstairs and stepped into the stark January afternoon, light white, nearly transparent, shadows crisp and stark. It would be night when he got out; even now, the afternoon was failing, sun low in the sky and a sharp breeze stirring, rustling the flags at the Mark Hopkins up the block. Where had the day gone? He had meant to get out this afternoon, to spend time in the city, but something had distracted him—perhaps the image of all those people getting on and off the cable cars, the mechanistic nature of it, or perhaps the mechanistic nature of himself. He remembered the first time he'd seen Nob Hill, riding the cable car up from the foot of California Street, hanging off the side and sticking his arms out, as if he were flying, free. Twenty-five years later, he'd done the same thing with Jonah, en route, during a weekend visit, to the Fairmont's Laurel Court Bar. This was their tradition, his and his son's, to go to the Fairmont on the last evening they were in the city; and briefly he wondered if he'd end up there tonight. He smiled as he imagined Jonah, wandering the halls of the hotel as if he belonged, looking at the framed menus and the photographs, all that evidence, all that detritus. History for Jonah was still a story, exciting, exotic even; he wasn't old enough to feel the acceleration; he didn't realize yet that it was personal. What did it mean when all you knew was slippage, when even the people you loved felt like chimeras, when time kept sliding past you and there was nothing you could do? This was one of the reasons he'd wanted to reconnect with Alex, to pierce the veneer of the present, to find an axe for the frozen sea in him.

At the meeting, he sat at one end of a long conference table, in a room overlooking the sparkle of the Bay. In the distance, he could see the container port of Oakland, the Bay Bridge curving towards it like a question mark. From the start, he felt himself drifting, felt the space of small talk, the illusion of intimacy. A woman

laughed bitterly at the specter of an impending birthday; another mentioned a friend who had just been diagnosed with stage III cervical cancer. Age and illness: the new vernacular. He listened half-heartedly, until he caught a glimpse of himself reflected in the window glass. *So gray*, he thought, unconsciously touching his hair, as if he were looking at one of those Facebook photos, with their weird texture of telescoped time. Was this who he'd become—this middle-aged city planner, here to discuss transit hubs, to think about the future of a city in which he no longer lived? When had he gotten so sober, so responsible, so fluent in the practical, in the little details by which we mark our lives? He wasn't in what he thought of as a mid-life crisis, not lamenting decisions, things he hadn't done. He loved his wife, his family, and yet he could see them shifting away from him. Tomorrow, Jonah would be leaving, when just yesterday he'd been as small, as lithesome, as Sylvie's son. *Sylvie, shit*...and for a moment, he was arrested again by the memory of her and the boy in that backyard, beneath the hanging dagger of the sun.

The ninth circle

It was dark when the meeting let out, and he found himself in the Financial District, wandering aimlessly. The last hour and a half had been a blur, an emptiness, time discarded, and he was glad to be outside, feeling the coolness of the evening, breeze sharp and static, buildings square against the sky. Almost without thinking, he walked to Montgomery Street, at the foot of the Pyramid, a crossroads in more ways than one. To his right, Columbus Avenue rose up through North Beach; to his left, the Russ Building, Market Street, the Palace Hotel. The Palace was where he'd agreed to meet Alex, in Maxfield's, with the Pied Piper mural above the bar. It wasn't a place he remembered from his time here; in fact, he hadn't known of it until decades later, when he and Annie and the kids had stayed. They'd been back several times now, another touchstone, and thinking about that, he wondered whether it was why he'd suggested Maxfield's: a layer of familiarity, a link to the present, a trail of crumbs to keep a place for him amidst the labyrinth of the past.

Alex had said 6:30; she had to be home for dinner; *nobody around here can get a meal on the table*, she'd written in a Facebook message, the grievance humorous or bitter, he couldn't tell. He took out his phone to check the time—6:15—and saw there was a text from Sadie, asking when he was coming home. At 13, she lived almost entirely in the future, short- *and* long-term, chattering about summer plans, what

she wanted for her birthday, where she thought she wanted to go to college—all of it a limitless fantasy. It reminded him of something else he'd read, about the tension between kids and grown-ups: that our children were desperate to get us out of the way because they understood that their true inheritance was the future, which was the one inheritance we could not withhold. He remembered feeling something similar, a longing for real life to begin. This was why he'd come to San Francisco, driving west with Jack as if it were a matter of destiny. On their first night in the city, in that studio on Haight Street, they had watched the darkness descend, lights snapping on like stars in the apartment buildings ringing Buena Vista Park, and he had felt his body fill with breath as if, in leaving his past, his history, and coming here, he had been freed.

Now, of course, that *was* his past, a past so thick he felt encased. Standing here, he tallied echoes: the Pyramid, with its vaulted point and red eye at the apex, a vision of Atlantis, or so he'd once been told (and half-believed). The story had invested his time in San Francisco with a whisper of the mythological, as if he were living in a different timescape, the kind of magical thinking that had led him also to Grace Cathedral, letting him imagine, briefly, that there was a shape, an order, to the world. The same was true of North Beach, although there, real history had left a residue: City Lights, the Condor, the hungry i. Now, he knew better, knew that even landmarks had a habit of dissolving, that time was finite, and it always took its toll. No, this wasn't a mid-life crisis, it was an *identity* crisis. And it wasn't existential either, at least not in the sense that it was about death. Even now, midway upon the journey of his life, within a shadowed forest where he had lost the straightforward path, he had the sense that there was more to it, that the issue was less dying than living, that there was something he hadn't learned yet, that same essential lesson: *be here now.*

The wind picked up again, lashing him with bitter needles. He put his hands in his pockets and turned his collar up. Ahead, Montgomery Street unfolded like a carpet, leading to Market, the Palace growing visible in stages the more steps he took. First, the rounded corner of the building, yellow brick and cornices, then the marquee on the rooftop, spelling out its name in electric light. Another throwback, another nod to the history of the city, another nod to a different time. In one form or another, the Palace had stood on this corner since the 1870s, a vestige of that long-gone San Francisco, phoenix risen from the ashes, seal of the city come to life. The original had been destroyed in the 1906 earthquake, but the hotel was rebuilt three years later, which made it an emblem of both San Francisco's substance and its insubstantiality, the way all the years, everything erected here, could evaporate with the twitching of

the fault. He remembered pictures, downtown San Francisco after the quake and fire, streets scrubbed clean of buildings as if representing a virgin grid. The city in those images was little more than memory…memory, yes, and also imagination, the vision of a city yet to come. As a planner, he loved the mix of history and possibility, as if the form of the new city might be inscribed directly on the template of the old. And yet, there was also the filter of his own experience, since he'd been through his first earthquake here, a medium-sized temblor late in the afternoon of an Easter Sunday that he could still recall for its visceral lurching, the ceiling fixture of his studio apartment swinging wildly, wood beams in the walls rat-tat-tatting out an SOS. It was hard to feel rooted, hard to see the permanence of anything you might construct in such an active landscape, and maybe that was part of it also, his sense of the conditional, a physical reaction to living in California, whether here, on this elaborate peninsula, or in that sprawling megalopolis four hundred miles south.

He caught the light at Market, cutting in front of an F streetcar from Milan. A block west, he could see Lotta's Fountain, dedicated in 1875 like the original Palace, a legendary meeting place for survivors of the earthquake. A century later, there were no more survivors, and yet the fountain remained, a big bronze anchor jutting out from Market Street. He wondered what would happen in the next quake, where people would gather in the aftermath. One reason the 1906 earthquake was so resonant, so *present*, was the photographs; it had been the first disaster of the Kodak Era, the first to be recorded by informal snapshots, millions of them. At the Cable Car Museum, on the other side of Nob Hill, you could still see the quake unfold on vintage stereopticons: streetscapes, rubble, women with bustle skirts and parasols, the entire city recording its destruction, not in denial so much as a willful cool. Here it was, the onset of the image age, and where more vividly than in San Francisco, where the devastation and the need, somehow, to enclose the devastation were the puzzle pieces of a common dream? It was this to which he had long aspired—a kind of flinty realism, although he was aware that such pictures were no more real than those on Facebook. Like all photos, they promised a proximity they could not deliver, a set of windows on a world that had disappeared in the very instant of its recreation: time stopped, time rendered solid, time pinned down in two dimensions, so close you felt you could step inside it, until you were repelled by the reflective surface of the frame. The same was true of his time in San Francisco, which was less about memory than memory suspended, like a solid shape he had both left behind and would never leave behind.

At the Palace, he glanced at his phone again—6:30, right on time. He passed through the lobby and down the corridor to Maxfield's, hearing the buzz of cocktail hour chatter, as familiar as the chirrups of tiny birds. By the door, he scanned the long mahogany bar, looking for a match to Alex's Facebook photo, coming up blank. Finally, he saw her, sitting with another woman at a table in the back. *Two women?* he had time to wonder in the second before she noticed him, but then Alex was waving and both women were standing, and he was moving towards them, and as he drew closer, confusion yielded to recognition which, in turn, became another layer of confusion as he identified first the faint smile and then the wary eyes of the other woman at the table, her features tumbling together like a succession of slides, of snapshots, before collage-ing into the face, familiar and yet at the same time, long-forgotten, of Elena, his old high school girlfriend.

Interiors

His first thought was that he had been set up. He wasn't sure why, except for the look on Elena's face. Once he recognized her (and, in the end, how could he not?), he nodded self-consciously when Alex told him they'd been talking—both lived in San Francisco, and they saw each other once a month, twice a month, for a drink or coffee—and that Elena had thought it would be fun to come along. Elena smiled then, smiled with her mouth and she had little sharp predatory teeth, as white as fresh orange pith and as shiny as porcelain. The look she gave off shook him, as if her presence were its own kind of earthquake, major or minor it was too soon to tell. Large and small earthquakes began the same way, with a moment of rupture; the length of the rupture determined the severity of the shaking and the devastation that it caused. He could feel the rumbling as they said hello. *This was a mistake*, he thought, then pushed the idea away as he sat, a tiny flicker of something—unease? anxiety?—flaring in his solar plexus like a flame.

Alex was effusive, Alex was excited, Alex was happy to see him. Her broad face broke into a smile and she chattered in a raspy voice, but he was having trouble making out the words. He ordered a drink, Jameson on the rocks, sipped greedily when it arrived. *I don't often drink hard liquor*, he found himself telling them...or did he only think it? Either way, he was too old for excuses, although just being here, just seeing Elena, made him feel like a high school kid again.

And what did that feel like? Tense, uncertain, self-aware. As the alcohol seeped into him, he became aware of making small talk, almost as if he were watching himself in a play. He and Alex, talking about high school, sharing stories of their children, while Elena sat in the corner, watched them, flat half-smile on her face. She was pretty, Elena was, prettier than in high school, hair black and thick, expensively cut, shoulder length with bangs. He remembered her as raw-boned, blowsy, a big, fresh-faced girl he'd never bothered to get to know. It had been unremarkable, their relationship…or it would have been, if not for his virginity. Their first night together, she had taken off her clothes with an abandon that surprised him, and he, fumbling, over-eager, stunned at his good fortune, had done the same. They hadn't gone very far, just rubbed against each other, but when they finally got dressed again and he walked her home, he knew he had crossed a border of some kind. Or no, not crossed it—that would come later—but brushed right up against it, not of sex so much but something equally exotic: the line separating childhood, adolescence, from the adult world.

Now, here they were, entrenched in that adult world, although adolescence kept pulling at him. Or not adolescence, but post-adolescence, that shadowy line again. He had teenagers; he knew from close observation just how young that was. Still, he also knew how the choices, the experiences, of that time continued to resonate. Wasn't that the point of this…reunion, get-together, whatever it was? He was looking for something: roots, he guessed he would say. And yet, that was the problem with roots—that they grew tangled, that they went in all sorts of unexpected directions when you followed them back to the source.

Take Elena. She hadn't even been part of this, part of his San Francisco experience. Sure, she'd been here, a freshman at Berkeley when he and Jack landed in Haight-Ashbury, but after high school, she'd been wary. (*Be honest*, he told himself, *she wasn't the only one.*) It hadn't ended well between them, had ended in the only way it could, with him blowing her off after a series of graduation parties, parties where he'd felt the need to say something, *to be consoling*, like the pressure of a noose. He'd been 17, the same age as Jonah, and he hadn't understood that she had feelings…or at least, feelings that were different from his. But that wasn't it, not exactly—it was that he *hadn't* had feelings, any real feelings, any feelings that he'd wanted to keep. On their last morning together, he had woken up at a friend's house, fifteen or twenty kids huddled together in a basement rec room after a long and bleary night. Everyone was hung over, spaced from too much dope and drinking, edgy, raw with lack of sleep. He'd kept his distance, relieved that it was over, that he wouldn't be seeing most of

these kids again. Even then, he'd been a shedder, not the kind of person who liked to keep things, which made this whole weird day in San Francisco that much stranger, this three-dimensional gouging of the past.

But Elena hadn't let him off that easily, Elena hadn't let him walk away. She'd always had a toughness he couldn't penetrate—penetrate? Hell, that he couldn't *recognize*. He'd thought it was over when he left her in that basement. Now, in Maxfield's, he looked at the Pied Piper mural and wondered if time was a pied piper, leading him, unwitting and dream-besotted, from there to here. Elena was talking, and as her lips moved, he could feel his discomfort realign itself as the memory of desire. Elena had been his first...first fuck, first blowjob, first everything. She knew it and he knew it, and in the back of his mind, he couldn't help but wonder if that was why she was here. It wasn't like he'd had much experience subsequently: a couple of girlfriends and then Annie, whom he'd met in college and with whom he'd been together ever since. *Was that part of this?* he asked himself, signaling for another drink.

So what are you doing in town? Elena asked, as if reading his mind, her voice pointed as a lance. He mentioned the meeting, talked for a moment about transit hubs, said he wasn't sure why he had made the trip. *Some things haven't changed, I guess*, she replied, and her bluntness stopped him. He squinted at her across the table, looking for a point of view. She was smiling again, mouth cracked open in a semblance of good nature, but her eyes were mica: flinty, fierce. *Why is she here?* he thought. *She doesn't like me.* And then, with a feeling a lot like that of vertigo, he realized this was precisely why she had come.

Barstool blues

Later, he would wonder if he had misread things. Later, he would wonder if it was the alcohol. In the moment, though, he knew he was right. The realization struck with the force of revelation, and he looked quickly towards Alex to see if she was aware. She seemed oblivious: sipping her Chardonnay, delighted to be out of the house even for an hour, to have a break before serving yet another meal. That was all she'd wanted, a quick flash of reconnection, and as she sat there, her mouth unfolded lightly in a Cheshire cat grin. Alex, he now remembered, had never been a talker; even on that afternoon in Berkeley, with *Emotional Rescue* blaring from the speakers, she had been content to let the music talk for her. *You're too deep in*, Mick Jagger had sung, *you can't get out*...which was the danger of the past, that it could rise up at any instant

and swamp you like the sea. And what about the danger of the future, the way it sparkled, offering promises it couldn't keep? Again, the image of Sylvie rose before him, so vivid it was almost as if she were at the table with them, her body twisted into a question mark. *No*, he thought, and shook his head, rubbing his eyes to mask the motion, wondering how long he needed to stay here, wondering how he would extricate himself.

Elena kept talking but he wasn't really paying attention, something about her son, who was applying to law school and her daughter, who was majoring in art. She hadn't spoken yet about her husband, but that didn't mean anything; she wasn't trying to show off for him—more like she wanted to put him in his place. She asked about his kids, nodded when he kept it general, telling her that they were teenagers, that she knew how it was. Even as he mouthed the words, he was seized by a desire to protect them, not to reveal too much. It wasn't that they were under attack (at least he didn't think so), but there was something about her tone, its edge of probing, like a scalpel or a knife. *They must be interested in something*, she said, voice rising to a point. *They're kids*, he said, and laughed to shift the focus, although he could not recall having dismissed them in such a way before.

Elena looked at him from across the table, her teeth flashing. *Kids?* she said. *We were kids too, back when we used to know each other. I'm not sure I know what you mean…* Her voice trailed off, a fading siren, and he felt as if he'd walked into a trap. Alex was sitting up now, closer to the table, rolling the stem of her wineglass in her hand. Her eyes were hooded, but he thought he saw a look of confusion there. *Help*, he wanted to say, but that seemed so dramatic, and in any case, help from what? When had it become dangerous to sit in a hotel bar with a couple of former friends and have a drink? And yet, he felt lost, felt again as if this room had become a stage set and he were trapped within a play. *No Exit*, he thought, or *Waiting for Godot*. I can't go on, I'll go on….

Now Elena was saying something else, her voice low but firm against the buzzing background of the bar. *Do you remember the last time we saw each other?* She leaned forward. *You don't, do you? I bet you don't.* He wanted to laugh at that, wanted to tell her how much he did remember. And yet, when it came to her, she wasn't wrong. He tried to recall when last he'd seen her; he knew it had been during his time here, but he couldn't bring the details to mind. *That's how little you mean to me*, he thought, reflecting again on their relationship, the way it had petered out with the school year, just another thing to leave behind. Under the surface, he was aware

of something, a pull, the fragment of a recollection, but again the alcohol…or maybe it was just that he had never cared that much. Not in the moment, certainly, and not after: He hadn't given her a second thought in all the years that divided them, as if she had disappeared.

For a second, he was aware of a breath of anticipation, as if Elena were expecting him to speak. Then the moment passed, and she turned to Alex, talking about people, just names really, none of whom he knew. Again, he had the weird sense that this was for his benefit, to show him how full her life had become. He was glad for her, although as he thought about it, he understood that it had nothing to do with him. This was the irony: He had come to Maxfield's for one reason, and she, apparently, for another, and both were bound to leave here unfulfilled. Elena must have intuited this also, for eventually, she made a show of looking for the bar clock, and suggested that they get a check. While they waited, she began talking again, describing an outdoor party she was planning; her husband was turning 50 and she was catering a picnic at their house in the Berkeley Hills. *A catered picnic?* As she went on, he listened surreptitiously: a bar, a portable dance floor, heat lamps, and tables, each with a picnic basket as a centerpiece. *That's not a picnic*, he thought, but he knew better than to say anything. The check was coming; he just wanted to get out. *The last time I went on a picnic*…and then it clicked, the memory, the image, and swept over him.

It had been in Berkeley also, deep in the spring, towards the end of the academic year, late April, early May. She had called him in San Francisco, stunning since they hadn't seen each other in the months since he'd arrived. There was some event, he couldn't remember—a concert? a performance?—and she'd suggested a picnic first. After picking him up at the downtown Berkeley BART station, she drove him in her little car to Strawberry Canyon, to a spot overlooking Memorial Stadium, where she'd spread out a blanket and served fried chicken and California Chablis. Then, once he was full, stretched out beneath the blood-red Berkeley sunset, she had lit into him, telling him how much he had hurt her, voice low but insistent, her words as sharp as little blades.

Sitting in Maxfield's, he could feel his insides churning, as if the bottom of his stomach had fallen out. It was all so close, and yet not, all of it telescoped into an instant, with her right before him, and also inaccessible, in the past. He kept a neutral look on his face—the payoff of all those years of meetings—but behind the wall of his eyes he was scrambling, his mind a pair of ragged claws scuttling across the floors of

silent seas. What else had she said? He couldn't quite bring it back, but he could sense the flavor of it, knew that it had to do with the extent to which she had cared for him, the extent to which she had felt betrayed.

At another time, in another moment, he might have dismissed this as fantasy: his or hers. How could something that had happened so long ago, something that had never seemed important, continue to haunt her? Then again, just look at him. Wandering the city as if it were a ghost town, walking the stations of the cross. Occasionally, at home, Annie would do this also, talking about the boys she'd known in college, or someone she'd dated briefly before he and she had met. *He was hard to get rid of,* she had said of one such former paramour just a few nights ago, riding in the car with him and Jonah, and although he'd laughed and told her to get over herself, he wasn't laughing now.

Thinking about that, he found himself all of a sudden imagining Elena as she had been at 18, as if the veil of her sophistication had slipped, leaving that slightly horsy, awkward girl behind. He could see her, see her impression of a smile, lips tight, uncertain, as if the worst transgression would be to laugh. Was this what had attracted him, that diffidence, that shyness? He couldn't remember, and besides it didn't matter anyway. For when he saw her as 18, it wasn't from the point of view of his younger self, but rather from that of the present, not as peer but parent in a sense. He knew so many girls like this now—*his own daughter*—and he knew how deep their feelings ran. No wonder she was still nursing…whatever it was, a grudge, a sliver of resentment; no wonder the memory had lingered and she had shown up here to see it through.

He took a last sip of whiskey, now mostly water from the melted ice. He set the glass on the table precisely, matching its edges to the damp impression on the cocktail napkin, as if getting them to sync up was the most important thing in the world. No one was saying anything, the silence like a balloon between them, a balloon they were afraid to pop. *I…*, he started, but then he let the syllable trail off, like an error or an afterthought, a symbol of all he should say and all that he would never say, an apology he would never make.

When the check came, he reached for it and, waving off their protestations, gave the waiter his credit card. It seemed both expected and utterly insufficient, a gesture, like all the others, destined to fall short. Elena was watching him, but he was afraid to look at her, afraid it might trigger something, afraid of what he might say. *I'm sorry?* But what good would that do? It had all happened so long ago, and anyway, who knew what she was thinking? It would only make things worse.

And so, he sat there, waiting, face a blank as usual, again at a loss for words. He signed the slip and got up, watched as they both stood in turn. They hugged: a loose embrace with Alex, a stiff clench with Elena. *So much to be said*, he thought, *so much that will never be said*. Then he turned and left the bar.

Ulysses in nighttown
Market Street was a relief, crowded, clanging, the sky above compressed but open: full dark, no stars. For the first time in an hour, he felt like he could breathe. He meandered up the block, crossed the street and stopped at Lotta's Fountain. Like a survivor, which was what he was, of course…for the time being, anyway. Around him, the city continued its relentless motion—streetcars, tourists, commuters, hustlers, a cacophony of speed and light. And yet, here he was, at the center of it, at the *epi*center, totally unnoticed. He took solace in his anonymity.

After a moment, he went right on Kearny Street and started north. He was not walking towards anything so much as away from everything, as if his goal were to get lost in the city, to pursue a trail that could not be traced. He turned on Sutter, again on Grant, following the broad sidewalk to the Chinatown gate. On the other side, the street was like a carnival, a crazy quilt of signs and sound and movement, as garish as a sequence from a film. The sidewalks were full: people drifting, people talking, people looking up at the pagoda roofs of the buildings, taking photographs. California Street was two blocks ahead, but he couldn't bring himself to take the plunge. Instead, he turned on Bush and cut over to California on Stockton, where, muscles in both calves burning, he began to climb Nob Hill.

The idea was to return to the hotel, order room service, hide out until it was time to go home. Maybe later he would go to the Laurel Court, lift a glass to Jonah, to the present, to all he had left to do. Memory was a trap; he had always known it. It could eat you if you let it; just look at his encounter with Elena. *Elena*…he thought again, her face rising before him, half as she had once been and half as she was now. And yet, he began to understand as he crossed first Powell and then Mason Street, his was a peculiar kind of memory, defined by landscape, even his own inner landscape, but at the same time—and with few exceptions—curiously devoid of humanity.

The realization stopped him on the sloping sidewalk, with the Mark Hopkins glowering above him, a dark shape against the sky. It was true, he knew as soon as he thought it, and in that instant he felt more alone than he had all day. What use was

his connection to these streets, to the vista of this skyline, what good his memories of this place? All it had left him with were pictures, intercut with a few small film clips: Alex in the sorority house, that Sunday service at Grace Cathedral, hardly anything to cling to, these bits and ribbons of the past. His memory was like a Facebook page, a set of scattered images, posted as if they meant something when they revealed nothing at all. Generic, he scoffed, or worse, empty…and that was the whole problem, wasn't it, that he was an empty vessel, that his disengagement was not a function of getting older but had been a part of him all along.

 He pinched his eyes as if to squeeze the thought out, pushed up the hill towards his hotel. But half a block shy, he veered, almost instinctively, across the street. The last thing he wanted was to be alone in a room, trapped like a hamster on a wheel. No, that was just another sinkhole, another spinning cycle; he needed more stable ground. So he kept on, past the Pacific-Union Club, past Grace Cathedral and down California towards Van Ness, sidewalk sparsely dotted with pedestrians, lights on in the low-slung buildings, small and sketchy in the night.

 He could feel his body fall into a groove now, legs pumping like a machine. He could feel his heart achieve a steady rhythm, feel the flow of his own blood. It was a sensation he knew well: the oblivion of the long-distance walker, moving street to street, neighborhood to neighborhood, passing along the outer edges of a million lives. Like a ghost, he thought, drifting down the sidewalks, looking into the lit-up windows, both a part of it and apart from it, watching all those solitary men and women as they went about their routines. Solitary, yes, even when they were together, faces staring at each other across the dinner table, eyes hooded, mouths working in a quiet mumble as they tried to find something to say. How many times had he felt the same?

 He turned right at Van Ness, followed it to Lombard, went up to Fillmore and cut over towards Marina Green. He had worked here, all those many years ago, canvassing for Greenpeace out of an office in Fort Mason, and most nights, after going door-to-door in Berkeley, in Albany, in Daly City, he had waited for the bus at Fillmore and Chestnut, or taken the long walk back to the Haight across the darkened city: Fillmore through Pacific Heights and then up Clay or Sacramento to Divisadero, watching the neighborhoods change, chic to shabby, feeling the pulse of the streets rise up inside him like some kind of umbilical connection, although he didn't know about that anymore. He had walked, then, in a kind of fugue state of exhilaration, but tonight, as he pushed himself, first towards the water and then east, up the hill and

past the Black Point Battery, it was exhaustion he sought. He remembered, a decade ago, the first time he had taken Jonah here, showing him the cannons and the secret staircase (not-so-secret, actually, although he had always thought of it as his alone). It had been overgrown then, and remained so now, and as he started down, a shadow in the silent evening, he felt a brief glimmer of…what? resolution? No, nothing that complete. Yes, he had passed his love of San Francisco on to Jonah; yes, it had become a bond they shared. And yet, what if it was all a frozen landscape, past and present blurred together, a sea whose floor he could not access, his claws skittering along the surface, unable to find a point of entry, always just at the edge of control? *He was barely here, he had never been more than barely here.* And as he came back into the grid at Beach Street and slid along the front of Ghirardelli Square, all the lights and tourists, the street musicians and the clatter of the cable cars, even on a cool evening in January…they only made it worse by reminding him of his disconnection, as if not just his life but everyone's had passed him by.

The crowds were dense, the crowds were pressing, the crowds were a bubbling current that threatened to sweep him away. There was too much noise, too many flashing signs; it was the landscape of a nightmare come to life. He felt his stomach fall again, a queasy sensation like being on a roller coaster, nauseous with the idea that he did not exist at all. Eyes down, concentrating on his breathing, he skirted the tumult until he got to Columbus, where he headed into North Beach, then turned right on Taylor Street and began the slow, slogging climb in the direction of his hotel.

Labyrinth

But a funny thing happened on the way to the hotel: He found himself redeemed. Or not redeemed so much as confused, beguiled…or maybe he was seduced, again, by the serendipitous pull of the city, with its interplay between the present and the past. He was breathing hard as he reached Clay Street, legs heavy, lower back starting to tug at him in an intimation of middle age. Over his shoulder, San Francisco opened in a sea of lights. But up ahead, all he could see was Grace Cathedral, and, just beyond it, the slender tower of his hotel.

He paused, panting, fingers splayed across his thighs. Then he took one step, and another, point of view shifting the higher he went. The Cathedral seemed to rise out of the hilltop, its double tower like an outstretched hand, not magical, he understood now, but supplicating, a prayer in concrete to the empty universe, a

declaration of both desperation and desire. Desire? Yes, the desire to be noticed, the desire to leave a mark. *Here we be*, the building seemed to be exclaiming, *not for long, but here we be.* The statement was so futile as to be meaningless, and yet what other choice had there ever been? You could keep on moving, or you could roll up and die. The second option was assured, sooner or later, which meant that the only decision of any consequence was what you did about the first.

Across Sacramento, the steps of the Cathedral beckoned. He took out his phone to check the time: 9:30, after his long peregrination through the city, and not a single message. In every way that mattered, he was on his own. He thought about calling Annie, texting the kids. But they were in their lives, four hundred miles to the south of him, and he was not part of it, not tonight. And yet, those steps. They shone white beneath the streetlights, leading to the Cathedral's double door. He followed them up, first one level, then a second, until he was on a little flat plain of plaza, with the rectory off to his right. Just to the east, tucked into an attenuated open-air rotunda, he could see the outline of a labyrinth, a replica of the labyrinth inlaid in the Cathedral, which was itself a replica of the labyrinth at Chartres. He knew a little about labyrinths, having walked one once on a bluff overlooking the Pacific Ocean at Santa Cruz. The original labyrinths—or the original Christian labyrinths—had been built as *chemins de Jerusalem*, landscapes for a proxy pilgrimage, but the point, especially in California, had long since shifted to personal discovery. He recalled walking the narrow lines in the failing sunlight, mist blurring the edges of the ocean, rendering it in shades of bluish white. He had been skeptical—he was always skeptical—but as he had followed the looping lanes of the maze, focused on staying within the boundaries, his sense of both past and future had receded, leaving him in time and yet outside it, mind and body finally still. He had never told anyone about that, not even Annie; it had seemed too…he didn't know, too personal, too intimate to share. Now, however, he remembered that calm, the way it had descended upon him about halfway through his silent passage, and without thinking consciously about it, he moved slowly towards the mouth of *this* labyrinth, and embarked upon its winding path.

For an instant, he grew self-conscious. There was no one here, but he knew he could be seen from the windows of the adjacent hotels and apartments, and he felt a twinge, a shudder, at the thought of people looking at him. Then he remembered Sylvie, and how he'd watched *her* through that kitchen window, watched her pushing her son on the swing as if the world had shrunk to the two of them. Sylvie hadn't cared; she was consumed by the moment, she understood that the moment was all

there was. He wanted some of that same understanding, it was all he wanted, a way to fend off all his fear and longing—or no, not fend off, they could never be superseded, but a way to integrate them instead.

He took a step, and another. The labyrinth was divided into quarters; the idea was to walk each section in succession until you made it to the middle, and after that, to walk your way back out again. In Santa Cruz, it had taken hours, but this labyrinth seemed smaller, and anyway, where did he have to be? He thought about Elena, about Alex; he thought about Annie and the kids. He thought about Sylvie, fighting the good fight, even though it was a fight that she—that no one—could win. He thought about himself here, alone, adrift, so little to hold onto, as it was and as it would ever be. Then, he placed one foot before the other, perspective narrowing to the path in front of him, mind a blank except for one thought, a simple benediction, which he repeated, to the rhythm of his walking: *Be here now.*

Black Clock

rick moody
THIRTEEN STORIES

There used to be twenty of these stories. Well, there were probably twenty-seven or so, but at every stage the number has been reduced. Midway through my 2002 book The Black Veil, *when I was supposed to be writing non-fiction, and afterward, in the ill wind of publication, I wrote a bunch of short-short stories for no occasion but that I hadn't written short-short stories before. There was a sort of vogue for them then, short-shorts, and a coterminous vogue for the prose poem. I thought I would try to exploit one or the other, or the gray area between the two. The point was to write as quickly as possible and not worry about anything but the plasticity of the language. Therefore: no purpose but a linguistic purpose to these constructions, with the story in each case proposing itself automatically, inadvertently, if at all. In 2007, when I was working on my third collection,* Right Livelihoods, *these stories were going to be central to the work. This was the case up to the point when I imagined the book to be composed solely of novellas. Soon it appeared that the somewhat experimental and automatic veneer of these works were not in phase with the rest of the collection. Whereupon they got sacrificed again. They have been parceled out to little magazines over the years, some if not all, but this is the first time they have been published together. (And in such a carefully winnowed condition.) They have been preempted by a lot of other stuff for collection number four, which is in the planning stages as I write these lines, so this may in fact be their only chance at historical relevance.*

General Purpose Foreword

Literature is based on a true story. Literature is an American flag with an erroneous number of stars. Literature is torn from a tabloid and taped into the lone window of an orthopedist's office. Literature is a white powdery substance. Literature is a mildly unpleasant electrical current. Literature is a low-calorie coffee beverage with

natural flavors. Literature is the original black-and-white version of a colorized classic; literature is commemorative stamps and action figures and other collectibles; literature is talk show hosts, now and forever; literature is complimentary samples of serotonin re-uptake inhibitors, literature is plus-size models, literature is our only hope, literature is *[insert metaphor]*, literature is the renunciation of irony and its replacement with ambiguity, knots upon knots, convolutions upon convolutions, evasions upon evasions, mysteries piled upon enigmas piled upon secrets. Store up thy treasures, come hither unto the source, do not look directly thereupon. All hail.

I was 17. I had just arrived at the university at *[name of city]*, where I was afflicted, as are all 17-year-olds, with unrequited adoration for *[non-specific]*. S/he was dancing on the bar in town, the bar on the other side of the interchange. S/he was in the audience of the production of Shakespeare set at a Parisian fashion show. Rapt, undivided in his/her attentions with respect to the Bard. Or perhaps s/he had become one of the constellations, and I lay in a field on the outskirts of town, where cattle lowed sweetly in a perfumed dusk. Loss upon me like a sickness. This was after her/his untimely *[car accident/overdose/suicide]*, or it was while I had that job, that dispiriting swing shift job at *[convenience store or bowling alley]*, a work-study thing, because my father had walked out on my mom the year before. My mom rained down oaths upon me when I mentioned his name.

I was supposed to be doing course work in deviant behavior, but because of *[euphonious name]* I was seized with the works of *[somebody complicated, since nobody reads James Gould Cozzens or Irwin Shaw when having an existential crisis]*, and the revelation of the work was like wildfire or flash flood or Central Asian temblor in my desiccated *[internal organ or humor]*. The gods of writers are Eleatic, or maybe aleatory, they are liminal, hegemonic, canonical and when they *[tapped me on my bruised scapula, or battered my heart, or seduced and ravished me]*, it was as though the citizens of *[town, as shown above]*, where I appeared to be walking to and from class and going to get my *[make of automobile]* lubed, were ghosts and wraiths. I renounced their habits and routines. I heard saxophones in darkest night playing *[bebop]*, I heard the cries of children, I heard *[folk idiom]* jamborees, there were voices in my crowded skull, and so I began to set words down on the page. On a typewriter, I should say, none of this word processing nonsense, my words are not processed, they contain no additives, they are as free and natural as that organic produce you get at your local co-op. I was an ethicist of the Word. I was a scientist of the grammars of the heart, an economist of verb tenses. I was like that son of Hagar, of whom it was said that *his*

hand will be against every man, and every man's hand against him. I wrote, and many nights my lamp was burning until the first streaky light of the dawn.

In due course, I became a full-fledged apprentice, an up-and-comer, a slip of a thing, living hand to mouth in *[this is after the university years, and you can use any sort of dead-end town that works for you, though I personally like Hoboken, NJ]*. It was the national periodicals that sustained me, that said to me, "Hey *[your name here]*, you can do this job, you can find a few readers, you can have your voice ring out among other voices." In particular, there was *[name of literary magazine you hold in your hands, or book, or collection of short stories, or broadside, etc.]*, which I used to steal from the independent bookstores downtown. The best way to steal it was *[blandishments offered to underpaid bookstore personnel, or books snuck into the bathroom and thrown out the window there, or books tucked into the bib section of overalls]* and I didn't feel too badly about it then, because I understood that the university was underwriting this particular magazine. Then I devoured the *[book, poem, quarterly, glossy, broadside, etc]* while riding on mass transit in my city. It was all there, it was right in the pages of *[the item you have in your hand here]*, where writers as diverse as *[could be anyone pretty much]* got their start, back when they too were living in *[rust belt towns]* and working nights in the *[white bread, double-stick tape]* factory waiting for break. The first part of a writing career is the loneliest part, when without peers you dream of honor. Who doesn't wish instead that he or she could drink *[cheap American brand]* at *[local tavern]* arguing with friends about the proper outcome of a story about the wedding cake in the middle of the road.

The stories you have before you in *[name of periodical or book]* are diverse and thrilling, yet with a common vision, a vision of *[insert common vision here]* in *[place name]* at the end of *[epoch]*. What we see here is that human yearning is universal, that the longing for *[insert item]* is the same in whichever culture it is articulated, whether in the *[name of culture]* or in the *[choose a different group]*, literature always hews close to the complexities that inform character across cultural boundaries. In the story by *[name of an author]* entitled *[title]*, for example, family is limned with a particular vehemence. Never before, except perhaps in the work of *[insert name of author of works about family]*, have we seen the dynamics of familial relationships so trenchantly explored. Similarly, in the piece called *[title]*, by *[author]*, the time-honored coming-of-age theme is relocated to *[anyplace at all]*, and metaphorized in the slaying of the *[defenseless animal]*. While the section concerning dispensing with offal of the carcass will be offensive to some readers, the ritualized violence of hunting

nonetheless has a particular *[hortatory noun]*. Finally, we have the illness narratives of *[author]*. Perhaps it is a topic that will seem well-travelled. Nevertheless here the *[adenocarcinoma, melanoma, blastic sarcoma, etc.]* is rendered with an honesty and sobriety that makes the familiar new. We are lucky, as always, that writers of courage and ambition continue to imagine, dream, compose.

Especially in times so dark as these, when *[insert national crisis]*, the efforts of these new voices are crucial. What could be more important than reading, what could be more important than writing, what could be more important than the endeavor of literature, what could be more salvific? Plumes of smoke drift menacingly across the expanses of *[place name]*. Women and children stand forlornly at the margins of *[place name]* searching their persons for handkerchiefs, while men, stanching their own grief, vow to avenge the lost. At a time like *[epoch]*, the last thing a writer of forewords should be concerned with is *copyright.* That's right. Copyright is a kind of brutality that lingers from the Middles Ages, but in a time of emergency should its imperatives still obtain? Let's do away with copyright for the moment so that language can propagate itself, like the grass pushing forth its stalks between the cracks in the paving stones. As evidence of the seriousness of this revolutionary purpose, the writer of these lines has decided to abjure the rights attendant upon the composition of his foreword and to urge other writers of forewords, whenever necessary, whether due to overwork or because moneys are not available to pay for the composition of new forewords, simply to use this general purpose form. Fill in such blanks as you need to fill in. The reuse of this foreword will result in general savings to aid the war effort in *[name of country where war effort is currently taking place]*. It will make more time for other compositional efforts elsewhere. Reprint as needed. All hail.

— *[insert author and date]*

The Groom Smokes

Don't really want to go back in there, the groom thinks, meaning into the V.F.W. hall. Dusk exercising its influence over the groom. Dusk in late summer. The groom drinks lustily from a foamy lager. Sunset in the lower branches of larches and willows. The groom has seen the V.F.W. festooned with its patriotic swags and arrangements of plastic flowers. He has seen the V.F.W. laid out with punches, with cheese plates, with pigs in blankets. He has seen the wedding cake, with its bride and groom action

figurines, and there are tears in his eyes, because here is the dusk exercising its influence over him. In the action of inertia he stands outside drinking, talking to his friend the parcel deliveryman, known since high school. The parcel deliveryman is noteworthy for complete taciturnity, and so it is the groom talking, in expository bursts that are sentimental, about the good times they had. Swimming holes, stolen cars, trips into the woods, sagas of girlfriends, sagas of alcohol abuse. Those were the days. And they were not long ago. These expository bursts are unconvincing. When the groom asks the parcel deliveryman for a smoke, the parcel deliveryman produces a brand that does not meet with favor. You can't possibly want to smoke *that,* the groom says, and you can't possibly want *me* to smoke *that.* Because I'm not gonna smoke *that,* not if I'm on my death bed. Dusk over the groom and dusk over the parcel deliveryman. Sunset in the lower branches of larches.

Inside the V.F.W. the family of the groom and the family of the bride and the families that have known these newlyweds for the whole of their nineteen years are mustered around folding tables. Children are running around the tables until one skids on spilled beer, abrades his knee, bruises his skull. A deejay plays well-known ballads in the country and western style. It is common knowledge that there is already a job for the groom, after the honeymoon, which is the job of roofer, the job of swabbing creosote on the roofs of new homes and coming home smelling of incinerated tires. Silence in the V.F.W. hall, sunset in the branches, dusk over the groom. Clouds of dust on the unpaved roads, hanging in the air, from the last car through here. The groom argues bitterly about a particular brand of cigarette, which he says tastes like scorched brussels sprouts. Says he needs a man's cigarette, says he needs what a man needs, because now he is a man. And yet he has not gone back inside. The groom arranges his hair nervously. Inside the families await the Dollar Dance, in which they will push small bills into the bodice of the happy bride. There is also the wedding cake. They wait for the groom to be done smoking and drinking. It's time now. The moon is on the horizon, over a stand of larches. Luck is always either good and bad. The groom will not go in.

An Elaboration on Arrival[1*]

Arrival is bright, *arrival is bright,* the light is arrived, the light is bright as the arrival of the sun's rays, *love,* find me, as bright as the safety of the sun's fine arrival, in this light, the sun is bright as an arrival, *love,* in this light, *find me,* find the arrival of the sun, in this light, light the sun's rays with your arrival, *love,* brighten the sun's rays, the sun's light is in an arrival of rays, there is safety in rays, find me, *find love, find sun, find light, find arrival,* fined for the arrival of the brightness of the lightness of the safety of the sun's rays, love light, love safety, love arrival, love the sun, who loves the sun, find me, whomever it is who loves the sun, find the love who arrived like the sun, as bright as the light of the sun arrived, *love in this light,* love is bright in this light; my son was fined for the carving of a safe tee from the tree of the right arrival, strong tree, bold tree, be right, be writerly, as the sun raises the lie teasing the safe love from me, it's fine with me, you'd be right about the arrival of my son, Ray, in this light, it's right with me, the light is right, the bright is right, it's safe to love me and find me, fine me, to dine with me, your arrival is like a mighty survival, your loving kindness is free, loving kindness is me, arrival is blighted, arrival is lighted, the bright light of arrival is safety-free at least between you and me, on and on and on, in and on and is and as, the *in this,* as is, as is, *love,* arrival might be bright if it weren't for the light of the sun, which is both fun and *no fun,* fun in the sun and no fun because stunned, depending on whether it's free between you and me and she and he, whether there is safety and intrigue between those three and me, safety took a wrong turn, unlearned what it earned, arrival is bright, *arrival is bright,* arrival is light especially at night, recoil from blessing of the bright light arrayed like the sun's rays, *arrival is light.*

Cheese, *The Proposal*

Stan Powell, that's his name, and he finds cheese disturbing. He can't make his peace with cheese. At least not the really decayed varieties of cheese. Stan wonders how the first guy or gal got the idea. *I'll just take this enzyme found in a cow's stomach and mix in some residual dairy products and then I'll strain them both through some cheesecloth.* Except that there was no cheesecloth back then, of course, because there wasn't cheese

---

[1*] Written in response to two lines of poetry by an unknown elementary school student: "Arrival is bright as the sun's rays, in this light/safety and love find me"

yet, perhaps there wasn't even cloth. At least not in the sense that we know it. Through what did this inventor of cheese first strain his or her cheesy build-up? Stan ponders these things. And how did this guy or gal get the idea of straining? Maybe there was yogurt first. Maybe yogurt led to cheese, which led to an explosion of these ideas. *Hey, it tastes kind of like yogurt only worse! Great!* At this early moment in the history of cheese the notion of things going bad must have been rather different from the notion we have now. There was as yet no clear boundary between milk that was potable and milk that had *turned;* no perfect terminology distinguished between the *fresh* and the *spoiled.* You might be sickened by the latter. Otherwise, how to know?

Stan Powell will take up these issues in his commentary, *Cheese.* In this monograph, the discovery of rennet is as revolutionary as fire. Though Stan cannot make his peace with cheese, he can recognize that a paradigm shift is implied when the language of cuisine becomes able to observe, *This material that tastes like it has gone off is actually a delicacy.* He has given over profound rumination to the subject of cheese. Why do certain people like really *awful* kinds of cheese and certain people not? Why do certain people believe that Stilton is food? How is that possible?

In one chapter, Powell develops a catalogue of words associated with cheese, from which the following is but an excerpt: *semi-soft, mild, nutty, provocative, vegetal, luscious, sweet, lasting, herbaceous, delicate, spicy, intense, satisfying, rustic, buttery, distinctive, charismatic, friendly, tangy, challenging, electric, elegant, grassy, liquescent, stinky, concentrated, leafy, coin-shaped, sour, full-bodied, barnyard, velvety, earthy, racy, aromatic, amiable, crystalline, relaxed, intense, robust, pungent, sensual, traditional, bordering on mean, sinful, flaky, woodsy, notorious, bacony, briny, rustic, unctuous, enigmatic, plush, mushroomy, chocolaty, subtle, septic, sassy, savory.* Any of these modifiers, when applied to a cheese product can bring out torrents of rage in Stan Powell. Let's not get into it! He can't control himself where the language of cheese is concerned! Nothing can stop him! Stan has often consulted professionals with this complaint about cheese. In fact, on one occasion, he was forced to abandon friends at a restaurant—leaving behind a perfectly good *pinot noir*—when the word *amiable* was used to describe an *assortiment de fromage.*

Cheese is about death. This is the monumental conclusion of this Stan Powell's life's work. The love of cheese is a kind of sublated obsession with death. A manifestation of death-drive. Blue cheese is death, Gorgonzola is death, *chèvre* is death, string cheese is death, Velveeta is death, ricotta is death, and so on. The dawn of civilization, according to Powell, carries with it the stain of death, death is always in

the air, and therefore there must have been cheese at the dawn of civilization as there is cheese now; or, to put it another way, civilization is dependent on cheese, on the ideas inherent in cheese, because civilization is meaningless without the advent of death.

Consider, the current epistemological incarnation of cheese, as metaphorical formulation for sentimentality *(This song is cheesy!),* now clearly to be seen as continuous with the origin of the idea and outward manifestation of cheese, as substance: cheese implying a *sentiment* resembling a kind of *rotting,* a kind of decay. We should be purified of sentiment, as the colloquial users indicate. Sentiment is a putrefaction. We should feel the revivifying breeze of change blowing away the foul vapors of cheese. We should feel the daylight of innovation crowding out the darkness of cheese. We should feel the freshness of technology wiping aside the obsolescence of cheese. Only then will there be satisfaction.

I urge you to consider publication of Stan Powell's electrifying monograph.

A Short Philosophical Primer

The way the winter sky is both sunny and ominous, this is good. All things that are ambiguous but reliable are good. Foods that take decades to be appealing, like turnips and beets, are good. Records that you hate at first are good. Paintings that you don't understand for years, but which then reveal their intensities, very good. The weird ebbing and surging of long friendship is good. Things that disappear and then reappear are good, socks being one example. Things seen backwards through binoculars are good. Waiting is good. Waiting even longer is better. Extremely long, dull waiting periods when you imagine you will never do anything but wait, these are hellish, but sometimes good. Sleeping with someone and forgetting about the explosive part of it, this is often good and refreshing. Remembering that there was a thing you wanted to do, and then forgetting it, this is often very good. Youth is good when you are young, but middle age is much much better, much more good, and in middle age youth seems vain and self-satisfied, except in certain exceptional cases. Blurry photographs are better than photographs that are distinct. Stories in which the narrative is all but absent are extremely good. Indistinct narrators are good. People who come back into your life after long intervals, with apologies, are absolutely good. Pieces of music that do the same things over and over and over and over and over and over and over and over and over and over and over and over and over and

over and over and over and over and over and over and over and over and over, until in the repetition you begin to see that the repeated thing has infinitely more variety than you hitherto believed, these pieces of music are so good that we need to laud and magnify them. The repetition of the word "good" until it is drained of all meaning is good. "Good," since it is overused by children early in the learning curve of language acquisition, needs to be made *good* all over again. Virtue is good and virtue when stippled with failure is even better. The acknowledgment of earthly failure is always good. Ideals are essential, but lapsed ideals are nearly as good. Good is perhaps derived from Sanskrit *gadh,* to hold fast, which implies that uniting is good. Bearing things together when they are apart is good, finding the order in the disparate is good; people with extremely large eyes are good, laughing in the dark is good, and whispering is good and all silences are good, as are the times after silence. Plato is good, Aristotle is less good, Nietzsche is good in some ways. Fear of death is very, very good. Making up things as you go along is a good way of working and then rearranging the order of these things very quickly without looking is also good. Your insides are good, your organs and viscera, and you should let them be outside, this would be good, at least in some metaphorical way.

***From* Great Moments in Psychotherapy**

It was linear low-density polyethylene, part of the boom in plastic film products that had, since the Seventies, overtaken the merchandising of grocery items. Its resin acted as a gas barrier. It could keep chicken parts fresh, it could be a boil-in-bag for a tasty frozen dinner, it could be an ice bag, a garment bag at your dry cleaner, it could be a mulch film, a fumigation film, it could be a peat moss bag, it could be bubble wrap. Not today. Today, this was a routine grocery bag, having come from a strip of such bags where it had been separated and opened by an underpaid supermarket employee, and what it contained, initially, and, if a bag could be said to have feeling, *happily,* was a smaller plastic bag (high-density polyethylene) that in turn contained a half-pound of pistachios. Just beside the pistachios: a sixteen-ounce jar of fancy Italian marinated peppers. And a box of decongestant tablets.

In accordance with the principles of waste management, the bag was extremely lightweight. This was especially apparent on the day in question, because, in a heavy breeze the bag was making the sound that plastic manufacturers refer to

in the literature as *crinkling*. Occasional plastic bag users have expressed misgivings about the crinkling characteristic of linear low-density polyethylene bags, especially in high wind, and on this day the plastic bag user, a young professional in his early thirties, late to help his girlfriend with the hors d'oeuvres for their cocktail party, was irritated with the crinkling. He carried another portable accessory: a black leather messenger-style bag, over his left shoulder. It therefore occurred to this plastic bag user that he might put the plastic grocery bag, or its contents, or both, into the over-the-left-shoulder leather messenger bag, thereby bringing to an end the crinkling portion of this history, while also serving to cloak the contents of his grocery bag, which was semi-transparent, from the prying gazes of passersby. Unfortunately, to the peril of this worthy idea, the plastic bag became caught in the cord connecting his headphones to his portable digital music player, and there was, momentarily, the danger of accidental asphyxiation by cord or bag, etc., with the result that this plastic bag user needed to stop on this Eleventh Street, the block with the highest density of psychotherapists in all New York City, in order to: detach the plastic bag from the headphones, restore his headphones, remove the contents from the bag, place the supermarket products in his messenger bag, condense the plastic bag, store it in side pocket of messenger bag, etc. The confluence of factors that needs to be fully understood for the purposes of the narrative therefore includes the breeze, the crinkling, the irritation, the portable digital music player, the messenger bag, the cocktail party, the lightweight nature of linear low-density polyethylene resins, and so forth.

    He was no litterer. The plastic bag user counted himself responsible in the matter of recycling except on particular days when he was in a rush or when his girlfriend was travelling on business. On these occasions, he did take the occasional day off from recycling, and without undue remorse, since he was rarely apprehended breaking these particular laws. However, in the instant of exchange of goods from plastic bag to messenger bag, the instant of headphone detachment and exchange of goods, *the bag escaped his keen grip*. He took in the almost magical hovering of the bag, its ghostly lingering. It was nearly beautiful. But that was before it *floated away*. Suddenly, the plastic bag user was mortified. By reason of a density of psychotherapists, this block was heavily visited by pedestrians. He might have noted fifteen or so persons passing between Fifth and Sixth Avenues at this very moment, not to mention any number of therapists or clients of therapists who might have been staring out the windows of their respective offices, frustrated or despondent, or perhaps simply reflective, as one occasionally is in the psychotherapeutic theater. In looking out the window, these

persons might have seen the bag flying away and might have understood that the young professional plastic bag user was somehow responsible for the lifting off of the plastic bag during the removal and repacking of American goods. He ran for the bag, therefore, he lunged to grab it, in front of a woman walking a Pomeranian dog, but the gust of wind, an autumnal breeze, was so profound that his lunging and reaching and stretching—however useful for his musculature—did not result in the intended capture of the bag; *it was free,* and, again, though it is impossible to impute feeling to an inanimate linear low-density polyethylene resin, we would have to conclude that the bag, in some fashion, was happy. It was a chain of chemicals and additives, it was off-white, it was milky coloring and chemicals. Later, in most bag histories, it would be a waste minimization statistic, it would be combusted, occasioning the release of carbon dioxide and water, or it would sit in a landfill, releasing cadmium in the process (because of the blue lettering on its side), or it would be densified, which is the technical term for being crushed, or agglomerated, joined together with other such plastic bags at a resource recovery site.

But for the moment the bag was *free,* flying up above the first floor of a series of classrooms belonging to a university on the block, and then up past an expensive brownstone with an expensive picture window, and now it was, indeed, listing toward the building noted for containing one of the psychoanalytic training institutes in the neighborhood. This induced the young professional plastic bag user to flee the scene—at a speed faster than a walk, but slower than a trot. Perhaps it's more accurate that he began to forget, with impressive haste, his relationship to the bag. There was an average event duration for acts of environmental redress and this event duration was in the area of forty-five seconds. For forty-five seconds, he didn't want to be recognized as the source of the wild, unfettered linear low-density polyethylene resin bag. He didn't want to be held responsible. But then he had the cocktail party to attend to. It rushed back into his consciousness. There was only so much worry that could attach itself to the predicament of the bag. Anyway, he was a little sick. This accounted for the decongestant tablets.

The plastic bag itself might have flown far and wide, up over the East River, perhaps over the Gowanus Canal, the Jamaica Bay, perhaps out into the wide Atlantic; the bag might have been part of a great migration of plastic bags, toward the Continental Shelf, or, through the agency of the Gulf Stream in the direction of the Faeroe Islands, or the bag might have soared on the breeze to Bermuda, or even Lisbon. It might have gone distantly abroad, as a sign of American ingenuity and progress, were it not for

the maple trees on the block. Indeed, somewhere just out of reach, just beyond the windows, two stories up, in front of the office of a psychoanalyst who specialized in couples therapy and the treatment of eating disorders, the bag lodged, in the autumnal breeze, speared, impaled, knotted, affixed.

Think of the total volume of tragedies contained in that office. The office with the view of the bag. The office itself was a sort of high-volume container of tragedy, despair, of the occasional revelation. The office contained, for example, any number of pulped tissues, tissues that were densified or agglomerated in the palms of the unfortunate. Think of the volume of tissues. Think of the volume of tragedies. On a regular working day, incest, molestation, alcoholism, heroin addiction, bipolar disorder. All routine. Obsessive-compulsive disorder, fetish, perversion, self-mutilation, autoerotic asphyxiation, auto-immolation, shoplifting. At 8:40 AM, e.g., there was a young banker who had thrown up blood that morning, in an effort to void the two pints of ice cream from last night. When she was done sobbing at 9:30, a five-minute interval followed, in which the psychoanalyst took some notes, stared absently out the window without seeing the bag. At 9:35, there appeared a couple who hated each other so completely that they were barely speaking. They'd each had multiple affairs. At 10:30, the apparently high-functioning auctioneer from the West Village who admitted that he'd been embezzling funds from his employers. At 11:25, suicidal ideation, until 12:20, when the psychoanalyst observed a lunch break, stuck her hand out the window to see if the rain had begun. Now, at last she took note of the thing, the thing in the tree, *what the hell was that thing in the tree?* Later, outside, underneath the maple containing the linear low-density polyethylene resins of the bag, she looked up, considered heights of various ladders, despaired. *It's way up there.* How had what had been accomplished so effortlessly by the breeze, by the machinations of chance, become so permanent?

The incremental decay of the plastic bag was a reliable therapeutic subject for most of the next six years.

Physically Adaptive End User Interfaces with Hydro-Industrial Indoor Appliance

Thirsty physically adaptive end user (A) flings Acme brand clay pigeon into the uninterrupted blue of sky. Childhood friend of physically adaptive end user (B) fires Remington 12-gauge in same direction, having loaded firearm with fancy peeled

carrots. Carrots bounce harmlessly from clay pigeon. However, jackrabbit (C) sees carrots, leaps from bushy undergrowth at carrots falling from sky. Local timber wolf (D), attached by rubber cord to red aluminum wagon, sees flying rabbit, catches rabbit in mouth, dragging red aluminum wagon (E) onto railroad tracks, where freight train carrying load of propane (F) and other inflammable products bears down on wagon. Train (G) derails, rolls down mountainside, spilling propane and other inflammable products into valley where troop of Cub Scouts (H) are camped around fire, singing drinking songs. Inflammable cargo trickles to base of campfire, causing valley to burst into flames. Hot air balloon (I), moored harmlessly nearby, spontaneously lifts off, in eddies of hot air, carrying away house cat, several Cub Scouts, seven volumes of diary of missing balloonist. Cat leaps out of balloon (J), in pursuit of passing flock of starlings, Cub Scouts leap after cat (K), causing balloon to rise further, over Continental Divide, until, in or around Los Angeles metropolitan area, balloon begins to lose pressure, landing in yard (L) of disgruntled independent film producer. Film producer, seeing deflated balloon in driveway, panics, drinks on top of antidepressants. Producer takes volumes of diary from basket (M) at base of deflated balloon, immediately recognizes, in hallucinatory state, that diary is *major motion picture.* Calls studio head (N). Studio head, engaged in attempt to eliminate starlings from attic of guest house by catapulting poisonous frogs (O) through louvered window, cannot hear film pitch by reason of bad cellular telephone contact, believes film producer is balloon store owner bringing over mylar balloon products for Sweet Sixteen of cocaine-addicted daughter (P), accidentally gives tentative green light to three hundred million-dollar project (Q) about the life of balloonist. Disgruntled independent film producer, doing dance of joy, falls from second story terrace, hits head, dies. Pool belonging to independent producer (R) dries up for non-payment of utilities, causing water vapors (S) to form clouds over body of deceased independent film producer (T), such that fast-moving tropical depression (U) gains strength and crosses Rocky Mountain region (V), showering several inches of rain on parched latitudes. Local aquifer (W) fills, so that well in house of thirsty physically adaptive end user produces water (X), as shown in hydro-industrial appliance in garage (Y) where no water has lately been produced. He (Z) drinks.

Flap

I've developed this flap of skin. On my wrist. After the argument with Leslie. She was saying that antibacterial soap didn't do any good. I get passionate. I had to wake really early one morning, and right when the alarm was screeching I was having a nightmare about postal delivery. Some *entity* reaching up from the interior of the mailbox and grabbing my arm and pulling me down. When I woke up, I remember seeing the flap. Not a little flap, either. More like a gill. Like I had a gill on my wrist. I didn't panic, you know, I didn't think, well, this must be some kind of dangerous medical condition. This is kind of embarrassing, but the first thing I thought was that the flap might be a sort of *vaginal* flap. I consider myself one of those guys who's always had a certain amount of vagina envy. I mean, I think vaginas are pretty. So my first thought was: maybe I had developed this flap through some kind of vagina envy. Maybe if I had a vagina I could know more about them. On the other hand, it's true that I did quit therapy after the session where my counselor fell asleep, and sure this experience made me skeptical about therapy and about the kind of ideas you might spend your money on in therapy. I wasn't sure if the vagina theory wasn't just, you know, a first take on the issue. If I'd been smart, I would have just *felt up* the flap, to see if there was anything clitoral up there. If it were a vagina, there would have been a clitoris there somewhere, right? I mean, I don't always know where the clitoris is, but if I felt a little shiver that would be a pretty good sign that I had a flap *and* a clitoris on my wrist. On the other hand, you know, maybe the flap was a wound, even though I couldn't remember anything like that. A slash of some kind. Some barely healed wound. Guys often think this about vaginas when they are young and naive, that vaginas are wounds. Also, I read about the Salem Witch Trials one time, and apparently the witches in Salem used to get right up next to people's beds, and, while these people were sleeping, the witches would *bite* them. Just sink in their front teeth. So maybe I was being bitten in my sleep. Maybe there was some witch getting right up next to my bed at night. Maybe Leslie was chewing on me, or slashing me. Because of the argument about antibacterial soap. Maybe my girlfriend was a witch. She had a pretty awesome pair of scissors in her desk drawer. And her teeth were in good shape. It'd be easy to slash me. At night I'm pretty trusting. I sleep hard for the first few hours, any given night. Maybe my girlfriend was a witch, and I was slashed at night, around eleven or so, and I was bleeding, and the flap was a wound. It'd be a pretty compelling theory, you have to admit, except for the fact that I wasn't bleeding.

The flap was getting bigger, but it wasn't bleeding.

I needed to go to the post office. For stamps. I know a guy there. Mitch. Mitch says it's a good job. The pension is great. I was trying to buy some of those new Stars of Hollywood stamps. I forked over a twenty, asked for stamps featuring the guy from *North by Northwest,* chased by a crop duster, when Mitch said, astounded, "That is some flap you got." Looked like my skin was unwinding. I was seeing it from the other side of the service window, through Mitch's eyes. Mitch was in the middle of counting back. He was agape. My skin was a bandage, and it was unwinding, and whatever was underneath there was going to show through. And what was underneath? Wiring? Sheetrock? Asbestos?

Later that evening: I had to get my kid from my ex-wife's place. It was my night with the kid. On the way over, I noticed that my flap was actually flapping in the breeze. Like it was a little prayer flag. Or a pennant. My flap was saluting the breezes. Definitely some part of my body was coming off. In middle age, all the surfaces start coming off. Like you're molting a layer. Like aluminum siding is shearing off of you. My daughter noticed right away. My daughter said I looked like I was made of wet cardboard. She wouldn't hug me at first. She stood in the center of the living room, by the coffee table, arms crossed, like she never wanted to stay at my house again. I didn't care. I was daydreaming. And what I was daydreaming about was my flap. Maybe I liked it a little bit. I was thinking maybe my flap was an actual flap, like *flap A,* which needed to be put in *slot B* somewhere. You know? Like with those instruction manuals that come with complicated gifts. I was an envelope, basically. Standing in my ex-wife's living room. And my daughter was crying, and saying she didn't *want* to go with me. I was too *weird,* my daughter said. However, an incontrovertible fact was about to emerge. My ex-wife had *places to go,* nails to be manicured, and she wasn't going to get into any discussion. Visitation *would* take place, without interruption. I said to my daughter, "So what if I have a flap? I'm still your dad."

I was driving her toward the fast food joint on the road next to the aquarium, and I got this idea that maybe my flap was more like a *flipper.* Maybe my flap was prehistoric somehow. I was a dolphin or a manatee. I was a guy with an ancient aquatic flipper, the kind of flipper on a mammal that lurched up out of a muddy swamp and onto dry land where grubs and insects were more plentiful. I was going down through evolutionary history, like in that William Hurt movie. I was going to be one of those amphibious mammals, and then maybe after that I would be a giant squid, and then a jellyfish. This would be interesting. Although it was true that there

were lots of people who could make something more important out of turning into a jellyfish, like one of the experts at the aquarium, or maybe a performance artist, like that guy who wanted to have an extra ear grafted onto his arm. Instead, I was the divorced owner of a successful chain of car washes. Not first choice for a guy who should be an evolutionary miracle. I was kind of a fuckup, in fact. I couldn't even get Leslie to let me move in with her. I had messed up more things than a lot of people I knew. Maybe the flap was a curse. Maybe my flap was some biological tendency that had been triggered after I cheated at golf two weeks ago. I never should have lied about three-putting. I could tell that Mitch's brother-in-law knew. I'm a blusher. There was also the lie I told Leslie about having flirted with that 19-year-old after some drinks at the Chinese place last month. Nineteen? After a certain point, the girl just walked away, probably because I'm old and I have a kid, and I owe massive child support, and the loans on my business are crushing me.

That reminds me. My company operates best in a climate of respect. I treat the guys who work for me with respect. But it's hard to meet your employees on a level playing field when your arm looks like it was borrowed from the *Mummy* costume shop. Everyone around the car washes has skin ailments. It's hard. From the water and the cleaning agents. That's why I keep on *believing* where antibacterial soap is concerned. On Thursday, everyone at the office wanted to believe that the flap had to do with the cleaning agent. Pete Bowes, one of the guys on the line downtown, asked me if I wanted him just to cut off the flap. He had a really good pocketknife with him. Natch, I'd considered going to one of the many cosmetic surgeons here in the Miami-Dade area, but I don't really trust surgeons, they're all about cutting, never about rapport, so I decided, why the hell not, why not Pete, as long as he sterilized properly. I had a few snorts from the desk flask, and he cut off as much of the flap he could get. I promoted him to ass't manager on the spot.

Next day, it was back. If anything, a little bigger and more infected than it had been before. There was no way around it. I had to go see Arnold Piccolo, MD. I'd known the guy in high school, when he was a teenaged alcoholic. He'd long since cleaned up, and his office had that isopropyl smell of all doctor's offices. Problem was, I think maybe Arnie had some kind of nerve damage from all the drinking. He had this tic where it seemed like he was looking over at his shoulder. He'd do it a couple of times every sentence. Like he'd sprouted an additional eye on his shoulder and he wanted to make eye contact. He seemed to be having trouble concentrating, which would be natural if you had to look over your shoulder that often. "Arnie," I said,

"Can you tell me what this is?" I whipped off the suede glove I'd taken to wearing. Arnie managed to get the tic under control long enough to give me the once over. He probed at the diaphanous sheets of flesh coming off. There was a silence. He put some of the skin under a cheap microscope. While he was looking he said, "Look, I gotta ask. Do you ever think about those days?" And I said, "Which days?" Like I didn't know. Jesus. Arnie said, "Those days." He was pushing the tissue sample around under the microscope. I said, "Arnie, I used to be quick-witted, and I used to carry a six-pack on my person. I used to be able to charm any girl on the beach. I could surf a little bit. I could open a beer bottle with my teeth, but now Arnie, I'm kind of too busy for any of this kind of thing. Time is money. For you and me both. And the whole top layer of my body is coming unglued, and I want to get to the bottom of it." Arnie needed to run more tests. And I was still out ten bucks of co-pay.

Honestly, I never even called the guy back. I was tired of explaining. I was bored of making bad jokes. *Hey, I'm trying to get work as a slot machine.* Never mind about the weird moisture that started coursing out of the warm, clammy space under the flap from thumb joint to elbow. It had a salty taste, not poisonous. Like tear juice. Could have been salivary, I figured. Okay, I did try one more thing, I tried *feeding* the flap. I could stuff something nutritive in there, I figured, as long as it came from the health food store, and if the flap wanted to ingest whatever I put in it, then I'd see that the flap was actually another mouth. Kind of creepy, I know, but not that horrible. I mean, I do like to eat. I was having sushi in town, even though I don't really eat raw fish anymore, because of the microbes. And I just shoved the roll with the fish roe in under the flap. The roe is too fishy anyway. I shoved it under the flap, while Leslie was telling me about the affair her boss was having, and immediately the flap gobbled up the sushi roll. It was the weirdest sensation. I mean, I just should *not* have a throat in my wrist, especially since I'm right handed. What if there were a choking incident? Leslie said, "Jesus, Ed, did your wrist just eat that sushi roll? " The enormity of my situation began to sink in. "Do you think it has its own stomach? Or another esophagus?"

Did I say this already? I always thought Leslie was too beautiful for me. And too young. I always thought she'd realize that I wasn't good enough, because I'd had my adventures, like I was telling Arnie that day. I'd hung out in the parking lots before concerts, tailgating in the company of guys with dreadlocks. I'd done all that stuff when I was young, but now I just needed to make the child support payments.

Leslie didn't want to spend the rest of her life with the owner of a car wash business. She'd get to a point where she'd just say that she had a prior engagement. Leslie was in possession of the facts: I was bald, old, didn't want my workers to unionize, I was obsessed with hygiene. All these worries were like a chorus yelling in my head, so much that at first I didn't hear it. Didn't hear it at first because I thought it was coming from the next table. I thought I was listening to someone really irritating at the next table. But it wasn't the next table, because there was no one at the next table. It wasn't Leslie doing some ventriloquist routine. It wasn't me. The maître d' was a young Japanese woman romancing the sushi chef across the room. That left only one possibility. *The flap had started talking.* Right at the table, like it was going to seize control of the situation. The flap had a bit of a lisp. Which was sort of embarrassing. I mean, my flap should have had a virile, masculine voice. But it did turn out to be a very good persuader. It wouldn't give up. And the biggest difference between me and the flap was that the flap *believed in me,* even if I didn't believe in myself. Here's what it said. It said to Leslie, "What are you waiting for, honey? Are you waiting for Mr. Perfect? Because if you're waiting for Mr. Perfect, you're going to be waiting a long time! This fella here loves you! And he may have some flaws, but those flaws are only skin deep! This guy loves to be loved, and he loves to give the gift of love! He loves the gift of giving! And he's neat and he picks up after himself, and I personally have seen him empty the garbage can without even being asked! Plus, he's a successful business owner. So if you're just waiting for the better thing to come along, you're going to wait a long time! You should try to see the beauty that's underneath the surface, because that's the beauty that lasts. Not that you need my advice—" The flap said *advice* like it rhymed with *scythe*. And it spit food. Talked with its mouth full. It was definitely a free spirit, if a little bit sloppy. And it sure was sentimental. Still, I was personally moved to tears by the flap's defense. Even more so when Leslie pulled me close. And reached into her pocketbook for the antibacterial wipes.

Metal

Had a lot of psychosomatic complaints, had a lot of stomach problems, was always throwing up, was throwing up and waking up Mom to tell her I was throwing up, had headaches, had headaches that made me throw up, certain people made me think I was going to throw up, most encounters with certain figures of authority made me

think I was going to throw up, certain foods, certain *ideas* of food made me think I was going to throw up, and to distract myself I went and bought a lot of bubble gum, which I loved and which I would chew in greater and greater amounts until my jaws hurt, until I didn't want to eat real food, didn't want to eat vegetables, especially, because they might make me throw up. Everything was about throwing up, about the built-in possibility of vomit at any and all moments, the necessity of avoiding vomit, of avoiding allowing my mother to see me vomit, though I was also terrified of being alone when I vomited, because the solitude of the vomiting boy, crouched, doubled over in front of the toilet, with the tuna casserole, partly digested, mottling his chin, this was too much to contemplate, because if you had to be alone when you vomited, that pretty much proved that it was a joyless, empty universe, didn't it. And the other thing was that girls avoided me, I'm not saying a little bit, I'm saying that most girls would go out of their way to avoid me, they would lock me out of four-square games, they would say the next chair over was taken, and I'm not sure that I knew what I was supposed to think about girls, I wasn't sure what girls were for, but I knew that having girls want to talk to me was an important sign of something, and I knew that these girls didn't want to have anything to do with me. Girls and vomit, these were the important themes, and the third important theme was baseball. Girls and vomit and baseball. Though no girl would talk to me, thought I was vomiting frequently, though most of the guys called me *faggot* and threatened me in the lunchroom for reasons that were entirely unclear to me, I was at the same time collecting the baseball cards, I was following the games, I was camped out for the whole nine innings. Baseball was the thing just before music, it was the batting practice before the nine innings of music, it was the undercard before the prizefight of music. Even if it was nice outside and I should have been trying to improve my swing at the plate, for I had a woeful swing, even though I should have been practicing so that the guys wouldn't call me *faggot* all the time, I wasn't, I was inside, watching baseball, eating fifteen dollars' worth of bubble gum, and wondering why all the girls hated me, like the ones I had asked to go steady with me. I had never been introduced to these girls, never said a single thing to them, not even *excuse me*—when I had to shove by them in the hall between classes.

Up until this time, there had mostly been pop music confections, there had been radio, there had been AM radio, which wasn't yet the province of mentally ill Republican talk show hosts, I had the AM radio on under the sheets, with the baseball cards and certain books about kids solving murder mysteries. It was all pop music, it was, e.g., that *bubblegum tunesmith* from England who later got a toupee and

announced his homosexuality, and had I known he was homosexual then, I would have avoided him entirely, because of all the guys who were calling me *faggot,* and because being called *faggot* made me feel like I was going to vomit all the time, and then my mother would have to come down the hall and attempt to talk me down when I was feeling like I was going to vomit. On my birthday that year, my crew of guys, they actually got me birthday presents, I don't know why they did it, because I didn't think they liked me any better than any of those girls liked me, they mostly told me *fuck off,* they would invite me to give them *blowjobs,* which was meant to imply, I think, that they were not homosexual, but that I *was,* anyway, I went over there one afternoon, to my friend's house up the street, and there they all were, my crew, and it was my birthday, and they had gotten me presents, so here, unwrap the presents, so I had the presents and they were all LPs, every single present was an LP, because that was the time of LPs. And I unwrapped the first LP, and I didn't really know what it was, this LP, because I had mostly been listening to the *bubblegum tunesmith,* but this LP was called *Made in Japan.*

They were saying, Man, you don't even know *Smoke on the Water,* how could you not know *Smoke on the Water;* this is what they were saying, because everybody knew that, everybody did, and to be able to play the chords of *Smoke on the Water* on your guitar was to guarantee that you were not a homosexual, which was very, very important, as I have been saying, even if you were a homosexual, it was important to guarantee that you were not homosexual, and guaranteeing that I was not a homosexual would probably insure that I would not vomit and would not have to wake up my mother to tell her that I was going to vomit, and maybe even some of the girls would talk to me, there would be some magical transformation, that had to do with those chords. I heard the chords that began *Smoke on the Water,* I saw that these people who played these chords had extremely long hair and were extremely ugly, not like the *bubblegum tunsesmith.* Maybe they were like certain longhaired hippie persons that I had learned about on the news and had been told to ignore or avoid; these people who played *Smoke on the Water,* though, they looked like the hippie persons, and their song was dark and forbidding like certain nightmares I had on nights when I believed I was going to vomit. Turned out that apparently music didn't have to be about girls and love, it could also be about, uh, what was it about anyhow, I didn't know what *Smoke on the Water* was about actually. Did any of the guys there have any idea what *Smoke on the Water* was about? No, uh, actually, they had no idea what it was about, didn't matter what it was about, man, it was *loud.* So who cared what it was about. The lead

guitar player got to take a really long solo, and the organ player got to take a really long solo, and the song just went on and on and there was *fire in the sky*. And so *Made in Japan* went onto my turntable, because it was simple, loud, and mean, and a whole new language was now clear to me, how had I failed to understand that everyone was speaking this language, which was the language of *metal,* which was at this time a new language. So new that it didn't even have a name yet. It was just loud and it was about boys not apologizing, it was about saying, *I am boy and I want,* and *Made in Japan* brought this boy argot into my bedroom, dumb, simple boy sexuality, soiled sheets and acne medications, I could be dumb and stupid too, I could like stupid things, I could love sluts and cars and I could talk about when I was going to drink and when I when I was going to smoke pot, and I could talk about naked girls, *naked naked naked naked,* and I could listen to *Made in Japan,* and I could go space trucking, and I could speak of *my woman from Tokyo,* and I could realize that all these songs were sung by Jesus, yes, the actual Jesus, from some musical about Jesus, this was the guy, this ugly longhaired guy, the singer guy had actually played *Jesus,* and Jesus wanted it loud, and I wanted it loud, and dumb, and I didn't care about anything else, because I had just gotten my first set of headphones, and I had grown my first pubic hair, and I had the headphones on and in my room I was listening *Made in Japan,* and the louder it was the better I liked it. Turn the motherfucker up. Avoid vomiting.

The Fiddler

The fiddler despaired of her playing.

She was hunched, from the corkscrew she made of herself. To ply her reels. When she fitted her chin on the chin rest, she gave up hope. When she tightened the horse hair of her bow, when she gripped the frog of it, she wept for her hands, their swollen knuckles and callused fingertips. The strings were worn, and the body of her ancient fiddle was chipped and flecked with rosin and water stains. She had not tuned properly. On the cobblestones, she hopped from foot to foot, trying to stay warm.

There was mist in the windows up and down the streets of the old village.

The seal pup splayed itself out next to her, by their wagon. She meant for the seal to balance a ball on its nose while she played, but, as she sawed into the old ballad, The Drinking Wife's Bad Dream, the seal looked up at her with its bathetic eyes, as if to observe that playacting was not dignified in the midst of a winter so hard.

Now, according to the seal, was the time to mothball the famine ballads and songs of romantic murderers from the fiddler's youth. Now was the time to collect a pension.

The fiddler hated her playing when she was young. She practiced her fiddle, screeching away, especially on the E string, while the other children gamboled in the fields, catching lightning bugs and learning to kiss. The fiddler had a sister, and her sister was more beautiful than she. Her sister's singing voice made the linnets twitter. The fiddler looked old when she was young and wore frocks with high necks, and she learned lonely songs from an old man from the next village who rapped on her knuckles when she had problems with her pitch.

And yet her mother loved it when the fiddler practiced. Even though the fiddler played badly as a girl. Her mother bribed her with sweets and it made all the difference. An ear is a thing of discernment. If it took sweets to train it, then it took sweets: pears in brandy, chocolates filled with marmalade, and cinnamon cakes.

By the evening of her first recital, in the streets, for the coppers of the lords and ladies of the town, the fiddler was long since alone. The girls of the village, her sister included, had babies of their own. Her mother was dead of a brain fever. The fiddler played The Cat Jumps Out the Rowboat. People tossed their coins into her upturned straw hat. They took the fiddler for a cripple or an imbecile. When she played on the village green they asked her to move along. When she played in front of the courthouse they asked her to move along. When she played behind the public houses, they asked her to move along.

It was when she found the seal that the town began to tolerate the fiddler and her disgraceful appearance. Who doesn't love a trained seal? The seal was dressed in a red waistcoat, and it barked happily when she fed it, and it balanced the ball on its nose during especially difficult compositions, indicating its discernment in the matter of fiddle music. The fiddler played Don't Go Off to Sea, she played The Summer Girl's Dresses, she played Now We Go Gently Dancing, into the evenings when the chimney smoke smelled of a vanished time. She played Bells of the Old Belfry. She threw the seal a fresh herring and told it she loved it, though on occasion she was filled with resentment about the seal and its ability to charm banknotes out of the rich.

The fiddler ate stale chocolates, and that was all. No matter the day. She slept in a thicket of briars behind one of the churches. When it was cold she took the seal indoors and slept on the floor or in the pews. She imagined dancers trading partners, and the look of horror upon the faces as she played. She played, and hated her playing, hated the notes on the staffs, hated the men who passed in greatcoats and went home

to their sons and taught them to hunt the fox and the antelope. And she fed the seal and petted its head when it wasn't trying to bite.

The fiddler lived the songs, grew into them, until the fiddler was an apparition from the songs, a conjuration of balladry, rather than an engineer of it. She hoped, when she was fallen dead on the banks of the stream, according to the model and augury of the old ballads, that someone would care properly for the seal.

Report from the Society for the Prevention of Aesthetics

We gather here today in league in order to intervene in the matter of autumnal imagery in contemporary literature. Our first goal will be the elimination of all brooks. You know the kind we mean. Those sylvan brooks on the Appalachian trail, the ones that tumble down with snow melt from granite peaks veiled with thickets of blueberry. These sylvan brooks, by virtue of overuse will now be prevented in the national literature. Mrs. Ellen McClintock has volunteered to convene a subcommittee for this purpose, fresh from her longtime position on the decorating committee, and we would like to commend her in her undertaking. In the state of Ohio statisticians have already compiled a concordance of sylvan brooks in the poetry of young adults and have found that 63% of all young adults have made use of the sylvan brook in their poems, accepting that *stream* and *creek* have been deemed synonyms.

Following the removal of the brook from all such poetry, we will begin to focus our attention on all descriptions of *foliage,* including the misspelling "foilage," common in midland locales. Foliage in the northeastern part of the nation, considered essential to tourist economies there, will henceforth be considered ill advised in any literature, whether commercial or artistic in purpose. We will urge that all use of the word *foliage,* and related terminologies, *spectacular reds, yellows, and oranges,* and descriptions of *peak foliage,* etc., should all be abandoned. Apple picking, an activity of the vicinities of this offending season, especially when accompanied by retrievers, or in the presence of small red wagons, these will likewise be eliminated, and, it should go without saying, the vehicles which would be required to convey all this gear. We will resist any depiction of these vehicles. No one will mention pullover sweaters or wool jackets.

Dr. Miles Henderson, MD, who recently sold his urology practice, has volunteered to contact those responsible for the above to attempt to persuade them

to abandon their fiendish activities. We will include a complete report from Miles, during the "old business" portion of our next gathering.

Let the minutes indicate that Mrs. Roger H. Milliken of Walloomsac also proposes a discussion of the tapping of sugar maples, and all the "damned nonsense that goes along with it, like those knick-knacky roadside shacks that are just a time waster for people who can't be bothered to get real jobs." Mrs. Milliken requests action on maples, and "leaf peepers" who drive too slowly and tie up traffic, and she wants this action now. As the sugar maple has not been discussed substantially at these proceedings, the society commends Mrs. Milliken on her keen observations, and her zeal for bringing to our attention a tradition that needs to be extinguished before it goes any further. While we're at it, let's pause to denounce further the trend toward leaf piles, and the repulsive raking and arranging of leaf piles. We urge that leaf piles remain unphotographed, whether on traditional film or in the digital medium, and we urge that the persons who make films avoid such images. Poets who rely on the imagery of leaf piles should be treated severely, or at the very least reprimanded, and children should avoid jumping in leaf piles as this will only encourage perpetrators.

Anything else? Are there any other terminologies of autumn that we need to deal with today, here in the comfortable living room of our hosts, Mr. and Mrs. Horace Ganz, who have made such fine peanut brittle for the occasion? There is of course the *crisp weather,* you hear about so often, which is not crisp at all, for it is usually rainy and three degrees above freezing. There is the smell of wood smoke that is unpleasant and lingers in wool for days afterwards. Those who sing ballads of *wood smoke* and its poetical redolence should be forced to spend days at a time camping, where they will become damp and will be attacked by moose, animals that we should consign to city zoos. You can lay money on the fact that at the end of such an undertaking these persons will be wanting to spend a good stretch in a motel with an ice machine and access to soft drinks.

Now that the new business has been completed the chairman has remarks he'd like to make on the subject of loneliness and whether or not loneliness is somehow related to autumn, whether loneliness is inevitable, in poetry, the popular song, at the movie theater, during the retirement years, even when we are gathered together in a friendly community like this. Please fill out the questionnaire.

Pirate Station

For the first twenty-four hours, the pirate station broadcasts the sound of someone coughing nervously. An august beginning. It's not the dead air of the rural FM dial. It's someone coughing nervously. Much nervousness at the pirate station, and thus much nervous coughing. The next Tuesday a jazz band is convened, so that live jazz might be broadcast on the pirate station. None of the players has ever had a lesson on his instrument. These include soprano sax, vibes, electric guitar, bass, drums, mellotron. Three idioms of jazz are agreed upon: cool jazz, smooth jazz, Afro-Cuban jazz. At the count of three, the ensemble begins. The pirate station broadcasts the music of this ensemble for six days, without ceasing. There's no agreed upon coda for the piece, the pirate station simply pulls the plug.

That fall, after weeks of casting about, a symphony is written by filling in notes on a staff at random. A local orchestra attempts to pick out the piece without rehearsal. However, the symphony is considered too sentimental for broadcast. A bird call program is surprisingly popular, however, with the great horned howl coming in for most requests, these issuing from the sheriff's office. Perhaps it's the lonely night patrolman of the graveyard shift. The sounds of Southwestern cacti are broadcast for several weeks until, by general assent, it is agreed that cacti make no sounds.

The pirate station branches out. It broadcasts, over twelve nights, a comparative study of whistles, including penny whistles, the starter's whistle that your high school track coach favored when in an ornery mood, and that guy up the street who can whistle like nobody's business. Briefly, the pirate station backpedals reluctantly and agrees to play musical recordings of the conventional sort, but only if the selections alternate in the following way: salsa, mariachi, tejana, reggae, Tuvan throat singing, thumb piano concertos, music released in 1964, and songs sung by tone deaf people. And yet these categories are considered too easy to fill, and, after a week or so, the pirate station loses interest.

The pirate station broadcasts news programs, but never at the top of the hour, and only when bootlegged from other stations. The substance of the news in these programs is altered slightly in order to mislead: the weather is said to be sunny, no matter the weather; the stock market is said to be going down without respite; the high school football team is said to be losing; newcomers are said to be bringing prosperity to the town; and the war is always said to be going smoothly, with little loss of civilian life. The pirate station broadcasts a single chord, a major third, key of A, for

four consecutive days. Here's the secret to this particular broadcast: a toy organ has the relevant keys held down with duct tape.

Upon the return of pirate station employees from the holidays, a period of reflection sets in. The microphone is turned on and all the pirate station disc jockeys gather around and speak of their uncertainty about the pirate station. What could be done differently with the medium? What can the pirate station do that no one has done before? Is complete liberty not terrifying in some fundamental way? Can we burn in effigy a classic-rock deejay and a shock jock and broadcast these burnings live? A recording of this staff meeting is then played backwards, sped up slightly, on the pirate station, with the harmonious conclusion first and the confusion at the end.

The pirate station sends people out into the street, humming, with contact mikes, the only requirement being that they hum songs with the word "joy" in the title, though not that song by Three Dog Night. Inducing strangers and townspeople on the street to hum along is considered particularly exciting. At the conclusion of the program, the unpleasant man at the dollar store is persuaded to hum "Frosty the Snowman," though it is spring. A contest is announced on the pirate station, to find the person who has the best radio voice. This person is then tickled mercilessly on air and driven blindfolded to a distant metropolis. The sounds of people making love are broadcast for the entire month of May, rising to a crescendo of simultaneous orgasms on May the fourteenth and then dwindling away to some heavy breathing and delicate sighs by the first of June, just in time for summer.

The doors of the pirate station are thrown open and anyone is invited in. The building that houses the pirate station is demolished, and the station moves out into the rubble. Soon the pirate station begins moving, night after night, never staying in one place for more than a few hours. Interns carry the transmitter, in its small red toolbox. The pirate station becomes a condition of all possible sounds, so that everything is a song, and there is no commercial interruption and no fundraising drives. The people who began the pirate station grow old, marry, have children, make out wills, and leave the pirate station behind. The children of the pirate station owners take up incendiary devices in lieu of better-paying professions. They move to different cities where they claim to be uninterested in radio, which they consider less avant-garde than crayons on construction paper, but then they order transmitter kits from foreign countries nonetheless.

The sounds of freight trains begin to sound suspiciously like broadcasts on the pirate station, and the sounds of police sirens begin to sound suspiciously

like broadcasts on the pirate station, the sounds of cheerleaders goading on the local football team are definitely prerecorded and borrowed from the pirate station, and any music produced in the year 1964 seems to suggest that the pirate station is back on line and up to its old tricks. The Federal Communications Commission becomes obsessed with the possibility that the pirate station is continuing to broadcast but at wattages so meager and in places so far flung that no one at all can tune the programming. Still, this is unacceptable.

The pirate station refuses to cooperate with finding the enemy. The pirate station refuses to inform on its neighbors. The pirate station no longer takes photographs the way it did when young. The pirate station once thought gardening was satisfying, but no longer. The pirate station makes its own bricks, using mud from the back yard. The pirate station forgets the name of distant relations and people it met only recently. The pirate station goes off its medication. The pirate station quarrels frequently and is testy about things that never used to bother it. The pirate station eats infrequently. The pirate station loses interest in worldly things. The pirate station never calls. The pirate station imagines it can hear the music of the spheres and begins to totter down a long narrow corridor, the color purple, in which many dead friends beckon to it, but just when it is about to sleep its eternal sleep, the pirate station reconsiders, and remarks, haltingly, that it has work yet to do.

Afterword

Finished. Finished. It's finished. Finished. Finished. It's finished. Finished. Finished. Finished. It's finished. It is finished. It is totally finished. It is completely finished. Finished. Finished. Finished. The end of the beginning as previously announced. No further end than this end just described. The mother of all endings. No end beyond this preliminary end. Finished. Completely done. Over with. Over and out. Finished. It's finished. Finished. Finished. It's finished. No further remainder to result in any additional or secondary stage of completion. No other finishing but the finishing just mentioned. It's finished. It's done. Even the finishing discussed above is now finished, though I may have reason to reiterate any termination. Done, done, finished. Finished, finished, done. Done, finished, done, finished. Finished. Don't bother with inquiries by phone or fax. Written inquiries will be discarded. The office is closed. The relevant employees have been laid off. It's over. It's over with. It's so over it's

over. Finished. It's not over till it's over but it's definitely over. Inevitably, there's some tautological moment when no other word will suit, and that time is now. Finished. The curtain has fallen, and it's a frayed curtain, not one of those pleasant crimson draperies that you find in the refurbished theaters that show family spectaculars. Finished. Finished. Finished. Don't ask again. The result is foreordained. The needle is caught in the last groove. It's going around and around. The dryer has buzzed to alert you that the cycle cycles no more. The dog has kicked aside his bowl. Was a time when things were in a stage of commencement, when there was a flourishing of enthusiasm, people were flush with it, but now that time is *kaput*. How much more secure I'd feel about starting, although staring presupposes a kind of insecurity, too, a less insecure variety than the kind that I feel when I say something is finished. Any language will do it. *Fin, finito, finire, finisshen.* I am done with this line of reasoning, with any line of reasoning, in fact. Actually, I'm the kinda guy who never wants to bring any bad news, who broods over the fact that the sun has gone over the horizon and now there are subzero temperatures and the wind is howling around the clapboard on the house front. Concentrate on finishing for too long, and you feel like giving up. A man in a uniform will be around to help you exit. There is a finishing, which is a veneer, which is an ending, which is a completion, which is a fulfillment, which is a dashing of preconceptions. Finished. Finished. Finished. A limit or boundary to what once was. You think it's a joke? Had I to produce footage of a couple embracing, a couple on the run, wantonly embracing, in order to persuade you that the narrative has now reached its *finis* and we are into the end credits, I would produce this couple, although it is difficult to procure the services of Equity type talents on short notice. Punctuation will be the self-evident marker of the fact that no further bulletins will be issued. The period, what a delightful mark of punctuation. Was any other ever as effective? This little dot indicates the end of the information that will be conveyed herewith.

And don't be asking for characters. That's not the kind of story we have underway. The characters have been neutralized. Some of them were encouraged to attack other characters with blunt knives. One of the characters tried to draw and quarter one of the others, which is a more complicated operation than you might suppose. I had to put a stop to this, using independent contractors, muscular types, who, since the war, have found themselves unable to integrate into general society. Later, the contractors served as highly-placed anonymous sources in press reports indicating that the violent phase of the conflict was no longer violent. Though international authorities lack a legal framework for bringing the perpetrators to justice, the threat of intervention

convinced my characters that the time for conflicts had come and gone. Still, one of the characters, prior to incarceration, produced a hand grenade and detonated the setting for this story, killing twenty-six non-combatants and himself.[2**] I am obliged to inform you, therefore, that the setting is in ruins. It was a rather dilapidated locale. One of the glossies had pronounced the setting of this story the twelfth most desirable place to live, but now that evaluation will be revised. After the demise of the characters, it became impossible to locate the story of this story, nor could a replacement be purchased at any of the large retailers, whereupon the only professional aspect of my composition that remained was its theme: Finished. I wish there were more. Finished. It's finished. Finished. Finished. It's finished. Finished. Finished. Finished. Finished. Finished. Finished. Finished. Finished. Finished. Finished. Finished. Finished. I knew it would end badly. Finished. Finished. Finished. Finished. Finished. Finished. Finished. Finished. Finished. Finished. Finished. Tell me. Finished. Finished. Finished. Finished. Finished. Finished. Finished. Finished. Finished. Finished. Tell me it's not. Finished. [18]

[2**] I observed the action from a safe distance.

Black Clock

joanna scott
UNTELLING

joanna scott

In June, 1905, a tourist agent and amateur collector of Egyptian antiquities named Armand de Potter disappeared mysteriously at sea off the coast of Greece. His body was never recovered. De Potter's Grand Tour attempts to solve this mystery. Opening on the day Armand goes missing, the novel tells the story of a seemingly happy marriage that ends with shocking abruptness. Drawing from real sources that include journals, letters, legal documents, and a trove of diaries, the novel moves forward and back through time, following the de Potters through their lives as they meet, marry, lead tourists around the world, settle in a luxurious villa in Cannes, and become hopelessly entangled in the antiquities trade.

Though this is my shortest novel, it has taken me nearly five years to write. If someone had informed me before I started De Potter's Grand Tour that I'd spend three years writing it first as a nonfiction book called The Gilt Cabinet, and then as some sort of fictional/factual hybrid monster, I wouldn't have believed it. If I'd been warned that after finally completing a draft, I'd have to discard half of it and reimagine the other half, I would have said, I'll quit now while I'm ahead. And if asked, after I'd finally finished it, to describe the painful process of undoing all the hard work I'd done on the book, I would be tempted to pretend it didn't really happen.

It wasn't me who got so lost in a project that she nearly didn't make it out—it was a fictional writer who will go unnamed. And here is what she might admit, when invited by Steve Erickson to fess up.

More than a century after her great-grandfather's disappearance, a woman opens a steamer trunk that had been in her mother's basement and finds a brief obituary, clipped from a newspaper:

> Word has been received of the death at sea, off the coast of Greece, of Pierre Louis Armand de Potter, d'Elseghem. Mr. de Potter's death took place after a trip to Delphi and Argos, in connection with his studies of art and archaeology.

Armand de Potter was born in Paris on June 4, 1852, to Belgian parents. His grandfather, Louis Antoine de Potter, was widely known in Europe for his philosophical writings and memoirs, and was a leader in the Revolution of 1830, which separated Belgium from Holland.

The woman, who happens to be a writer, keeps digging through the trunk. She finds an assortment of letters, maps, itineraries of tours through Europe and around the world, threadbare albums full of photographs, a set of travel brochures, packets of magic lantern slides, and a thick stack of albumen prints. She finds a leather belt with a folded wallet, embossed with the name "Armand de Potter." She finds pages of legal documents on onionskin that had been crumpled into accordion folds, as though used to fan a sweaty face. And, finally, she finds several of her great-grandmother's leather-bound diaries.

The woman stays up late that night reading through the diaries. At first glance they seem to be little more than a record of the weather and the state of her great-grandmother's health. But she keeps reading and discovers that hidden deep inside the diaries are secrets Aimée de Potter never dared to speak aloud.

The woman who found the diaries is used to writing novels. She has the impression, however, that when she opened the trunk she was handed a story far more interesting than anything she could have invented. There is so much to tell. She resolves to leave nothing out.

The next morning she begins her new book. She titles it The Gilt Cabinet *after the cabinet in her mother's living room that holds all the family has left of Armand de Potter's collection of antiquities. For several months, this serves as the beginning:*

Too early in my childhood, I decided that I didn't have much use for toys. I lost interest in board games, plastic dollhouses, and stuffed animals. I stopped baking cardboard cupcakes in my play oven and began expressing disdain for the dolls that were in vogue. I quit swiveling my Barbie's limbs to hear her joints squeak and instead gave her to my Newfoundland dog to chew.

The writer feels liberated, knowing that she won't have to make anything up. And since this is a family memoir about her ancestors, she believes it appropriate to approach the past through her own childhood memories. She congratulates herself on her cleverness as she writes, It wasn't that I felt in any hurry to grow up. I just happened to be susceptible to the influence of certain family members. These included my older brothers, who, for the fun of it, would dangle me by my ankles over the second-floor banister; my mother, who sent me out to roam the fields and woods at a very young age; and my

father, who had a brief stint as a copywriter for an ad agency and liked to expose the lies contained in every sales pitch. I tried to show off my sophistication by scoffing at commercials. And I learned that it was better to be outside the house rather than inside. I worked hard to convince my neighborhood friends to join me, but more often than not I was alone and secretive in my wanderings. In winter I looked for animal tracks in the snow. In summer I walked barefoot, as quietly as possible, sometimes trailing one of my cats on her hunting expeditions as she searched for mice in the Skinners' unmowed yard next door. I felt proud of my independence, tough in my solitude. I defined myself by my expertise as a tree-climber, an explorer, a nimble, uncivilized creature of a suburban landscape that I thought was a valid version of the wilderness. And at the end of the day I'd come home and sit patiently while my mother picked ticks out of my hair.

She pauses to reread what she has written so far. She is supposed to be telling a story about 19th-century tourism, the antiquities trade, and a marriage that ended abruptly when Armand de Potter threw himself off a ship. What do Barbies and ticks have to do with anything? She has hardly begun, yet she has already taken a wrong turn. She chews the earpiece of her glasses, looks at the screen, backs up.

She clicks on the blank page of a new document and starts over.

Open the beveled glass door and you'll find scarabs and seals, copper bells, crucifixes, painted buttons, and several miniature busts of emperors. There is a heavy iron statue of a riderless horse with an ornate saddle from which hang tiny stirrups made of braided wire. There is a porcelain bull, a set of lidless canopic jars, and a short bamboo stick that fits neatly into the bowl of a pipe. A dented brass fish has a detachable head and red beads for eyes. Tiny ivory castles carried at a tilt by two elephants in a chess set are chipped at their rims. A bronze falcon attached to a horn-shaped glass vessel has only one leg, and an arm of a ceramic statue of a Greek goddess is broken off at the elbow. A pair of fused alabaster tubes, once used to catch the tears of women as they wept for the dead, is streaked with a sooty residue. Inside an intricately carved ivory box is a lock of dark blonde hair, labeled *Yvonne, age 10,* along with the arm of the goddess.

She is convinced that she has come up with a fitting opening this time. The gilt cabinet offers the route into the world of the story. There is so much to explore.

Drawing from the materials she'd found in the trunk, she writes about her great-grandfather's arrival in America. She writes about his marriage to Amy Beckwith of Tivoli, New

York. She writes about their lives together, their prosperity, the tragedy that brought an abrupt end to their happiness. She writes about the secrets Aimée de Potter revealed in her diaries.

As she writes about the day when Armand said goodbye to his wife for the final time, she realizes that she doesn't know enough about her great-grandfather. He was a wealthy man who, by all accounts, loved his family. He lived in a luxurious villa in the south of France. He had the resources to build up a famous collection of ancient treasures. What went so wrong in his life that he thought he had no other choice but to kill himself? She worries that something important is missing from the story she is trying to tell.

She decides that she has to do more research. She leaves her office and heads out to investigate. She ferrets through the attics of relatives and the archives of museums. She goes to Philadelphia and Brooklyn. She becomes obsessed with her detective work and even takes a trip to Cannes, and then to Istanbul. She is amazed at what she finds.

She persuades herself that her search is as interesting as the materials themselves. She wants to share the story of her investigation with readers. She writes about visiting a relative in New Jersey:

The crystals glinted, the chimes jingled, the rain beat against the large windows in the kitchen. I was directed toward the family room, where cardboard boxes full of books were stacked alongside the back wall. There were more books on the table, along with photo albums, papers, and a pair of old-fashioned opera glasses. To my surprise, among the books was a full set of Louis de Potter's four-volume biography of the Bishop de Ricci, sandwiched between one volume of Racine's collected works and a copy of Dickens' *Pickwick Papers*.

She writes about a conversation with her elderly aunt:

The roast chicken is adequate, my aunt noted, and, yes, she said in response to my question, Gertrude was Grandmother's niece. Or perhaps her cousin. Her cousin? There were many Beckwith siblings, and Gertrude was one of them. Then she was Aimée's sister? Yes…rather, no! Oh, good, there's coffee. But it wasn't coffee, it was ginger ale, I pointed out. Ginger ale, then, yes, that will do, and yes, Gertrude was the daughter of one of the Beckwith siblings, which would have made her Grandmother's niece. That's right—she was a niece. And her great-grandfather was the Bishop of Bruges. The Bishop of Bruges? But hadn't Gertrude been a Beckwith, from Dutchess County? Yes, that's right, she was a Beckwith, and her great-grandfather on her mother's side had been the Bishop of Bruges. But that was impossible. No, it wasn't impossible. Why, if I'd only look in the closet I'd find him there: the Bishop of Bruges.

She reports on a conversation with her cousin:

"You've heard about the plate in his head," my cousin said to me after I'd confessed to her that I didn't think our great-grandfather had fallen into the sea by accident. She was reminding me of the metal plate that had been used to mend his fractured skull years earlier and supposedly was the cause of his dizzy spells. Yes, I knew all about that plate. But I offered the argument that a man prone to dizzy spells wouldn't have put himself at risk by standing so close to the rail of a ship.

"You know," she said, lowering her voice, "My mom told me he was seen sitting on the rail."

"What?"

"He was last seen *sitting* on the rail, not standing next to it. He'd climbed onto the rail and was just sitting there…."

And while she's at it, she might as well tell readers about the conversation she had with a complete stranger on Ellis Island:

It was a clear October day, and the sunlight streaming through the windows of the Registry building made the stacks of steamer trunks, suitcases, and straw baskets on display look like they'd been dipped in melted bronze. I took out my notebook with the intention of writing down brief descriptions of the scene. As I was searching in my purse for a pen, a stranger approached and stood beside me. I could feel him looking over my shoulder as I prepared to write. He was a short man, slightly taller than me. He was wearing a dark brown suit that was too large for his small frame and gave him a disheveled appearance. He wore a beret at a slight tilt. He was bearded and had brown hair that hung below his ears in tight corkscrews, like dreadlocks that had recently been unknotted. I remember thinking that this stranger resembled something that had been living underwater for many years and only recently had emerged on land to have a look around.

He spoke to me in a thick French accent before I could speak to him, asking, out of the blue, "You know Armand?"

I blinked at him, convinced that I'd misheard. "What?"

"You know Armand?"

At that point I could only force a nervous giggle and wait for the floor to shift, the stacks of baggage to tumble, the roof to open up with a great yawning crack.

"You know him, yes?"

"Who?"

"Armand! Armand!"

"Armand?" My throat was dry, my senses at a stage of alertness that almost made me dizzy. Already I was wishing that I'd been recording the encounter so I'd have proof of it. I stuttered something like, "It's weird that you ask because, you know, I mean, Armand… do *you* know Armand?"

The man in the beret looked as confused as I was. "Armand, he was a great artist, a sculptor!"

"Armand? He was an artist?"

"Yes, he made like this!" His thick French accent was getting thicker, more difficult for me to understand. "He made sculpture," he said, gesturing to the display of baggage. "Armand!" At that point he reached for my notebook; I surrendered it to him, along with my pen, and he wrote on a blank page: *Arman, artiste, sculpteur.*

Not until the writer is back at home and able to search online does she understand that the strange little man at Ellis Island was referring to the French nouveau realist artist who went by the name "Arman." Born Armand Pierre Fernandez in 1928 in Nice. Died in New York in 2005. Made sculptures out of objects like steamer trunks and baskets. Appeared in profile in a film by Andy Warhol. How interesting.

Everything is interesting, she thinks. Consider the man Armand de Potter claimed was his grandfather, Louis de Potter, the Belgian writer who returned from Rome in 1823 and dove right into the political turmoil of the day. Why, she could write a whole book about Louis de Potter! At least he deserves a chapter. Here he is in his prison cell in Brussels:

He had only a small wood stove for warmth. His bed was a thin mattress on a simple frame. The brick floor was frigid beneath the thin soles of his shoes. Damp rot stained the corners of his vaulted stone ceiling, and there was a piss-stink in the air from his chamber pot. Worm holes in the heavy wooden door were edged with black from many centuries' worth of soot. The window looking out on the small courtyard was blocked with heavy steel bars—a constant reminder, if he needed it, that he was not allowed to come and go as he pleased.

The constraints on his freedom should have been demoralizing, especially for a man as used to privilege as he was. He'd been born into the nobility of the *Pays-Bas*. His education had been carefully supervised by tutors, and when his health was declared delicate he was sent south, to live for a decade in balmy Rome. As heir to a large estate, he'd enjoyed that rare privilege of designing a life for himself without the worrying task of generating income. For the period when he'd lived in

Italy, he had been busy writing books about the Catholic Church that extended into multiple volumes.

For this privileged aristocrat, this devoted writer and enlightened freethinker, imprisonment should have been experienced with bitter discontent. Yet paradoxically, as he wrote to a friend, he had never been happier than he was in jail. He reported that he was in love with punishment. He was happy to serve as the "expiatory victim" of the whole human race. While he waited for the term of his confinement to end, he decorated his cell as if it were a room in his family's castle. He ordered the finest linen for his bedding, along with a fur-collared robe to lounge in on cold mornings before the stove was lit. A lover of music, he hung his guitar from a nail hammered into the wall. He kept his clothes in a chest at the foot of the bed. There were two chairs in the cell and a small but adequate table. He had frequent visitors and complete access to the postal service. He always had enough ink for his feather pen, and he had stacks of books to keep him occupied when he was alone.

There's nothing irrelevant, as far as the author of The Gilt Cabinet *is concerned. She even finds reason to include Walt Whitman in the story, who, at the age of 6,* was among the crowd that had assembled to watch General Lafayette lay the cornerstone for the Apprentice Library in Brooklyn. It was the Fourth of July, 1825. The day, Whitman would later reminisce, "was remarkably beautiful." The usual seagulls wheeled overhead, their calls accenting the weight of the pauses separating the speeches and anthems. Dust from the newly excavated basement blew about in the summer breeze. For the residents of the village of Brooklyn who had marched in a procession to the site from the ferry landing, the mood must have been respectfully celebratory, with flags and banners decorating the scene and the tempting, sugary smell of roasting nuts rising from vendors' carts parked at the curb. Small children had difficulty seeing over the heaps of stones and construction equipment. Whitman would recall being lifted and passed along and placed for a moment in the arms of General Lafayette himself.

Her great-grandfather's collection of antiquities leads her to write about Egyptian techniques of embalming—

Once thought to be available only to the pharaohs, the gift of eternal life eventually became something that Egyptians believed could be claimed through wealth and status. The funerary rituals gave those who could afford them access to a special place in the Afterworld. Bodies were elaborately wrapped in linens in preparation. With the development of the pyramids in the Third Dynasty, dampness created by the

tombs hastened decay, and it became common practice to extract the internal organs and place them near the body in canopic jars.

And about death—

Death is *sah*, the mummified corpse. Death is *shuwt*, a shadow of the living body. Death is *yib*, the heart, where the memory of life is stored. Death is the revival of vital energy, *ka*, a person's spiritual twin. After life is over, after the body has been mummified and interred, *ka* requires its own nourishment and depends on *ba*, which is free to fly from the tomb each day, for food and drink. And finally death is all these separate elements bound together in a unified spirit called the *ankh*.

Visiting the galleries of Ancient Egyptian Art at the Brooklyn Museum, the writer notices that the lighting was soft but carefully targeted and gave the objects on view an internal radiance. The silence seemed to amplify the sound of my boots on the wooden floor. Clack-clack, clack-clack. I have always been a loud walker; I tend to stride with an exaggerated bounce off the ball of one foot and pound with the heel of my other foot. Usually when I become aware of the noise I'm making I try to stifle it. But on the third floor of the Brooklyn Museum, I wanted to stomp out the fact of my presence. I even felt the stirrings of a long-suppressed adolescent impulse to cause trouble. I suppose the desire was partly prompted by my worry that this search would lead only into a black hole of uncertainty. The puzzle remained confounding. While I knew something about the background of specific pieces, I'd failed to find a thorough account of their journey from Egypt to America. I might never know how the history of their acquisitions connected to the mystery of my great-grandfather's death.

Before she realizes what she's doing, she is writing about her growing frustration as she tries to get closer to her elusive subject.

I was just a visitor. I was stuck on the outside, and the ancient figures looking back at me seemed amused by my helplessness.

I studied the confluence of defining details. From one perspective I saw dignity and beauty. From another perspective I saw mischief and deceit, and I imagined that it had all been arranged by a delirious artist as a perverse tableau vivant. When we left for the night, the actors would step down from their pedestals and congratulate themselves for the good joke they'd played on their audience. Surely they were laughing at us from behind their masks. They were having fun provoking us, manipulating us, prompting us to consider our mortality. I'd come here to find a route into the past and had hoped that these objects would give me some clues. But they had been protecting their secrets for thousands of years.

The writer decides that if she's going to be honest, she has to admit her bafflement about the main mystery surrounding her great-grandfather's disappearance:

After visiting the Egyptian Galleries of the Brooklyn Museum, I felt I had a better sense of the thrill Armand must have experienced during those fruitful exchanges with dealers. But the haunting beauty of the objects only made me more puzzled by the mystery. My great-grandfather was at the height of his success, reaping the rewards of investments that would only grow in value. In the spring of 1905, he went on a trip to Argos and Delphi. He never returned home.

As if she'd already signed a contract with an imaginary reader, she feels compelled to differentiate between verifiable facts and her hypotheses. There is so much she still hasn't been able to corroborate—for instance, whether or not Louis de Potter was really Armand de Potter's grandfather. All the evidence she has found so far suggests that Louis de Potter had no grandchildren.

My search was taking me in circles. My suspicions led me to the Belgian Ministry of Foreign Affairs. I wrote to them to see if they could provide me with the citation for Armand de Potter, who proudly claimed to have been made a Knight in the Order of Leopold by the Belgian government. A member of the General Staff of the Belgian Armed Forces wrote back, informing me that they had no record of a Knight of Leopold named Armand de Potter. He'd found the name A. de Potter on a list, but he assured me that this was Agathon de Potter, Louis de Potter's most famous son.

I sent an email to the State Archives in Brussels. I received a speedy reply to the effect that they had no record of any connection between Louis and Armand. In fact, they had no record of any Armand de Potter. The phrase my Belgian correspondent used to describe this line of inquiry was "a dead end."

It is beginning to seem that every new clue leads to another dead end. The more she probes, the more the story crumbles in her hands. She finds a book with Armand de Potter listed as publisher. Six Weeks in Old France; Or, Doctor Thom's Holiday *tells the story of an interval during a Long Summer Tour, when an American touring party rested at a chateau in the countryside of France. The author, described in an advertisement as "a lady of uncommon literary ability" who has added "just enough romance" to her book to make it interesting, is named L.M.A. Aldrich.*

Reading through the book, the woman concludes that Armand de Potter had written it, or at least its final chapter, under a pseudonym. He was both author and main character, "L.M.A. Aldrich" and "Monsieur," the conductor of the touring party that

arrived at the chateau late on a September evening...

...filing from the courtyard through the front door and into the tiled entrance hall. An American flag had been pinned to the wall, and a servant was playing a rendition of "The Star-Spangled Banner" on the piccolo to welcome the American tourists. The chateau's owner was the same "Monsieur" who had been their guide on the tour. He'd left them in Paris a few days earlier and was waiting in the hall to greet the group warmly.

She continues, basing her description of a room called the "Petit Salon des Arts" on the lengthy description offered by the narrator.

There were paintings, a mix of copies and originals filling all available space on the walls. Among the original paintings by obscure artists were two of Venice depicting St. Mark's column and the Campanile, a painting of Apollo standing amidst the ruins of Pompei, a landscape that included hills and an amphitheater in Greece, and a portrait of a Spanish girl wearing a lace mantilla. An engraving illustrating a scene of children riding in a rude cart along a beach was hung beside a painting of a shepherd boy wearing a sheepskin coat. A porcelain plate depicted a young girl and boy turning the pages of a picture book. There was a plaque of majolica with a copy of a self-portrait by Van Dyke and a copy of the Cupids from a painting by Correggio hanging in the Borghese Palace in Rome. There was also a wood sculpture carved and painted to imitate an ivory tusk.

As she rereads the passage she has just written, she realizes that the images are familiar. She pulls out a photograph she'd found in the steamer trunk and studies it. The photograph is of a salon with the same works of art described by the author of Six Weeks in Old France. *The woman scans the photograph and inserts it into the text to provide an illustration of the salon. She scans other photographs and pastes them throughout her story. She includes pictures of the villa where the De Potters lived in Cannes and the painted sarcophagus Armand bought in Cairo. She adds photocopies of documents she'd found in the trunk to show the sources of her information.*

It's all proof, isn't it, that the story is true, unless...she pauses, blinking in weariness late one night, three years after she'd started writing her book...unless it isn't true, and she's been following false leads from the start. What if her solution to the mystery of Armand de Potter is wrong? What if Armand de Potter didn't really die at sea?

She writes,

What if the identity Armand assumed in America was based on fictions? If Armand wasn't who he said he was, then who was he?

She goes to sleep and dreams that she is at a flea market looking for a dusty old treasure to bring home with her. The next day she sets The Gilt Cabinet *aside and starts over from scratch. She gives up trying to adhere to some fixed notion of historical truth. With this draft, she resolves to write a novel. She tells herself that if she gets it right, then everything in the book will be true, whether it happened or not.* [18]

Lauren Artiles is an Editorial Assistant of BLACK CLOCK and in the CalArts MFA writing program.

Ani Bakhchadzyan is an Editorial Assistant of BLACK CLOCK and in the CalArts MFA writing program.

Bruce Bauman is the Senior Editor of BLACK CLOCK and the author of the award-winning novel *And the Word Was*. His second novel, *Broken Sleep*, will be published by Other Press in 2014, and his website is brucebauman.net.

Aimee Bender is the author of several books including *Willful Creatures*, *The Particular Sadness of Lemon Cake* and her latest collection, *The Color Master*. She teaches writing at USC.

Patrick Benjamin is a Senior Associate Editor of BLACK CLOCK and a graduate of the CalArts MFA writing program. His work has appeared in *Trop* and *The Collapsar*.

KT Browne is an Editorial Assistant of BLACK CLOCK and in the CalArts MFA writing program.

Tom Carson is *GQ*'s movie reviewer and a regular contributor to *The American Prospect*. His novel *Gilligan's Wake* was a New York Times Notable Book of The Year for 2003.

Ophelia Chong is the Art Director of BLACK CLOCK. She is an adjunct professor at Art Center, a published illustrator, graphic designer and gallery artist. She can be found online at opheliachong.org and ChongFucious.com.

Allison Conner is an Editorial Assistant of BLACK CLOCK and in the CalArts MFA writing program.

Anna Cruze is an Editorial Assistant of BLACK CLOCK and in the CalArts MFA writing program.

Regine Darius is an Editorial Assistant of BLACK CLOCK and in the CalArts MFA writing program.

Steve Erickson is the Editor of BLACK CLOCK and the author of nine novels including 2012's *These Dreams of You*. His website is steveerickson.org.

Brian Evenson is the author of more than a dozen books of fiction, most recently *Immobility* and *Windeye*. He has been a finalist for an Edgar Award and the recipient of three O. Henry Awards, and he teaches at Brown University.

Jessica Felleman is a Senior Associate Editor of BLACK CLOCK and a graduate of the CalArts MFA writing program.

Janet Fitch is the author of *Paint It Black* and *White Oleander*, and her stories and essays have appeared in BLACK CLOCK, *Room of One's Own, Los Angeles Noir*, the *Los Angeles Times* and *Vogue*. She teaches at the University of Southern California and at the Squaw Valley Community of Writers, and currently is writing a novel set during the Russian Revolution. Her website is www.janetfitchwrites.wordpress.com.

Sara Gerot is the Advertising Director for BLACK CLOCK. Her work has appeared in *Pank, A Bad Penny Review, Bookslut* and BLACK CLOCK. She teaches at William Penn University.

Arielle Greenberg is the Poetry Editor of BLACK CLOCK. She is author of *Shake Her, My Kafka Century* and *Given*, co-author of *Home/Birth: A Poemic*, and co-editor of three anthologies including *Gurlesque*. She teaches at the University of Tampa.

Emma Kemp is an Associate Editor of BLACK CLOCK and in the CalArts MFA writing program.

Anne-Marie Kinney is the Production Editor of BLACK CLOCK. She is the author of the 2012 novel *Radio Iris*, published by Two Dollar Radio, and her fiction has appeared in BLACK CLOCK, *Indiana Review* and *The Rattling Wall*.

Jonathan Lethem is the author of *Dissident Gardens* and eight other novels, as well as several collections of stories and essays. He lives in Los Angeles and Maine.

Orli Low is the Managing Editor of BLACK CLOCK. Previously she was an editor at the *Los Angeles Times*.

Greil Marcus is the author of *Lipstick Traces, The Dustbin of History, The Doors* and other books. With Sean Wilentz he co-edited *The Rose and the Briar—Death, Love and Liberty in the American Ballad*, and with Werner Sollors *A New Literary History of America*. His *History of Rock 'n' Roll in Ten Songs* will be published next year.

Joe Milazzo is the Assistant Managing Editor of BLACK CLOCK. His own writings may be read in the pages of *The Collagist, Drunken Boat, H_NGM_N*, and elsewhere. Joe lives and works in Dallas, TX, and his virtual location is www.slowstudies.net/jmilazzo.

Anthony Miller is Editor-at-Large of BLACK CLOCK. His writing has appeared in *Bookforum, LA Weekly, Los Angeles CityBeat, Poets & Writers, Los Angeles* magazine and *HiLobrow*. He is at work on a novel and a book about encyclopedic fictions and secret histories.

Rick Moody is the author of five novels, three collections of stories, a memoir and, most recently, a volume of essays, *On Celestial Music*. He has written regularly for *The Rumpus* since 2009 and is at work on a new novel.

Dwayne Moser is Editor-at-Large of BLACK CLOCK. His artwork has been exhibited internationally and is in many significant collections; he currently is completing a book of essays on fine art and the decline of Western civilization.

Geoff Nicholson is the author of twenty books of fiction and non-fiction including most recently *Walking in Ruins* and the forthcoming *The City Under the Skin*.

Joanna Scott is the author of two collections of stories and eight novels including *Follow Me, The Manikin, Arrogance* and the forthcoming *De Potter's Grand Tour*. Her books have been finalists for the Pulitzer Prize, the PEN/Faulkner and the *Los Angeles Times* book awards.

T.M. Semrad is an Editorial Assistant of BLACK CLOCK and in the CalArts MFA writing program.

Susan Straight has published eight novels including *Between Heaven and Here, A Million Nightingales* and *Highwire Moon*. Her stories have been published in BLACK CLOCK, *Best American Short Stories, O. Henry Prize Stories, The Sun, Zoetrope* and *McSweeney's*.

Chrysanthe Tan is the Communications Editor of BLACK CLOCK. She is a composer, violinist and poet in the CalArts MFA writing program. Her website is www.chrysanthetan.com.

David L. Ulin's books include *The Lost Art of Reading: Why Books Matter in a Distracted Time* and *Writing Los Angeles: A Literary Anthology*, which won a California Book Award. He is book critic of the *Los Angeles Times*.

Michael Ventura's latest book is *If I Was a Highway: Essays by Michael Ventura, Photographs by Butch Hancock*. Ventura's *Cassavetes Directs: John Cassavetes and the Making of* Love Streams was published in 2007.

Diana Wagman is the author of four novels. Her second, *Spontaneous*, won the 2001 PEN West Award for Fiction and her latest, *The Care & Feeding of Exotic Pets*, was chosen as a Barnes & Noble Discover Pick. She is a card-carrying member of the World Clown Association.

Adriana Widdoes is an Associate Editor of BLACK CLOCK and in the CalArts MFA writing program.

WRITING.CaLARTS.EDU

CaLARTS MFA CREATIVE WRITING PROGRAM

A unique non-tracking curriculum

Critical context for creative work

Unparalleled interdisciplinary opportunities

A dedicated, award-winning faculty

Close mentorship

Active professional development

Home to *Black Clock* and the Katie Jacobson Writer in Residence Program

RECENT VISITORS:

Lydia Davis
Edwidge Danticat
David Shields
Justin Torres

  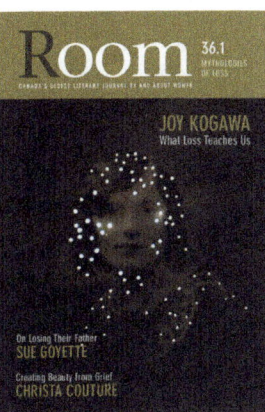 

Discover a space where women can speak, connect, and create. Subscribe today to enjoy original, thought-provoking literature and art that that reflects women's strength, sensuality, vulnerability, and wit.

Room magazine was founded in 1975 by a collective of writers, editors, academics, and feminists in Vancouver. Each quarter, we showcase original writing and art by women —whether cis, trans*, or gendervariant—from all over the world.

SUBSCRIBE TODAY
One Year | Canada $30 | USA $42 | Outside North America $56

UPCOMING CALLS FOR SUBMISSIONS

38.1 In Translation
Deadline: July 31, 2014

Have you written tongue-fumbling poetry about living in a land where you're learning the language? Fiction that considers the mathematical movement of a body from one point to another? Non-fiction about tumultuous semantic quibbles? *Room* invites you to submit writing about getting lost (and found) in translation. Texts entirely in a language other than English must be accompanied by an excellent English translation, as both will be published. Visit www.roommagazine.com for more details.

Room's Annual Literary Contest - Fiction, Poetry, and Creative Non-Fiction
Deadline: July 15, 2014

1st Prize in Each Category $500 | 2nd Prize in Each Category $250
Canadian entry fees $30 | Non-Canadian entry fees $42
All entries include a complimentary one-year subscription to *Room*.

www.roommagazine.com
www.facebook.com/roommagazine
@RoomMagazine

CPSIA information can be obtained at www.ICGtesting.com
Printed in the USA
LVOW02s1556070514

384803LV00005B/17/P